# DEATH GAMES

By the Same Author

NIGHT RITUALS

THE QUARK MANEUVER (Edgar Award Winner)

ARMADA

# DEATH GAMES

*A Novel*

MICHAEL JAHN

W · W · NORTON & COMPANY
*New York · London*

Published simultaneously in Canada by Penguin Books Canada Ltd., 2801 John Street, Markham, Ontario L3R 1B4.
Printed in the United States of America.

The text of this book is composed in Times Roman, with display type set in Benguiat. Composition and manufacturing by The Maple-Vail Book Manufacturing Group.
Book design by Jacques Chazaud.

First Edition

ISBN 0-393-02465-2

W. W. Norton & Company, Inc., 500 Fifth Avenue, New York, N. Y. 10110
W. W. Norton & Company Ltd., 37 Great Russell Street, London WC1B 3NU

1 2 3 4 5 6 7 8 9 0

*In memory of my father*

# DEATH GAMES

# ONE

On Memorial Day weekend and on the crest of a glorious evening, the street outside the Plaza Hotel gleamed with crystal and steel.

Diamonds reflected the gold of the lions and ladies' heads that decorated the black enamel standing lamps that guarded the hotel's doors. Priceless evening gowns and tuxedos were draped with the utmost care on bodies that slipped in and out of limousines or hansom cabs. Thousands of dollars were poised to be spent on bits of French this-or-that served with snifters of cognac in the many two- and three-star restaurants that dotted the side streets of midtown Manhattan.

Central Park South, the Via Vendetta of the American Dream, where people came to get even with the world for slighting their ability to make money, unnerved Frankie Rigili. The wealth stretched out before him, most of it earned honestly or at least not at the point of a gun, was alien. He was used to strutting his stuff in Bensonhurst, Brooklyn, where he could feel big and strong simply by leaving his car double-parked with the motor running while going into a store, knowing that no one would dare steal it.

In Bensonhurst Rigili was a man to be feared. Outside the Plaza Hotel he was out of place and aware of it, his pastel suit and rented limousine the objects of sly smiles of derision. He wanted to be anywhere but on Central Park South, where the razor blades were no sharper than in the old neighborhood, but a lot better hidden.

If only she would *hurry*. If only she wasn't so irresistible.

Just the night before he was sitting at the bar at l'Attesa, the busy Italian restaurant at Eighty-third Street and Columbus Avenue that served as a hangout for that part of the Mancuso crime family that controlled much of the Upper West Side. Practicing his smile in the backbar mirror, he waited for some randy stewardess to fall into his life.

The *she* walked in—right out of a *Town & Country* advertisement—and sat next to him. Not only was Andrea Jones beautiful, she was a true blueblood from Virginia, who owned and bred racehorses. Her thoroughbred stable was often represented in major races at Aqueduct and Belmont. Rigili remembered seeing its name in the sports pages of the *Daily News*. He thought he might even have bet on one of her horses.

But to have her sit next to him at the bar and ask him for a light—such an occurrence was inconceivable. Things like that didn't happen in his life, or in the life of anyone he knew. He lit her cigarette, smiled his smile, and, after a brief conversation, asked her out to dinner.

When she said yes, and when she asked him to pick her up the following night, Rigili thought: if the boys in Bensonhurst could only see me now.

As gangster executives go, Rigili was quite far down the ladder. He was, in fact, merely an arm-breaker for Vincent Ciccia, the *caporegime* charged by the Mancusos with running the rackets on the Upper West Side. But what Rigili lacked in power, he more than made up for in machismo. He could look in a mirror and see a jewelry store; that many gold chains, rings, and watches adorned his body.

Andrea Jones had no trouble spotting him as he paced the pavement, chain-smoking and frequently checking a gold Rolex wristwatch. She came down the Plaza steps and tossed her head so her hair caught the soft May breeze just in time for him to see it.

Rigili saw her, and he also saw the envious male eyes around him. He welcomed her with an expansive gesture: open arms, and a smile that told everyone she was his.

She walked into his expansive gesture and kissed him on the cheek.

"Hi."

"Hey, you look great!" he replied, wrapping her in his arms.

Jones smiled, neither an artificial smile nor a real one. It was a nice smile from a well-bred country girl.

"You look good, too," she said softly, giving his coffee-colored suit a quick once-over; "a bit like that actor on 'Miami Vice'—the one who doesn't shave."

"You really think so?" he asked, beaming.

"Except you're much taller."

"A compliment like that calls for a special evening," Rigili said. Without being aware of it he brushed back his hair, a habit born of many years of staring in mirrors.

He let her into the back of the limo, then climbed in alongside her. The car pulled out into traffic, and its space was quickly filled by another limousine, rather like beads sliding along a string.

Rigili said, "I got us the best table in the place and the cook is gonna make something really nice."

"What place?"

"L'Attesa, where we met."

She took his arm. "Let's go somewhere else tonight," she said.

"What's wrong with l'Attesa?"

"I've seen it already. Now I want to see something else: the restaurant under the Brooklyn Bridge. I've read so much about it."

Thrown off his well-rehearsed pace, Rigili scrambled for a name. "You mean the restaurant on a boat?"

"It's a barge, actually. The Bridge Café. The magazines have made quite a fuss about it. It's on the Brooklyn side. You must have been there."

"Oh, *that* place. I never got around to it."

In fact, it was located in a part of Brooklyn that was undergoing serious gentrification, as wealthy New Yorkers continued their expansion into the outer recesses of the city. Rigili felt uncomfortable around the Bridge Café. Again, money earned honestly made him nervous. But at least the Bridge Café was in Brooklyn.

"If there's something wrong with the restaurant . . ."

"No, no," he said quickly. "If that's where you want to go, we're on our way."

She smiled. "I called and made reservations for us," she said.

Rigili told the driver to take them down the East River Drive and over the Brooklyn Bridge to the Café.

"This is kind of fun," he said. "I never been out with anyone who knew exactly where she wanted to go and made reservations without asking me."

She squeezed his arm. "Do I hear the sound of manly pride being bruised?"

"Huh? Come on, I was just caught off guard, that's all."

His explanation, though not at all convincing, was uncontested by Andrea Jones, who kept hold of Rigili's arm as the car moved down the Drive, past the United Nations, the radio spewing elevator music, which Rigili had read was sexually provocative.

To the left, the East River displayed the lights of Brooklyn as reflected pearls. The images moved queerly with the violent motion of the currents. To the right, Manhattan shone as always; even to Andrea Jones the sight of Manhattan lights were familiar, the stuff of a million postcards. It was a light sculpture, unreal and holding an undeniable fascination; neon and fluorescent beams hurtling toward the sky, never to reach it.

As the car neared the Brooklyn Bridge off-ramp, Rigili toyed with her auburn hair. He became bolder and let his fingers slither over the monogrammed silk scarf that was tied loosely about her neck, over an antique linen blouse and inside a currently fashionable red-and-brown rag-texture jacket.

As his fingers neared her breast, she whispered "Frank" in a soft voice that told him "no," or, at least, "not now." He withdrew his hand.

"Sorry."

She patted his hand and then clasped it. She let her head rest on his shoulder and gazed out the window. The limo moved quickly across the span, which rumbled with the weight of the cars, trucks, and pedestrians crossing it. The theme from *Midnight Cowboy* came on the radio, and she quietly sang along.

The limousine took the first off-ramp and made a right-hand turn onto Old Fulton Street, which dead-ended in Fulton Ferry Landing, where commerce between Manhattan and Brooklyn was conducted by ferry before the bridge was built. Just south of the Brooklyn side of the bridge was the Café. Other limos and expensive private cars were parked in a lot paved with marble chips and bounded by white-painted chains.

The driver let them off by the door, then parked the car. Andrea Jones kept a firm hold on Rigili's arm as they went inside the Café. Like Central Park South it was bristling with money—designer money; money that bought clothes meant to be worn by models, not by mere mortals. There were few tuxedos and no furs. Rigili felt slightly more comfortable, and he relaxed. Jones watched as he slipped the maitre d' a hundred-dollar bill in exchange for a table on the patio—by the ledge directly overlooking the river.

They were escorted to their seats, from which the Manhattan skyline and the river sprawled before them. A large yacht, a yawl that looked a hundred feet long, was making its way downstream. Even under diesel power, the helmsman had to struggle to maintain rudder control, which is easy to lose when the current is pushing the boat nearly as fast as it can go. He managed, and within a few minutes the yawl made a turn to starboard and headed up the Hudson.

The menu looked exquisite. Rigili went on about the attributes of various Italian foods on it. Jones paid courteous attention, but she seemed to have little interest in food that night. Instead, she switched her attention from the yawl to the immediate surroundings: the parking lot, the expanse of Fulton Ferry Landing, and the row of carefully tended evergreens ringing the patio.

Several tall ships—majestic sailing ships with three masts each and what seemed like as much rigging as there was on the Brooklyn Bridge—were moored nearby, waiting their turn to participate in the 1986 observance of the Statue of Liberty Centennial. Small tenders moved between the ships and shore, ferrying men and supplies. Food was being taken off a truck at the ferry landing, which lay just beyond the low patio ledge.

The waiter brought the wine list, which Rigili pondered for a while, trying to make sense of the French names and wondering if he could get away with just asking for a carafe of *vino rosso.* Jones noticed his dilemma, and asked to help. She took the wine list, and, after a brief glance, ordered a respectable Bordeaux.

"Thanks," Rigili said. "I got to admit, I don't drink much wine. Just on holidays, you know?"

"I see that you have a holiday coming up," she replied, nodding at the tall ships and then going to the patio wall and looking at them.

"Yeah, are you sticking around for that? It's only a month off, and there's supposed to be forty or fifty thousand boats in the harbor. I can get us on a tour boat so we can see the parade of the tall ships."

He stood beside her, leaning against the wall with his back to it.

Andrea Jones said, "This was a good idea, coming here. I love it by the water."

"But you come from horse country."

"The Shenandoah Valley is named after a river, a very beautiful one. And it's not a long drive to the sea. I used to go there quite often."

The patio was filling rapidly. Chairs scraped against the floor and silver rattled in the service racks at the waiter station. Two women came in and took a table. Rigili watched one of them, convinced that she was somebody famous and trying to figure out who.

Jones said, "It's beautiful here tonight, and I want to remember it forever."

She went to her seat, and, with her back to him, opened her purse.

"What are you gonna do, take my picture?" he asked.

"Something more lasting," she said.

What happened next went so fast that it was etched in the memory of but one man, and only the Almighty knows if Frankie Rigili lived long enough to make sense of it.

She turned and leveled a massive revolver at Rigili's chest. The revolver was very old and looked like it might have been worn by a frontiersman. She fired two shots, both of which caught Rigili in the middle and nearly cut him in half before hurling his body over the ledge and into the churning currents of the East River.

People screamed and dived for cover. Tables were overturned, and in the confusion Andrea Jones moved swiftly to the carefully tended evergreens ringing the patio. She pushed her way through the trees and out onto Fulton Ferry Landing.

The general panic had spilled out onto the landing. A man who had been unloading the truck stopped Jones. "What happened?" he asked.

"Somebody's been shot," she said. "The man who did it ran up the street."

She pointed up Old Fulton Street, which had a few pedestrians but nobody resembling an assassin. Nonetheless, the man who had stopped Jones ran up the block.

Andrea Jones went a different way, walking swiftly across the landing and up Hicks Street to the intersection of Cranberry Street.

A gray BMW stood by the curb outside an antique book shop, the motor running. One of the back doors opened. She got in and the car drove off.

## "DIDYA EVER SIT ON A TOMATO?" DONOVAN ASKED

George the Bartender scowled at Lieutenant Bill Donovan, who had left work just in time to catch the last half hour of George's shift. It was during the last half hour that the man was sure to be in his finest mood.

"Do you want a Blatz or not?" he asked. "It's only a buck-fifty."

"I'm not drinking anything that sounds like a tomato being sat upon," Donovan said.

George sighed. " A Schmidt's, then?"

Donovan was wary. The price of booze at Riley's had, in recent years, been rising faster than an MX missile. "How much?"

"A buck seventy-five."

"Jesus H. Christ, what have you done? Gone to work for AA or something? You're driving everyone to sobriety with these prices."

George replied in the digital manner, elevating his middle finger and waggling it at Donovan, who was undaunted.

"Five years ago, Schmidt's went for sixty-five cents in this joint. Four years ago it was seventy-five. Three years ago it was ninety-five. After it topped a buck a bottle I lost count."

"Donovan . . ."

"How much is Jack Daniels now?"

"You didn't drink Jack Daniels then, and you don't drink it now."

"Tell me the price and I'll give you the reason," Donovan said.

"Two-fifty," George said reluctantly.

"Charging two dollars and fifty cents for seven-eighths of an ounce of Jack Daniels will get you five years in the hoosegow in any state in the Union."

Donovan brandished a pocket calculator and quickly tapped out some figures. "That works out to seventy bucks a quart. You're under arrest. You have the right to remain silent . . "

"Donovan," George interrupted, "have you ever considered entering the priesthood?"

"Yeah, but only for the sacramental wine. I'll have a Blatz."

A bottle was duly presented to Donovan, unopened and without a glass. "I hope you drown in it," George said.

Donovan and George Kohler had been fast friends for a dozen years or more, though it was hard to tell at time. Donovan was the head of the West Side Major Crimes Unit, a growing police presence whose members contributed heavily to the customer roster of Riley's Saloon. Riley's was located directly beneath the unit, or "house," as police outposts were routinely called. The two institutions were so closely linked that there was occasional talk of putting in a fireman's pole between the second-floor offices of the unit and the bar at Riley's. The talk never came to anything. Donovan, with the division commander's wholehearted approval, thought it would look bad in the press.

Riley's was a neighborhood bar on the west side of Broadway between Eighty-seventh and Eighty-eighth streets. The building had only two stories. The unit shared the second floor with a gym-turned-health-spa that served an increasingly upscale clientele. The ground floor held a sporting goods shop, a Chinese restaurant, a candy store that was really a numbers joint, Riley's, and an army surplus shop. A doorway separated Riley's from the

Chinese restaurant and also served as the entrance to the stairwell leading up to the unit.

George wandered back down Donovan's way, drew himself a mug of beer, and stared at the lieutenant. "Did you have any money on the Yanks last night?" he asked.

"Are you out of your mind? I'd rather waste my money in here."

"I bet on the A's," George said. "I lost ten bucks."

"Sorry to hear it," Donovan said.

"Don't you like gambling? What's the matter with you?"

"I like gambling. I put a buck a day on the single-action number. I wanna keep Ciccia in business long enough for me to kill him."

"You're a sweet guy, Bill," George said.

"Absolutely."

George said, "Did you at least watch the Spinks fight?"

"Anytime I wanna see two guys beatin' up on one another all I got to do is come in here about three in the morning," Donovan snapped.

"Whatever happens on Keane's shift is no skin off my ass."

Donovan poured some beer down his throat. "Not bad," he admitted.

"It's good enough for *you*."

The slug of beer had barely cleared Donovan's larynx when Sergeant Jefferson came in, looking like a stockbroker in one of his many Brooks Brothers suits.

"Oh shit," George said, upon spotting Donovan's black chief aide and best friend.

"What's with him?" Jefferson asked Donovan.

"He lost a sawbuck on the Yanks and has been using it as an excuse to insult the customers."

"When did he ever need an excuse?" Jefferson asked.

George was indignant. He was good at it. "Ah . . . I *am* addressing the poor man's Eddie Murphy, am I not? Well, get the fuck outta here and take Oscar Madison with you."

Unlike Jefferson, Donovan was hardly known as a flashy dresser. Donovan called his clothing habits "shabby genteel." The division commander had many other and more colorful words, but found it politically unwise to bitch at the unit chief with the best arrest record in the City of New York because he sometimes forgot to wear socks.

"Are you drinking or did you just come to collect the trash?" George asked Jefferson.

"The latter, m'man."

"Yeah, you colored guys are good at picking up trash, ain't ya? I see your brothers on the back of garbage trucks all the time." George was proud of the way he had set Jefferson up.

The black sergeant, having heard George abuse the ethnic diversity of the entire Upper West Side, and having done some of the same himself, just laughed. "You remember the time I came in here on a Saturday morning and there was this other black guy, some stranger, sittin' at the far end of the bar?"

George said, "I was sitting down having my morning coffee and reading the paper, and Jefferson came in for his morning orange juice. I love the way you guys feel free to use my place as a snack bar. Anyway, when he came in he sat at the middle of the bar, by the taps."

"George ignored me," Jefferson said.

"I did not. I said, 'Oh shit' and went back to reading the paper. So Jefferson sits there five or ten minutes, then finally stands up and shouts, 'Hey honky, what the fuck you gotta do to get served in here?' "

"I think I see this developing," Donovan said.

"So I stood up and yelled back, 'Whaddya want, ya black bastard?"

"The other guy didn't know we were friends, y'see," Jefferson said, "and he bolted down his drink and went running out the door. We cracked up. You could almost hear him thinking, 'Feet, don't fail me now.' "

George said, "The poor bastard felt whatever was going on in here, he didn't want to be part of it."

"Did he ever come back?" Donovan asked.

"Would you?" Jefferson asked. "What's that shit you're drinking, by the way?"

Smiling, George went off to service some other customers.

"Blatz is a very good beer. Premium. I recommend it highly."

"That's all fine and good, so long as you drink up. We're all ready at the garage."

Donovan chugged the rest of the bottle.

"I haven't done that since high school," he said proudly.

"I didn't think you'd want to miss this one, knowing how fond you are of Ciccia."

"Let's went," Donovan said, and was on his way out the door at the same time as Irving Nakima, another Riley's regular, who had given himself the job of making the runs to the numbers joint down the block. George had given him the name "Irving" after finding that Nakima's Japanese name was unpronounceable.

"Last chance for the number," he said.

Donovan slapped a dollar bill in the man's hand. "*Tres,*" he said.

"You wanna split it sixty-forty?"

"Nah. Shoot the works."

"See you later, Bill," Nakima said, but by then Donovan was on the run to his car.

# Two

Donovan admired the copper-jacketed lead obelisk. It had a somber majesty all its own, the .44 magnum did: something about the cool green of the jacket and the soft gray of the slug. When he was a young, uniformed officer, Donovan had filled a glass jar with spent copper cartridges and kept it on a table where the setting sun would flint off the green.

He threw the cartridges out a few days after killing his first man, but the fascination lingered. Somber majesty, Donovan thought: cool green discharging gray death. He studied the gray and the green in the quarter-light of the surveillance van before slipping the cartridge back into its chamber. He clicked the chamber back into place.

Jefferson turned at the sound. ''Are you done playing with that thing?'' he whispered.

By way of an answer, Donovan shoved the Smith & Wesson revolver into his shoulder holster.

''You get yourself a heavy-duty handgun and spend all your time starin' at it,'' Jefferson said.

''Shut up and go get me a sandwich and a Coke. And I want the old Coke, not the new Coke.''

"I hope you don't mind if *I* work while *you* sit there and play with your .44 magnum, do you? Wouldn't surprise me if you started comin' on like you was Clint Eastwood soon."

Donovan did a very bad imitation of Clint Eastwood. "Why sergeant, that sounds like a mighty fine idea to me," he hissed.

Jefferson chortled and went back to fiddling with the controls of his video and audio recorders.

They were parked in a corner of an underground garage on West 106th Street, which some years back had been renamed Duke Ellington Boulevard. Donovan liked Duke Ellington's music but not his boulevard. It had all the lack of charm of most major crosstown streets on the West Side. The apartment houses were all alike, dull gray tombstones. There were few stores, few pedestrians, and all that stopped the taxis from turning the strip into the straightaway at Le Mans were the many potholes.

The garage was no improvement. It was dark and stank of mold, machine oil, and urine. It was also largely empty. Most Manhattan garages emptied on Memorial Day weekend, when a good part of the population departed for three months in the mountains, the Hamptons, or assorted fashionable islands. The emptiness of that particular garage was being used by three separate groups. A local crime family was sending several of its warriors to sell guns. A Puerto Rican street gang from the Bronx was sending a few of its members to buy the guns. And the police were waiting to arrest the whole lot.

"What do you make the odds of Ciccia showing up personally?" Donovan asked.

"About the same as the Yanks making the World Series," Jefferson replied.

"I want that bum."

"You also want a sandwich and a Coke. Take it easy, Bill, you'll get him."

Donovan grumbled. In the two years since being made a *capo* in the Mancuso family, Vincent Ciccia had been number one on

Donovan's list. It wasn't his control of illegal gambling on the West Side that irked Donovan, who was known to drop an occasional buck at the numbers joint. Donovan was after Ciccia for selling MAC-10 submachine guns to teen-agers, and, as the lieutenant put it, for being "a grade-A lout."

Ciccia thumbed his nose at Donovan by regularly showing up at Riley's and trying to buy Donovan drinks. Ciccia also liked to hear himself referred to as "the Animal," although his best claim to toughness was a paunch the size of a small Caribbean nation. Donovan was often tempted to see personally if Ciccia wasn't just another stuffed animal, but his better judgement and the division commander talked him out of it.

Donovan checked his watch. "The sale was supposed to have gone down half an hour ago," he said.

"Twenty minutes," Jefferson corrected. "Maybe they got stuck in traffic."

"More likely mugged."

" 'Ricans can't get mugged. You ever go into one of those bodegas they run? They got these little cans of Mug-Pruf that they spray on themselves. It make 'em immune."

"I must pick up a can," Donovan said idly.

"Mug-Pruf don't work on white guys. It don't work on brothers, either, Only on 'Ricans."

Donovan didn't know why Jefferson disliked Hispanics. He was sure that there were at least ten thousand sociologists on the West Side who could explain it. But Donovan preferred to allow people their eccentricities, as long as they didn't use them to create a disturbance. Besides, Donovan had enough eccentricities of his own.

The radio, which had been dormant for some time, crackled into life. The detective watching the street from a second-story window had spotted a black Oldsmobile, known to be one of Ciccia's cars, heading west from Columbus Avenue.

"We have a target," Jefferson said gleefully.

''What's in it?'' Donovan asked.

Jefferson repeated the question into the microphone of the van's radio.

''Two male Caucs,'' was the reply.

''Does one of those Caucs resemble a small, Caribbean nation?'' Donovan asked.

''Is one of 'em fat?'' Jefferson asked his spy.

''Negative, 'kay.''

''Shit,'' Donovan said.

''Take it easy, m'man. We'll get Ciccia sooner or later.'' Jefferson pressed some buttons on his video and other machines. The date and time of day appeared in the lower, left-hand corner of a monitor that offered a wide-angle view of the garage's interior. The garage was even drearier on the monitor, which made the shadows cast by the cement pillars even darker and gave the two bare light bulbs dangling from the ceiling the sickening, yellow-green color of old flypaper.

Donovan glowered at the sign that announced the prices of renting a garage space in Manhattan. ''Two hundred bucks a month to park on 106th Street,'' he said in disgust.

''Duke Ellington Boulevard,'' Jefferson replied. ''When the signs went up, so did the prices.''

The radio spoke again. ''The car is turning into the garage.''

''Affirmative, 'kay,'' Jefferson replied. Then, turning back to his electronic equipment, he pressed another button and said, ''Roll tape . . . roll sound.''

Donovan smiled and shook his head.

The Oldsmobile came down the ramp.

''The gun bust, scene one, take one. And . . . action!''

Jefferson turned down the volume on the radio. Donovan took his gun out of its holster. The car rolled to a halt against the back wall of the garage and two men got out. One wore a dark suit, the other tan slacks and a white dress shirt open nearly to the waist.

''Where the fuck are they?'' one said.

"We're late, they're late. Big deal." The speaker was Tan Slacks, whom Donovan took to be the man in charge.

"I hate these punk kids."

"The man likes their money. You wanna argue with him?"

Donovan whispered, as if he were coaching them: "What man? Say the name, dammit!"

Jefferson shushed him. There was another radio message coming in. "I got a red Trans-Am with yellow flames painted on the hood. It looks like the car from the Bronx, 'kay."

"Ten-four, 'kay. Everybody get ready. The second the money and guns change hands I'm gonna give the go signal."

The Trans-Am came down the ramp and pulled alongside the Olds. "Would you look at that Spicmobile? I've seen better taste on Tenth Avenue hookers."

Two young Hispanics got out of the car and swaggered over to the men. The teen-agers, who looked hardly more than sixteen, both wore black jackets the backs of which were decorated, like the car, with painted-on flames. "Meet the cream of the Melrose Avenue Flames," Jefferson said.

The buyers and sellers, less than twenty yards from the surveillance van, began talking money. All four punctuated their speech with wild arm motions.

"Are you sure you're getting all this on tape? Both audio and video?" Donovan asked.

Jefferson was miffed. "You're talking to Mr. Microchips. Don't give me no grief over my technical expertise."

"Just checking."

"If you got to worry about something, worry about blowin' your foot off with that Clint Eastwood Special."

Donovan said, "Tell the troops that if any of those four clowns so much as touch a MAC, assume the goddam thing is loaded and get ready to open fire."

"Yo, boss," Jefferson said, and did as he was told.

"I don't want to see one of those things cut loose in a confined space. A couple hundred rounds a minute with a muzzle velocity over a thousand feet per second. Jesus!''

"I'm with you. Hold it! The goods are coming out!''

Ciccia's two warriors opened the trunk of the Olds and removed a heavy wooden crate. They set it on the floor and cut the straps that were holding down the top. Tan Slacks hefted an angry-looking machine pistol with a short muzzle and a folding shoulder butt.

"MAC-10,'' Donovan said.

Jefferson spoke into the radio: "They're selling a crateload of MACs. Everybody stay sharp.''

Donovan listened hard to the monitor. "Twenty pieces, two thousand per, right?'' Tan Slacks said.

"Yeah, that's it, man,'' a Hispanic voice replied.

"Let's see the money.''

Jefferson whispered, "How do a couple of kids from the Bronx come up with forty grand?''

Donovan shrugged. "Tax-free municipals?''

"These guys gotta be the same bunch that's been hittin' banks along the Grand Concourse.''

The two teen-agers pooled money from their wallets, counting hundred-dollar bills as if they were shuffling cards.

"When do you want to go?'' Jefferson asked.

"I'll let you know. I just want to have the whole transaction on tape.''

Counting and handing over the money took five minutes that seemed like an hour. That whole time, Donovan figeted with his revolver. Finally, Tan Slacks said, "Nice doing business with you,'' and shut the trunk of the Oldsmobile.

The two teen-agers put the cover back on the box of guns and were about to pick it up when Donovan said, "Now.''

Jefferson hit the button on the radio. "Everybody go! Go!''

Donovan kicked open the rear door of the van and leaped outside. Jefferson went out the side door, brandishing a megaphone. The four astonished suspects whipped their heads in the direction of the van.

Jefferson said, "This is the police! Stay right where you are and don't move!" The electronic voice roared in the underground garage. There were sirens outside, and the sound of feet running down the ramp.

The man in the suit dived behind the wheel of the Olds. He threw the car into reverse and floored the accelerator. The car shot backwards and slammed into a parked Dodge. Tan Slacks scrambled for the door handle, couldn't find it, and the car roared forward without him and made the turn up the ramp.

One of the teen gang members tossed off the cover of the crate and fumbled for a MAC.

"Don't!" Donovan shouted, raising his revolver.

The kid didn't listen or didn't care. Donovan saw the bulky machine pistol come up, and he recalled a briefing film in which a MAC cut a Toyota in half. He raised his magnum and fired one round.

The kid was hit squarely in the chest and thrown right over the trunk of the Trans-Am. The other teen-ager stood stock-still, frozen, but Tan Slacks produced a Colt Commander Auto Pistol.

Donovan heard the roar of Jefferson's regulation .38. Hit in the shoulder, Tan Slacks spun to the floor, the Colt skittering away from him.

Unseen by Donovan and halfway up the ramp, there were a handful of shots and the crash of a car.

Jefferson joined two other detectives who were handcuffing the dumbstruck teen-ager and tending to the man who had just sold him enough materiel to equip a small guerilla band. Then Jefferson bent for a moment over Tan Slacks, who was writhing in pain.

"He'll live, Lieutenant," Jefferson reported.

Donovan holstered his gun and walked slowly to the body of the kid he had shot. The MAC was resting a few feet from the corpse, the torso of which was splattered across enough garage space to house two Mercedes.

He stared at the round, hairless face that still showed some baby fat. "This is just a kid. A baby."

Jefferson joined Donovan. "A baby who was about to start a war."

"He can't be a day over fifteen."

Yeah, fifteen going on fifty. They grow up fast on the streets."

Donovan looked away. The scene about him had become a familiar blend of sirens, cries of pain, radio talk, flashing lights, and the reading of rights in both English and Spanish.

Jefferson said, "The one in the car is dead. What do you want done with the other two?"

"Take Al Capone to St. Luke's, patch him up, then have him sent to the prison ward at Bellevue. Take Che Guevara to the house and see what you can get out of him. Notify Bronx Detectives that we have one of their civic leaders in custody. I'll meet you later."

"Where are you going?"

"Where do you think?" Donovan replied, and left the scene in the garage.

He walked down Duke Ellington Boulevard, waited for the light, then crossed Broadway. Just to the north, the Olympia Theater was featuring a Sylvester Stallone retrospective. Donovan began across Straus Park, heading for where his car was parked.

Straus Park was a small triangle that marked the point where West End Avenue merged with Broadway. It had a small monument, and benches that, like those in many New York City parks, had been taken over by homeless people drinking cheap, sweet wine. Four of them were having a noisy argument, about which Donovan could learn nothing.

He paused to read the inscription on the monument, something he had been meaning to do for twenty years. Like most old-time New Yorkers, Donovan paid scant attention to the city's famous places and monuments, and had no idea why Straus Park was so named. The inscription read: "In Memory of Isidor and Ida Straus, who were lost at sea in the Titanic Disaster April 15, 1912. Lovely and pleasant were they in their lives, and in their death they were not divided.''

A sculpture of a reclining woman, her head supported by one hand, her eyes gazing sadly down into what once was a fountain but since had become a stagnant pool holding leaves, bits of paper, and wine bottles, caught Donovan's attention.

A thirtyish man, whom Donovan pegged as a junkie, eyed the lieutenant suspiciously. Donovan walked to his car, wondering all the while what Isidor and Ida Straus could have had in common with Duke Ellington.

## LIFT A JOWL AND THE NAME OF A HOOKER FALLS OUT

Vincent Ciccia's jowls drooped like those of a basset hound, and Donovan wondered if the man didn't keep things tucked away beneath them. Lift a jowl and the name of a hooker falls out. Donovan smiled at the thought, an action that Ciccia took as a welcome. He and his two black-suited goons smiled back.

Ciccia said, ''Lieutenant, how you doin' tonight?''

''Better than you.''

Ciccia looked perplexed. *He hasn't heard,* Donovan thought.

''Lemme buy you a drink,'' Ciccia said, helping himself to a barstool near Donovan.

''Save your money for your lawyer,'' Donovan said.

''Come on. Don't you like me?''

Donovan gave Ciccia a hard stare. ''I'd rather drink with Hitler,'' Donovan said.

Ciccia's two goons had less of a sense of humor than their boss. They stepped forward, but retreated when Donovan pulled his lapel aside, revealing his Smith & Wesson.

Gus Keane came down the bar, moving faster than Donovan had ever seen. ''Any problem here?'' he asked.

Donovan used his Clint Eastwood voice again, better this time: "Nothing that Smith, Wesson, and me can't handle."

Ciccia got up off his stool, with some difficulty, and moved halfway down the bar. His bodyguards followed. One of them sat next to Irving Nakima, who proceeded to relocate himself next to Donovan.

"I see your old friend is here," Nakima said. "Man, he's fat enough to cause an earthquake when he sits down. When he comes in here every night . . . just about this time, come to think of it . . . I can feel the floor shake."

"You're gonna feel a real earthquake in ten or twenty minutes, unless I miss my guess," Donovan said.

Nakima, the only avid horse player Donovan knew who had never picked a winner, missed Donovan's remark.

"Hey, I nearly forgot! *Tres!*"

"No shit!" Donovan exclaimed. He seldom hit the number. In fact, he only played it for the hell of it and also to give Ciccia the impression that his numbers parlors were being tolerated. Still, Donovan was elated.

"Seven bucks," Nakima said, and laid the money in front of Donovan.

"Is that all he's paying these days? I ought to bust him right now for unfair business practices."

"You can't do that," Nakima said, genuinely panicked. "If you shut down the numbers joint I'll have to walk all the way over to Amsterdam Avenue."

"You're right," Donovan said. "I can't have you ruining your legs on my account. After all, you did help me out with that business in the park a few years ago. I guess I owe you. Innkeeper!"

Augustus Keane, the current night bartender at Riley's, was a tall, thin man with a Harvard education that made him smart enough to realize that tending bar was easier on the spirit than, say, being a member of the bar.

"May I get you gentlemen something?" he asked.

"Two Blatz," Donovan said.

"Working," Keane replied.

Keane was the most eccentric person Donovan had ever met, and that in a city where eccentricity was almost a requirement. Unlike George, the day bartender who blustered like a fighting bull, Keane was an ethereal presence. He floated above his surroundings, ofttimes on a cloud of marijuana smoke, dispensing wit and wisdom accumulated during ten years' experience as a war correspondent, mainly in Southeast Asia. Keane had studied Zen, Jungian analysis, and cultural anthropology, and combined them with his war correspondent experience over the course of a two-year stint tending bar in Australia.

From it all he brewed a philosophy that taught him that the only way to handle a problem was to float above it, observing it and hoping it would go away. If the problem didn't go away, Keane would convince it to mend its ways.

Donovan thought that Keane's philosophy was just a fancy excuse to get drunk or other wise high and talk to inanimate objects, thereby attracting interesting people. That was until one wet and cold February when Donovan's car wouldn't start despite the efforts of three NYPD mechanics. Keane said, "Bill, the problem is that your car is happy where it is in the alley, and doesn't want to go out and get colder and wetter. We have to convince it of its civic responsibility. We must make it understand that it simply must take you to the scene of the crime. A car is not an island, and a disgruntled distributor or a wet generator is no excuse for absenting oneself from society."

Keane talked to the car and fiddled with it some, and within five minutes Donovan was tearing up Broadway toward a holdup scene near Columbia. Shortly thereafter, a suspect was in custody. Donovan stopped doubting Keane's philosophy, and even accepted his claim to be a direct descendant and namesake of the British ethnologist, geographer, and professor of Hindustani. Donovan accepted the two beers and gave one to Nakima.

"Gracias," Nakima said.

''De nada.''

''Just don't close the numbers joint.''

The pay phone rang, Keane picked it up, listened for a second, then said to Ciccia, ''It's for you.''

Ciccia grunted as he got up and walked the five feet to the pay phone.

He listened to the voice on the other end for less than a minute, then hung up. He looked at the bare wall, then turned and glowered at Donovan. The lieutenant formed his fingers into the approximation of a gun, aimed it at Ciccia, and mouthed the word ''bang.''

Ciccia tossed a five dollar bill onto the bar and rumbled out. As he neared the door, he stopped to glare at the lieutenant. Once again, Donovan opened his jacket to reveal his revolver.

''Donovan . . .'' Ciccia said, in controlled rage.

''Have a pleasant evening,'' Donovan said.

''What was that all about?'' Keane asked, when Ciccia was gone.

''He just found out that we busted one of his operations a little while ago. The man just can't take bad news with dignity.''

''He obviously is no gentleman,'' Keane said.

''Obviously.''

''On the other hand, I will be gentleman enough to share some information with you.''

Donovan asked what it was.

''The most beautiful woman I have ever seen in my life just came in here, saw your 'discussion' with Ciccia, and walked out.''

''Which way did she go?'' Donovan asked.

''South.''

Donovan ran out the door and looked south, but Andrea Jones had rounded the corner and was out of sight.

When Donovan returned to the bar, the look of disappointment on his face was obvious.

''You could have been gentleman enough to tell me sooner,'' he said.

# THREE

"Leonard Bernstein is behind the whole thing," Donovan said. "Him and Jerome Robbins."

Jefferson looked confused.

"They wrote *West Side Story,* which was about teen gangs on the West Side. There aren't teen gangs on the West Side anymore, but there seems to be a renaissance in the South Bronx."

"Yeah, can you imagine a couple hundred punk kids fightin' over a few square miles of burned-out buildings? Shit, if I was gonna grab me some turf, I'd make it fuckin' Beverly Hills."

"That's because you have taste, my friend."

"Thank you, Massa, thank you," Jefferson said, bowing at the waist. He liked to do an Uncle Tom act every so often to amuse his boss.

"I feel kind of grubby," Donovan said. "Why don't you handle the press tonight."

Jefferson beamed, and said, "You're puttin' me on."

"I'm tired, too."

"You're a star. Bill. They expect you."

That was true enough. The combination of the Left Bank romance of the West Side with a couple of major arrests had made William Donovan one of the best-known cops in town. He had stood before too many TV cameras to recall. Let Jefferson do it for a while, he thought.

"I'll take the credit when we get Ciccia."

"I knew there was an angle."

"Come on, I'll introduce you."

The interrogation room had been turned into a showplace for the arsenal captured that day. On the long Formica table, the boxy machine pistols were laid out in a row, along with cartridges and boxes of ammunition. Two TV crews, six reporters, and four photographers were gaping at the guns and enjoying the free coffee and danish.

Jefferson eyeballed the scene, then said to Donovan, "I've never been on TV before. Do I have to clean up my act in any way?"

"Talk normal English," Donovan advised, straightening Jefferson's tie. "No unflattering references to anyone's parentage, please."

"You got it. Do I look okay?"

"Sensational. Let's go."

When the reporters spotted Donovan, the TV lights snapped on. Donovan walked to the table and said, "I'd like you to meet Sergeant T. L. Jefferson. He developed the information that led to this evening's arrests. He ran the surveillance, and he's the best man to explain what happened."

Then Donovan went back to his office, leaving Jefferson to demonstrate the captured weapons before the TV lights. He looked good and handled himself well. Donovan was more convinced than ever that Jefferson was a rising star in New York City.

Donovan glanced outside the window at the traffic on Broadway and saw a clutter of ethnic neighborhoods linked by a crumbling old four-lane highway identified by downtown tourists with bright lights and stage plays but by West Siders with Spanish bodegas, Korean fruit stands, Szechuan restaurants, numbers parlors masquerading as candy stores, nouvelle cuisine restaurants that seemed to serve only quiche, and ice cream parlors with odd foreign names that sold cones, one scoop, for $1.10.

The West Side was bounded by Columbia University on the north, Central Park on the east, Riverside Park and the Hudson River on the west, and Lincoln Center for the Performing Arts on the south. It was Donovan's job to make the streets safe for the citizens. To be sure, there were the beat cops of the Twenty-fourth and Twenty-sixth precincts for routine matters. But as the West Side grew in wealth the crime got more serious. A few prominent civilians were killed, there was a series of ritual killings in Riverside Park, and abruptly the West Side Major Crimes Unit had doubled its budget, office space, and manpower.

There were more computers, which Donovan regarded with suspicion, and special parking zones. There was even a sign on the window to inform the public that what once had been a billiards parlor now was an elite NYPD unit.

Donovan got himself a cup of coffee and closed the door to his office. It was nearly eleven o'clock, and still the streets were filled with wandering couples. The gentrification of Columbus Avenue had begun to spill over onto Broadway, and chi-chi restaurants and shops with outrageous prices lined the street as far north as Ninety-sixth Street.

Donovan eyed the pile of paper on his desk. "You bring money into a neighborhood and this is what you get," he muttered. He turned over a few leaves. Corrigan and Bailey had a new lead on the coke dealer who was giving his rich Columbus Avenue clients the wonderful opportunity to grow extra nostrils. Bonaci and Tieman were getting no place trying to catch the guy who had raped three women in the same building on Seventy-second Street, curiously enough the same high-rise where the "Mr. Goodbar" murder happened. Masterson thought he had a name to hang on the bunco artist who was working the rich old ladies on Central Park West. As far down the pile of paper as he could see, Donovan saw more cops chasing more crooks.

On impulse Donovan opened a desk drawer and pulled out a

fading Polaroid picture. There they stood twelve years earlier, in bathing suits, arms around one another, beside her father's pool in Croton-on-Hudson. Donovan was a brash young sergeant with a jaunty mustache and the determination to eliminate crime in New York all by himself. Rookie officer Marcia Barnes was just out of the John Jay College of Criminal Justice and learning the life of a cop. Her silken black hair poured across Donovan's shoulder, and her cocoa skin was only a bit darker than his tan.

Donovan caught himself humming the main theme from *Camelot.*

Then he felt silly. He hadn't seen Marcia in a year, and then only for lunch. He didn't even know if she was still working out of Midtown South. Who was he to wax what-could-have-been over a fading snapshot?

He told the paperwork to do its own work, and went home.

But there was nothing on television that Donovan felt like watching. "Rat Patrol," long his favorite show, had been taken off the air, and its star, Christopher George, had died. "Doctor Who," the British science fiction series that ran on public television, had been pre-empted for a discussion of the latest Mideast crisis. All that was left was an episode of "Hawaii Five-O" that Donovan had seen half a dozen times.

He went into his study and switched on the desk lamp. Donovan sat and flipped through a copy of *Popular Mechanics,* and read the first half of an article on building your own submarine.

There was a splashing noise in the guest bathroom. The turtle was growing restless of late. In the several years that Donovan had the critter, he had grown from the size of a salad dish to the size of a turkey platter. Donovan went into the kitchen, got two whitefish bought at the fish store on Broadway, and brought them into the bathroom.

The turtle had fallen into Donovan's possession during the Riverside Park murder case. The animal was fairly benign then, capable only of inflicting a mildly severe flesh wound. Now he had grown into the monster that several hundreds of millions of years of evolution meant him to be. As Donovan approached, the snapper opened its mouth to reveal a pink tongue and razor-sharp jaws.

"Clint, my friend, you're getting to be a pain in the ass," Donovan said.

He tossed the whitefish into the tub. Clint snaked out his long neck and bit a fish in two.

"Mangia," Donovan said.

He went into the living room and put on a Duke Ellington record. He leaned back in his old armchair and dozed off. At about two in the morning he awoke, shut off the record player, and went to bed.

## "THE CISCO KID COLORING BOOK," FIRST EDITION, 1953

Donovan was buttoning his shirt when the doorbell rang. "It's open!" he yelled, but Donovan's apartment was so big and rambling that his voice got lost in it.

The bell rang again. "I never should have gotten that fixed," he said to himself, as he walked to the door.

Jefferson looked like an advertisement in *Gentleman's Quarterly,* as usual.

"Yo, bro' . . . I dig the drip-dry shirt," he said.

"Immigration finally caught up with my laundryman," Donovan replied, returning to the master bedroom with Jefferson following.

"Not Mr. Yin? He's been here ten years."

"Nonetheless, he's starchin' collars back in Hong Kong now."

The bedroom was filled with memorabilia from Donovan's life. Jefferson always delighted in picking through the tangle of softball bats, sailing trophies, infielders' mitts, the football program signed by Joe Namath, and the other icons too numerous to count. One item, however, caught Jefferson's eye. It was framed and hanging on the wall near the closet.

*"The Cisco Kid Coloring Book?"*

"It's a first edition," Donovan said proudly; "1953."

"You gotta be kiddin'."

"I was offered a hundred bucks for that book one time. It's a hot item amongst collectors of cowboy memorabilia."

Jefferson laughed.

"It's also how you got your nickname," Donovan said.

He often called Jefferson "Pancho," after the Cisco Kid's sidekick and also to get even with Jefferson for his constant abuse of Hispanics.

"Man, I wish you'd stop callin' me that," Jefferson said.

"No habla Ingles, Pancho."

"Yeah, that's what Che Guevara has been sayin' all night."

"What about Al Capone. Was he any more voluble?"

"He knows only one word. The only word you gotta know to get along in New York: 'lawyer.' "

"Why am I not surprised?" Donovan said. "So what's so important you have to pick me up personally?"

"Frankie Rigili, Ciccia's arm-breaker. He's in Sheepshead Bay."

Donovan consulted his watch. It was seven in the morning. "What's that to me?"

"Rigili bought the ranch and then went swimming," Jefferson said. "Some guy on a party fishing boat outta Sheepshead Bay hooked him while tryin' to land a flounder. The bum thought he had a fuckin' shark on the line."

"Where'd they find him?" Donovan asked, tucking in his shirt and pulling on his sports jacket.

"Off Breezy Point in the Rockaways. The body's on ice at the dock."

"The nerve of the bum to deposit his corpse off an Irish neighborhood! So, tell me why I have to go out to Sheepshead Bay just to look at the remains of Frankie Rigili?"

"The Mex says you won't fuckin' believe it."

## "I DON'T FUCKIN' BELIEVE IT," DONOVAN SAID

"I told you this was a weird one," said the Mex. He was the Medical Examiner, had seen a lot of strange doings in his time, so when he said that he had a hot one on his hands Donovan tended to listen.

"The slug is a *what?*"

"Beats me, Lieutenant. It looks like a .45, but it could be a .44. In any case, it's like nothing I've ever seen."

"You've seen every bullet ever made," Donovan said, handing back the plastic evidence bag containing the slug.

"I thought I had. But this one . . . I'm gonna run a lotta tests on it. For one thing, it looks old."

"Old? You mean like ten years?"

"I mean like a hundred years. The lead looks too soft to have been poured in this century. I can't be sure until I run the tests. And these tests are gonna set the lab back a couple thousand bucks. You got any spare change in your budget, Lieutenant?"

"I'll put a check in the mail. How long has this jerk been in the water?"

"*That's* easier to tell. Rigili was shot to death between seven and nine o'clock last night."

"Where? Never mind, I can figure it out. Pancho?"

"Yeah, Lieutenant?"

"There's a bait-and-tackle shop a block down Emmons Avenue. Go and get me this week's issue of *Long Island Fisherman* and a copy of the latest NOAA chart of New York Harbor. That way I can figure out the tides and work back to where Rigili was shot and dumped in the drink."

"Noah as in the Ark?" Jefferson asked.

"NOAA as in the National Oceanic and Atmospheric Administration. Don't you know *anything?*"

"I don't go fishing. Fish smell. Besides, we already know where he was shot—at the Bridge Café. He was dining with a fine-looking lady when somebody nailed him. Everybody was too busy ducking to spot the perp, but it may have been Rigili's date. She disappeared."

"She must not have liked his cologne. Get me the stuff I asked for anyway," Donovan said.

He turned his attention back to the body and to the Mex. "What the hell's going on?" he asked. "I can see Rigili getting shot. He wasn't exactly the best-liked kid on the block. Buy why *now*, and why with this weird bullet you're telling me about?"

"There's more," the Mex said. "Look closely around the entrance wound."

Donovan pulled the body bag open far enough to see the hole in Rigili's torso. Both skin and clothing were covered with a dusting of fine powder.

"Power burns. So he was shot from close up."

"That's not an ordinary powder burn," the Mex said. "That's *black* powder."

"Black powder! Aside from gun hobbyists, nobody's used black powder since the Civil War!"

"Bingo," said the Mex.

"What pro hit man would take out his target with black powder and a hundred-year-old bullet?"

"You're the detective. I just pick up the pieces and do the best I can to figure out how they got that way. And I got one hell of a puzzle this time."

## VINYL SLIPCOVERS, BLEEDING HEARTS, AND A PICTURE OF THE POPE

"That's about all we found, Lieutenant," Jefferson said.

"Nothing to link the bum with Ciccia?"

"The guy lived in Queens. He had a Queens house. There was

pictures of these hearts with blood drippin' off 'em on every wall. The sacred heart of Jesus or something.''

Donovan smiled. ''That's why they need the vinyl slipcovers. To keep the blood from spoiling the living room sets.''

''I guess you have to have been raised Catholic to understand,'' Jefferson allowed.

''It sure do help. You went through the whole place and didn't come up with *anything?''*

''An address book. We're checking out the names, but at first glance I don't see anything useful.''

''Ciccia's men must be better trained than I thought. What was the guy's name?''

''Dominic Palucci,'' Jefferson said, reading from his ubiquitous clipboard, ''Age forty-seven, wife, two kids, occupation listed as carpenter.''

''He could have made his own casket and saved his widow some money,'' Donovan said.

''Palucci was arrested six times, Lieutenant. Three for armed robbery. Two for assault with a deadly weapon. One suspected homicide.''

''What happened to the homicide?''

''It was plea-bargained down to manslaughter. Palucci was sentenced to three years at Attica. He served a year and a half. The guy got out on good behavior two years ago. Until Corrigan blew his brains out in the garage yesterday, Palucci kept clean.''

''What about Tan Slacks?''

Jefferson flipped over a page. ''His name is Peter Bono, single, age thirty-four. Lives in a new building on Third Avenue in the sixties.''

''Expensive territory.''

''We're getting a warrant for his place. It should be here pretty soon. Bono was a real nice guy, too. He was picked up twice for assault, once on a gambling beef, and once on suspected homicide.''

''And?''

''The witness to the homicide failed to show up in court. She's still missing.''

''Fish food,'' Donovan said.

''Yeah, probably halfway to Bermuda by now,'' Jefferson said. ''Anyway, Bono listed his occupation as construction foreman.''

''How's he doing in Bellevue?''

''He'll live, like I said, but don't waste your time talking to him. He still only knows one word.''

''At least we've got his place to go over. Do we have a watch on the door?''

''Two guys are sitting there waiting for the warrant. You still have time for breakfast, or to get cleaned up.''

''What do you mean 'cleaned up'?''

''You forgot to shave this morning.''

Donovan rubbed his lip. ''I'm thinking about growing a mustache,'' he said.

''No kiddin'? You'd look good with a little brush under your nose. When did you get this idea?''

''Twelve years ago. I had one then.''

''I didn't know that.''

''You were in diapers at the time.''

''I was twenty years old,'' Jefferson protested.

''As I said.''

''Okay, okay.''

''What about the car?'' Donovan asked. ''Did we find anything in that Olds, other than bits and pieces of Palucci?''

''Nothing relevant, unless you consider the daily papers with the day's line on the Mets and Yanks underlined.''

Donovan shook his head. ''What about the MACs?''

''They're down at Ballistics. The guys are using X-ray spectroscopy to bring up the serial numbers, but I wouldn't hold my breath. Ciccia runs a pro shop . . . you got to give him credit.''

''What I got to give him,'' Donovan said, ''is early retirement.''

## WHERE FIVE THOUSAND YEARS OF CIVILIZATION HAD BROUGHT US

"All my tenants are good people," said the rather agitated janitor. "Hard-working, professional people. Who else could afford two thousand dollars for a one-bedroom apartment?"

Donovan pressed a fingertip to his temple and thought out loud: "Drug dealers, pimps, rock stars, and guys who sell machine guns to teen-age kids."

The janitor nearly dropped his ring of keys.

"You aren't saying that Mr. Bono was one of those guys in the paper this morning? I didn't read the while story, but . . ."

"Read the whole story."

"Jesus . . . I never thought . . ."

"If you're not gonna open the door, give me the key," Donovan said.

He slipped it soundlessly into the lock. The long hallway of the high-rise, carpeted in blue-gray, muffled slight sounds.

Donovan asked Jefferson, "You think there's anyone there?"

"Maybe a broad, no more."

"How good do you feel about this perception?"

"Pretty good," Jefferson said. "I'll take the low position."

"Cute," Donovan replied. The low position, with the officer crouched as the door was flung open, was the safest.

Donovan drew his .44 magnum and turned the key in the lock. The janitor was way down the hall, ready to duck into the elevator. Donovan shoved the door quietly open. "On three," he said, and counted.

As one, Donovan high and Jefferson low, they swung into the apartment, to be met only with silence. The place was devoid of life. Moving from living room to kitchenette to bathroom to bedroom, Donovan and Jefferson secured the apartment. The forensics team was already on its way to the site.

Donovan sat on the white corduroy couch and surveyed all he saw. Most of what he saw was white, with the exception of stainless steel floor lamps that curved out in long arcs and illuminated this-or-that white chair, white table, or white footstool.

"Signor Bono must be in his white period," Donovan said.

There were two exceptions in the living room: a framed poster advertising a Frank Sinatra appearance at Carnegie Hall, and a neon wall sculpture that, when switched on, glowed pale blue. It was shaped like a spray of cattails, and measured five feet from top to bottom.

"Tasteful," Donovan said.

"Eminently. Come and have a gander at the boudoir."

Bono's bedroom was little more than bed, a king-sized monster that quivered when Donovan sat on it.

"Another lover of aquatic life," Donovan said. "Rigili and he must have been related."

"Pure fuckin' H-two-O," Jefferson said. "If you press that red button over by the right you can make waves in it."

"Son, the day I need a button to make waves in bed I'm gonna hang up my spurs."

Jefferson lifted the cover of a large Lucite box that gave the impression of being a dresser without drawers. It was, like nearly everything else, white. When he did so, motors whirred, gears churned, the front slid open, and, from the top, a five-foot TV screen emerged.

"Well, looky here," Jefferson said, "the man likes to watch the box from the bed. I wonder how his taste in home movies runs."

Donovan slid off the edge of the bed and onto the thick, white carpet. Below the videotape machine was a long row of cassettes.

"Did you notice any *books* in this place?" he asked.

"There's a copy of *Hustler* in the throne room."

"What a surprise. Well, let's see where five thousand years of civilization has brought us." Donovan ran a finger along the row of taped movies. "*Debbie Does Dallas.* Off to a flying start. *Deep Throat,* a classic."

"Absolutely," Jefferson said.

"*The Devil in Miss Jones,* another classic. The boy's got taste. *Wayne Newton in Concert.* So he's a music buff, too. *A Tribute to Frank Sinatra.* What else? *Rocky, Rocky II,* and *Rocky III.* Come on, where the hell is *Rocky IV?*"

"It's not out in cassette yet, Bill."

"Glad to know you're on top of these things. Why don't you sit on the water bed and make waves?"

Jefferson chuckled and resumed his search of the apartment.

"*The Magnificent Seven, The Dirty Dozen,* and . . .*The last eight Super Bowl games!* Well, awright!" Donovan got up off the floor and brushed the lint from his pants.

"That's it?" Jefferson called, from inside the walk-in closet.

"No. There's plenty more. A couple of *Rambos* and three Chuck Norris movies."

"No *Dirty Harry?*"

"Bono doesn't have that much class. And while we're on the subject, what's in the closet?"

"A whole lotta polyester and leather," Jefferson replied, emerging from the closet. "This guy must have the same tailor as Mr. T."

"Hold on, Mr. T is one of the three black guys I'd have to my place for dinner."

"Not that he'd be fool enough to go there. Hey, wait a second! Assuming I'm one of the black guys and he's another, who's the third? No, don't tell me . . ."

Donovan looked away.

"Aw, come on, Bill . . . I warned you. If I get the slightest hint that you plan to hook up with *Sergeant* Barnes again, I'm gonna lock you in the basement and keep you there till the howlin' stops."

"She's an old friend, no more."

"Where have I heard that before? Christ, I don't even want to think of it. Come on, there's nothing here that we can find. Forensics has to scan the joint before our guys can peek in the corners."

"That's some TV," Donovan said.

"We'll get one for the office tomorrow."

"Can you imagine what *Raiders of the Lost Ark* would look like on that thing?"

"Lieutenant . . ."

# Four

Andrea Jones didn't take much time making herself up. In the dressing room of her suite at the Plaza, she slipped on a lime-green running outfit: nylon shorts and matching top, with eighty-dollar running shoes and a small, lightweight backpack that was designed to hold running gear and other supplies.

She looked at herself in the mirror. She wore no makeup, and her hair, held in place by a headband that bore the markings of the Boston Marathon, was not its natural auburn but light blond and pulled back into a ponytail. Her eyes, not the vivid blue that was natural to her, were muted gray, the result of tinted contact lenses. Jones covered her hair with a light scarf and her eyes with dark glasses and left the suite.

As she walked through the hotel lobby, she could sense the male eyes on her. The bell captain even got in a word: "It's a good night for a little run, Miss Jones."

"I think so," she replied.

"Going around the park, are you?"

"Twice tonight, if it doesn't get too cold."

"You be sure to stay with a group, now. There are some parts of Central Park where a young woman like yourself doesn't want to be alone."

"I'll be all right," she said, and walked out onto Fifth Avenue.

She crossed the street and went up to the low granite wall to do her stretches. After five minutes spent playing the part of a serious runner, she went into Central Park, but instead of heading north along the joggers' and cyclists' line, she turned west and jogged straight across the south end of the park.

When she reached Columbus Circle, she slowed to a walk, and, not even breathing hard, walked through the circus that confronted commuters at that corner of the park. On the park side, a reggae band was raising a ruckus, while in front of the Coliseum across the way, a mime was attempting Marcel Marceau's man-trapped-in-an-invisible-box routine. On the corner of Eighth Avenue and Central Park South, a bearded young man with a portable electric guitar was singing "The Night They Drove Old Dixie Down."

She shook the scarf from her head and put it and the dark glasses in the backpack. Jones walked casually west along Fifty-eighth Street until she reached the rundown hotel that had been her true headquarters since coming to New York. The desk clerk, who was also the owner, was an elderly black man who had seen it all and understood the value of money, a great deal of which he had gotten from Andrea Jones.

He got up from behind his creaking old cashier's desk at the sight of her. "Hi, miss," he said.

"Any messages?"

"Just one. Here it is." He handed over the slip of paper.

"Been out joggin'?"

She gave him a naughty-child look. "Now, what is our arrangement?"

He quickly said, "I don't see nothin', I don't know nothin'."

Jones gave the man a fifty-dollar bill. "Silence is golden," she said.

"You can count on me," the old man said, pocketing the bill.

"That's good," she said. "I'm going up to my room. I don't want to be disturbed."

The woman could have been any of the bag ladies who made their homes in the nooks and crannies of the side streets, and their money by poking tireless fingers into the coin returns of phone booths in search of forgotten change. She could have been thirty or sixty; the dirty face hid sallow-looking skin that appeared to be stained with the remnants of donuts and pizza crust pulled from garbage cans. A torn old trenchcoat several sizes too big hid whatever shirt she might be wearing, but from beneath the coat emerged woolen pants too hot for Memorial Day weekend.

She limped north up Broadway, stopping at each garbage pile and phone booth. In the trash heaped curbside in front of a fruit stand, the woman found two apples and an orange that were too spoiled to sell, and put them in her pockets. The old pillowcase that served as a carry all weighed heavily on her shoulders. She stopped in front of a liquor store, let down the bag, and fumbled through pockets for money. She came up with three dollar bills and some quarters and dimes. With a smile, the bag lady bought a half-pint of Jack Daniels before resuming the slow trek uptown.

It was just past eight in the evening when she came to a halt in front of Riley's. She set down the bag, then peered in the saloon's big front window. A ball game was just getting under way on TV. The woman had a clear view of it from the sidewalk. She dragged her old pillowcase over to the curb, sat down, and leaned against the side of a car—Donovan's car. She took a bite of apple and washed it down with a slug of whiskey. Robert Merrill was singing the national anthem, and the America flag was flapping in a fresh spring breeze.

Gus Keane nudged Donovan, and, hooking a thumb in the direction of the bag lady outside, said, "One of your relatives has come to call."

Donovan swiveled away from his coffee and corned beef sandwich long enough to catch a glimpse of the person outside. The woman had put aside her supper and was spit-polishing her belt buckle, using an old rag. Donovan smiled and turned back to his meal and the ball game.

Traffic was light. A white Cadillac cruised slowly by, then made a right-hand turn onto Eighty-sixth, circling the block. Another Cadillac, this one black, double-parked alongside Donovan's car.

Ciccia, with the help of his driver, squeezed out of the back seat. "Here he comes," Gus said.

"I got the parking ticket ready," Donovan said. "It's been a long time since I gave one out."

Donovan didn't bother to look at Ciccia, but the bag lady did. As soon as the car door closed, Andrea Jones slipped her hand into the bag and cocked the trigger on a very old and special gun.

Ciccia lumbered onto and across the sidewalk, his driver looking nervously from side to side but staying by the car. Jones raised the pistol and aimed it at Ciccia's huge frame. He pushed open the door to Riley's, and in that instant Jones pulled the trigger three times, firing through the bag. Three slugs tore into Ciccia's body, hurling it through the swinging doors and slamming it against the pinball machine. The roar of the pistol echoed up and down Broadway.

Ciccia hit the machine and slumped over it for a few seconds, then rolled onto the floor. His chest was nearly ripped open, and blood dripped from the pinball machine onto his face.

"Jesus Christ!" Donovan said, pulling his revolver. Nakima and the other customers huddled behind their barstools. Keane stood tall, having seen a lot worse in Southeast Asia.

Donovan leaped to a position alongside the door, his magnum held in front of him with its barrel upright. He looked a bit like a priest carrying a crucifix. "Call my office," he snapped.

Keane hefted the big wrench that George used to intimidate troublesome customers and gave three stout whacks to the water pipe that ran up from the basement, through Riley's, and to the johns in the West Side Major Crimes Unit.

Within seconds, footfalls could be heard coming down the stairs. Donovan swung through the door and out onto the sidewalk. A woman shopper let out a yelp at the sign of Donovan's gun. Policemen, led by Jefferson, poured onto the pavement.

"What's the matter?" Jefferson asked.

"Somebody shot Ciccia. Look in the bar."

Jefferson ducked into the bar, then back out. He barked orders, and men moved into Riley's to seal off the crime scene.

Donovan ran to his car and ducked behind it, looking for a sniper in one of the buildings across the street. Following his lead, Jefferson had men fan out from Eighty-sixth to Eighty-ninth streets, scouring the building tops.

Andrea Jones was gone. The second she rounded the corner onto West End Avenue she found a dark spot beneath the steps leading up to a brownstone. She shed her bag-lady clothes, beneath which was her jogging outfit. Jones stuffed the costume into a trash can. She used a Handi-Wipe to rid her face of the makeup that made her look like a veteran of the streets and trash bins of the West Side. Soon she was back on the pavement.

Within two minutes of having taken a life, Andrea Jones was just another well-off and attractive young woman jogging down a West Side avenue.

Donovan grabbed Ciccia's driver, who was frozen in place beside the black limousine. "You! You see anything?"

The man shook his head.

"Come on, you bastard! You must have seen something!"

"I swear, Lieutenant. I didn't see nothin'. And I was looking up and down the block. All I saw was the boss gettin' hit and then a lot of people running."

"Against the car, asshole. Bonaci!"

"Yo, Lieutenant," the detective replied.

"Check this guy out, then take him upstairs and hold him."

Bonaci nodded. "Okay, scumbag, assume the position."

"Check out the car, too. And put this on the windshield." He handed over the already filled-out parking ticket.

"Sure thing."

Donovan called in help from the Twenty-fourth, and for the rest of the evening policemen stopped passersby, questioned shopkeepers, and inspected rooftops. Nothing was revealed. Three television crews arrived, but all were denied access to the area surrounding Riley's and the Unit.

Donovan was furious. Not only was his prime target killed before he got the chance to send the man up the river, it happened in Donovan's favorite watering hole while he was in it, eating a corned beef sandwich. He refused to give interviews, perferring to write up a one-paragraph statement that Jefferson Xeroxed and handed out to the press. It went on about plans to continue the investigation into Ciccia's operation despite the sudden departure of Ciccia. Donovan wouldn't speculate on who might have done it. In fact, he didn't have a clue.

## THE CASE OF THE KILLER BAG LADY

"She was only a hobo," Donovan said, "or so she made it look."

Jefferson began taking notes.

"She limped up a few minutes before Ciccia arrived. There was something wrong with the right leg, though I'm sure she was faking it. She looked in Riley's, figured out she could see the TV from the curb, and sat down to have a few jolts of hootch and an apple."

Donovan bent to look in the gutter beneath his car. "That apple," he said, pointing at it. "Have it put in an evidence bag and taken downtown."

"Prints?"

"Everything. Prints, saliva, blood type, genotype. Everything the whiz kids from Silicon Valley can think of."

"You got it."

"The way I make it, our hobo friend waited for Ciccia to arrive, then fired from the hip through a pillowcase she was using to carry her junk in. That's why nobody saw a gun. And that's why the angle of penetration was below the horizontal—she fired from a sitting position."

"Are you saying that you saw this woman?"

"Yeah, I saw her. So did Gus. We'll work up a description. And, since she got away so fast, I have to assume that she dumped the bag-lady duds someplace nearby. Have every corner and every garbage can gone through for five blocks in each direction.

Donovan gave Jefferson the description of the woman, then told him to get Gus's. Finally, Keane and Donovan sat down with a police artist to make a composite drawing of the suspected killer. The result was pretty much what Donovan expected: a white woman who looked thirty going on sixty, but given the probability that she was a hit lady, the younger age was more likely.

Donovan rummaged through his brain. Was the bum really the killer? If so, she was probably a professional. Why would a professional killer use such an extraordinary disguise just to bump off a mid-level West Side hood? The old sawed-off in the hallway was usually good enough. Then, Ciccia had pretty good security, which would require something fairly original to get at him.

And there was the white limo that Donovan had seen circling the block. Maybe the shots came from it. He pondered these things until Jefferson stuck his head in the door to Donovan's office.

"Go home, boss," he said. "it's been a long day."

"Have the composite drawing reproduced and shown to every shopkeeper from Seventy-second to 110th, Broadway and Amsterdam."

"Sure thing. Tomorrow. Go home."

Donovan turned off his desk lamp, pulled on his jacket, and turned the helm of the West Side Major Crimes Unit over to the nightwatch officer. "Buy you a beer?" Donovan asked as Jefferson followed him down the stairs.

"After today, why not?"

An officer guarded the door to Riley's. The television crews were gone, but a small crowd lingered outside the police barricades. Most were Riley's regulars. Keane sat on the stool by the front end of the bar, sipping a beer and working on a crossword puzzle.

Jefferson said, "Okay, everybody, it's Miller Time."

"Not here it isn't, " Gus said. "The cops closed the place for the night. I'm just standing guard."

"The cops just re-opened it," Donovan said.

"You mean I can let my customers in?"

"No. Just Pancho and me. We'll have two Blatz."

"I can't do that, Bill. Look at them out there. They're like a pack of hungry wolves. There's only six or seven now, but they're growing by the minute. Soon there will be a few dozen. It'll be like the storming of the Bastille."

"Two Blatz."

"If they think that you two have got a private party going, it's going to get really ugly out there."

"Okay," Donovan said, "we can have a party in the park."

"Can we do that?" Gus asked.

"As long as this is my neck of the woods, we can."

Gus looked happy for the first time since a leg collapsed on Donovan's barstool, sending the lieutenant head over heels into the peanut machine.

"Do you remember that time . . . I think it was ten or fifteen years ago . . . that we had forty people by the Soldiers' and Sailors' Monument after closing time?"

"Bill, public drinking is illegal now."

"I just rewrote the law. If the 'Ricans can have picnics at Riverside and 108th, and the blacks can have barbecues at Riverside and 119th, I can throw a party by the monument."

"I'll get some cases of Blatz," Gus said.

"I'll go chase off the winos," Jefferson said.

Donovan beamed. "It will be just like old times on the West Side. Remember? . . . Guys used to come from as far north as the West End, Balcony, and the Marlin."

Gus went off toward the back room, singing "Those Were the Days."

## THE ADVENTURES OF CAPTAIN COOK

"Three hundred and fifty bucks should do it," Gus said.

Donovan looked over at his friend. "What?"

"That's what you owe me."

"What do I owe you money for?"

"Three hundred for the pinball machine. In case you hadn't noticed, Ciccia bled to death all over it."

"So what? You were getting rid of the thing anyway."

"I was trading it in. I think the vending machine company will frown on the machine's new condition."

"Buy a bottle of Lestoil and clean it up," Donovan said. "What about the other fifty bucks?"

"Forty to replace the two panes of glass from the door. Ten for beer. *That* I'll split with you."

"How generous."

"Look, I'm not the only one who lost money on account of you."

Irving Nakima chimed in, saying, "Yeah, I finally picked a winner and Ciccia got bumped off before he could pay me. I been trying to pick a winner since the end of the war."

Donovan was irked. His friends were blaming him for a murder that had been his profound embarrassment to watch.

"Fuck you all," he muttered.

"Not to mention lost business," Gus said. "Let me have that paper back. I want to tack on a couple hundred bucks."

The party had swollen from six or seven Riley's customers to eighteen or nineteen within an hour. The odd patrol car that wandered by was shooed off by Donovan's men. He watched the trees of Riverside Park shake in the gentle wind blowing off the Hudson. He wanted to think of open skies and blue seas.

Gus sat back down next to Donovan and Jefferson and handed the former the revised casualty figures for the evening.

"Seven hundred bucks?" Donovan asked.

"We lost a lot of business while Ciccia was being hauled away. It took two hours, six guys, and a tow truck to get him to the morgue wagon."

Donovan gave the paper to Jefferson. "File this," Donovan said.

Jefferson crumpled the paper and tried a snappy foul shot at the trash can. He missed.

"You're never gonna make the Celtics shootin' like that," Donovan said.

"Not every black guy can play basketball, Lieutenant," Jefferson replied. "*You're* better than I am."

"Shooting baskets is my therapy," Donovan explained.

"Mine is reading," Gus said.

"I thought it was time-travel," Jefferson said.

"What sort of stuff?"

"Nonfiction, mostly. History . . . I like history. I just bought this book called *Great Explorations of the World* from the guy who sells used books in front of Zabar's."

"I know him well. I've picked up a few bargains there myself."

Keane went on: "It's fascinating how adventurers like Captain Cook navigated hundreds of years ago. They followed the trade winds. It's so simple. You can zig-zag all around the world just by following the trade winds."

Donovan nodded. "That's why they're called the 'trade winds.' Commerce naturally followed the exploration routes."

"Do I get any credits for taking this course?" Jefferson asked.

"No, but you can get me another beer."

Donovan crumpled his can and hit the trash basket with a perfect sky-hook.

While getting the beer, Jefferson said, "See, I told you that you're part brother. There's a little bit of Afro blood in your veins, Lieutenant."

"Nope. I'm pure WASLC." He pronounced it "waselk."

"What's that mean?" Gus asked.

"White Anglo-Saxon Lapsed Catholic," Jefferson translated.

"There's a lot of you guys around," Gus said.

"It has its advantages. You can sleep late on Sunday, and Jewish girls find you irresistible."

"Really?" Gus asked.

"Yeah, you know that chick in Central Records . . . the one from the Bronx who's had the hots for you for ten years now," Jefferson said. "How come you never followed up on that?"

"Who says I haven't?" Donovan said smugly.

"I know everything you do."

"Wrong. You know what I want you to know. And she's not from the Bronx. She's from Riverdale."

"That's in the Bronx."

Donovan replied, "Riverdale is in the Bronx like Columbus Avenue is in the real world."

A thirtyish couple, dressed very well, crossed Broadway on their way from an expensive Thai restaurant to their condo on Riverside.

"I don't understand the gentrification of the West Side," Donovan said.

"Trade routes," Gus chimed in. "Just like Captain Cook."

"What?"

"These are all baby-boomers who grew up in the rich suburbs like Riverdale and Westchester. They came to Manhattan twenty years ago, made their money, and now as they enter middle age are working their way back to their ancestral homelands."

"I never thought of Riverdale as an ancestral homeland," Donovan said.

"It is to them. You see, the West Side is a natural migration route from the traditionally wealthy parts of Manhattan to Riverdale and Westchester. Think of Persia.''

''You guys are losing me,'' Jefferson said.

''So drop the course,'' Donovan snapped. ''You mean that the Persians . . .''

''. . . being on a natural migration route to and from the Holy Land and the Far East, were trampled on every hundred years or so by one or another army of zealots that had set out on a mission handed them by God. That's why the Persians—I should say the Iranians—are so insular and paranoid,'' Gus concluded.

''Interesting,'' Donovan said. ''In other words, the West side, like Persia, is a natural migration route.''

''And you're the Ayatollah,'' Jefferson said, finally able to get a word in.

''The Ayatollah can have snotty subordinates shot at dawn,'' Donovan said.

It was then that the limousine pulled up. It was a gray rental job, and stopped right by the monument. A uniformed driver opened the back door. Donovan beamed when Sergeant Marcia Barnes stepped out, looking elegant even in a blue workshirt and fading cutoff jeans.

Jefferson moaned, ''Not again,'' and buried his face in his hands.

Marcie walked over, put a foot up on the concrete barricade, and smiled. ''Donovan, you're reached your level at last—unshaven and drinking beer on a park bench in the middle of the night.''

He called, ''Hiya, kid! What brings you over to the wrong side of the tracks?''

Donovan nearly flew across the pavement, past the ancient cannons and the memorials to Farragut and Sherman, brushing aside Nakima, to embrace Marcie. Many envious eyes followed Donovan. With the exception of Nakima and Jefferson, none of the Riley's regulars had ever set eyes on the legendary black beauty out of Donovan's past. Some of them had even come to believe he had made her up.

"I came to get you," she said. "I need some help, and your nightwatch man said you were down here."

Donovan wasn't listening. He framed her face between his hands and looked at her. Her cocoa skin gleamed like polished bronze in the lights of the tall, columned monument. Her hair, normally straight and long, was curly and just touched her shoulders. It made her look a bit like the girl in *Flashdance,* a movie that Donovan caught on cable a few weeks earlier, only a lot more classy.

"What did you do to your hair?" he asked. "I think it looks great." He took her hands and stepped back to survey all of her. "I think *you* look great."

"You're not so bad yourself, Donovan. I was afraid you'd have a pot belly and gray hair by now."

"I work out nearly every day. I still shoot baskets on Sundays."

Marcie looked around the party, and saw only men. "Where's Rosie? Do you think she'd let me borrow you for an hour or two?"

"She's history . . . six months now," Donovan said, "and you don't need permission to borrow me. What's up?"

"I'm moving."

"To the West Side? But you're not from Riverdale."

"Croton-on-Hudson is in Westchester," Jefferson shouted.

She looked at Jefferson. "I see you've still got *that* millstone around your neck. Donovan, I don't know what Westchester has to do with it, but if it makes you feel any better I'm only moving to the Seventy-ninth Street Boat Basin, and only for the summer. I rented a boat. I'm going to sit on it evenings and weekends and pretend I'm at Marthia's Vineyard."

"A rich girl's vacation on a sergeant's pay," Donovan said, "not bad thinking."

"Wait until you see the boat. It's sensational."

"The limo isn't a bad touch, either."

"I know it's expensive, but you don't think *I'd* trust *my* wardrobe to some guy's moving van, do you? Especially since you can be counted on to handle my clothes with care.''

''Let me bid farewell to these clowns and I'll be right with you.''

Before Donovan could address the clowns, he heard the clinking of handcuffs. Jefferson dangled a pair in front of Donovan's eyes.

''Down in Riley's basement, fool,'' Jefferson snarled.

''What?''

''I *told* you that if you went anywhere near her I was gonna lock you in the basement and keep you there till the howlin' stops. These cuffs will fit around one of the steam pipes real nice.''

Marcie nodded at Jefferson and asked, ''What's with him?''

''Food poisoning,'' Donovan said. ''He had some bad ribs for dinner and has been like this all night.''

''Yeah, yeah. Let's go. It's for your own good.''

Donovan pushed Jefferson's hand, and with it the cuffs, to one side. ''I'm just gonna help her move some clothes onto her boat.''

''Sure. If I could put lyrics to that tune, I'd sell more records than Michael Jackson.''

Donovan said, ''Let these guys hang around the monument for another hour or so, then send 'em home. Make sure Riley's is locked and guarded all night.''

''Bill . . .'' Jefferson pleaded.

''Clothes,'' Donovan said softly, ''boat.''

''Bull . . . shit,'' Jefferson replied.

''I'm going now,'' Donovan said. He put an arm around Marcie's waist and walked her to the waiting limousine. A chorus of whistles followed them.

''I'm not gonna pick up the pieces this time!'' Jefferson yelled.

# FIVE

Even past midnight, Donovan could tell that she was quite a boat. The *West Wind* was forty-two-foot wooden ketch, traditional in styling, with a bowsprit extending a sharply defined bow, and teak decks that, while carefully tended, had just the right amount of wear in them. She was a racing boat once, and probably had had quite a few Newport-to-Bermuda races, if not multiple circumnavigations of the globe as Marcie insisted. Now she was in retirement, berthed in the third slip from the end of marina's southernmost pier.

Carrying the boxes of clothes all the way from the parking lot took an hour, and getting them stacked in the main saloon nearly as long. Marcie stayed below, trying to figure out where to put her considerable wardrobe.

Donovan grasped the wooden wheel and closed his eyes. He was Jack London in the Solomons, Lord Nelson at Trafalgar, Ted Turner winning back the America's Cup.

"Ready about," he snapped to his imaginary crew, "hard a'lee!"

Marcie's head appeared in the companionway door. "*What* are you doing?" she asked.

"Don't interrupt me. I'm in the middle of a hot tacking duel with Dennis Conner."

"Who?"

"The guy who lost the America's Cup in '83."

"Donovan, have you ever heard of the Peter Pan syndrome?"

"Go forward and check the set of the jib, would you?"

"Donovan!"

He took his hands off the wheel and opened his eyes. A party was raging on a boat across the marina.

"Come downstairs," she said.

"It's called 'going below,' " he replied, and went below.

Marcie handed him a glass and filled it with champagne. She offered a toast: "To a quiet and restful summer."

They clinked their glasses together and drank.

"To the restless sea," he said, in a toast of his own.

She winced. "I should have let Jefferson lock you in the basement after all."

Donovan waxed haughty: "Do you recall exactly when it was that you lost your sense of humor?"

Marcie's shoulders slumped and she set her glass down on the chart table. She hugged him, nestling her head against his neck. "I'm sorry. I must be more tired than I thought. I've been at this all day."

"You're forgiven," he said; "let's sit down."

He led her to an L-shaped couch that was built into the port side of the main saloon. Donovan sat, put his feet up on an oak coffee table that opened to form a dining table, and encouraged her to wrap herself around him. That she did, again resting her head between his neck and shoulder. They were silent long enough for Donovan to begin noticing the lapping of the water against the hull and gentle creaking of the timbers.

He absorbed the warm tones of the teak, mahogany, and varnished oak, while listening to the song of the wooden hull. "No wonder they call ships 'her,' " he said; to himself, he thought.

"What?" Marcie asked quietly.

"You were right. She *is* sensational."

"I'm sorry about what I said up on deck. Please don't ever grow up on me."

Donovant smiled and squeezed her hand.

"Promise?"

"Okay."

She kissed him on the cheek, then sat up and reclaimed her champagne. "You haven't called me in a year."

"Come on, we had lunch on your birthday."

"My birthday is in July. That was almost a year ago."

"I've had a lot on my mind," he said.

"Especially of late. You really made a splash on the eleven o'clock news. Were you really eating a pastrami sandwich when Ciccia bought the ranch?"

"It was corned beef," Donovan replied testily, "and I don't want to talk about it."

She laughed. "Donovan, you *do* have a way of getting your name in the papers. If I weren't so tired, I'd run up to the corner and get an early edition of the *Times.*"

"Thanks anyway."

"Who do you think did it?"

"I don't know, and I don't want to know . . . at least not until morning."

She draped her arm across the back of the couch and played idly with Donovan's hair. "What *can* we talk about? How's your love life?"

"Nothing worth writing home about. What about you?"

"The same," she admitted. "Like you, I've been too busy."

He smiled and set down his glass. Quite instinctively, she did the same. "Now *that,*" he said, "is something we can talk about."

"Start talking," she said, and let her lips part slowly, inviting him. He touched them gently with his, teasing, tantalizing, remembering how good it was.

She licked a corner of his mouth, and he pressed his lips against hers. They kissed until they were breathless, and he pulled back.

''Donovan . . .'' she said, her voice deep and dark.

He took the front of her skirt and ripped it open. Buttons flew around the compartment. Then Donovan took one of her breasts and gently wrappped his lips around the nipple.

She sucked in her breath and pulled him against her, kissing the top of his head, and, finally, just leaning back and whispering his name over and over.

Donovan picked her up and carried her into the main cabin.

## "CAPTAIN BLIGH IS IN THE SHOWER," SHE SAID

Donovan opened his eyes to see Marcie's face. It was longer than he could remember that such had happened. She was fully dressed, made up, and wearing a linen suit.

''Coffee, sailor?'' she asked, handing him a mug.

''What time is it?'' he asked, sitting up in the cabin's large bed.

''Seven-thirty. How was your sleep?''

''The best in years. And yours?''

''The same. You were wonderful last night.''

''Thanks. Your contribution was likewise notable.'' He sipped the coffee, and then nodded appreciatively. ''Mountain grown.''

''Only the best is served on my yacht.''

She extended a slender finger and idly poked Donovan's pectoral muscles. ''Looking good,'' she said. ''I forgot to mention it last night. I was kind of busy.''

Donovan said, ''I've been pumping a little iron lately. I'm told that it's a phase men go through when they're pushing forty.''

She laughed. ''God, I forgot that you're going over the hill in two months.''

Donovan said nothing, but continued to sip his coffee.

''Well?'' she asked.

''Well what?''

"No outburst of outrage? No yelling and screaming?"

"Forty is just another birthday."

"I can recall you being rather touchy on the subject of turning forty when you were thirty-eight."

"It seemed a whole lot more important then," he said. "Now I don't care. I feel healthy in mind and body. I am at ease with myself and the world,"

Marcie kissed him, and said, "That's great."

"And I'm gonna tell everyone I'm thirty-nine for as long as I can get away with it."

"Donovan! Christ, what am I going to do with you?"

"I was just kidding."

"No you weren't. Look, would you take some advice? Try creative lying. If you tell people you're thirty-nine, they'll know you're over forty. You can get away with saying that you're thirty-two, but don't. Eventually you'll slip up and mention your twenty years of service and blow the whole thing. Tell people that you're thirty-seven. People will believe that. You may even get compliments about how young you look."

He agreed: "Okay, I'll be thirty-seven forever. And you?"

"Thirty-two. I think I can get away with twenty-eight, but I don't want to push my luck either."

Donovan yawned. "You don't look bad for a thirty-two-year-old broad."

She stood and straightened her suit jacket. "There are bagels and cream cheese in the fridge. I have to go. I'm wrapping up a case today."

"You're dressed well today . . . not like a hooker."

"I'm not doing undercover vice anymore," Marcie said proudly. "I'm a buyer for a major department store chain."

"Are you now?"

"Yes, and I'm on the verge of buying nine miles of hot broadloom from Arnie the Carpet Maven. He's taking me to breakfast at a very expensive place."

"Where's the wire?" Donovan asked.

"In my bra."

"The first place I'd go for."

"It may be the first place *you'd* go for," she replied, "but Arnie the Carpet Maven is a leg man. I really have to leave. You can find your way around. I left a razor in the sink so you can shave." She leaned over and kissed him.

He finished his coffee and lowered his feet to the floor.

"See you tonight," she said, as she went up the companionway and into the daylight.

Donovan suspended his longtime dislike of being taken for granted. He *wanted* to see her that night, and many other nights as well. He thought of the fading snapshot in his desk drawer as he made his way into the shower.

Marcie stepped off the stern of the *West Wind* and walked briskly up the pier. Halfway to shore she encountered Thomas L. Jefferson, who stopped to talk and expected her to do the same. She brushed by, pretending that plucking a bit of lint from her lapel was more important than him.

"Captain Bligh is in the shower," she said.

"I don't want to hear it," Donovan said, and went back to humming the main theme from *Camelot*.

He hoped that the rush of the shower would drown out Jefferson's voice. Donovan was wrong.

"Man, I don't believe you. Every coupla years she comes around, just like that bad water deal in the Pacific that messes everything up."

"El Niño," Donovan replied. "It's called El Niño."

"Yeah, that thing. She comes along with some sweet talk and a soft bed and you hop right in."

"It's none of your damn business."

Donovan rinsed the suds from his hair and shut off the water.

"It's my business when you go runnin' off in the middle of the night with your allegedly black mama to sleep on some damn boat when we got a hot case goin'. I'm supposed to be able to find you when I need you.''

''You found me, didn't you? Hand me a towel, and knock off this 'allegedly black' crap.''

Jefferson handed him the towel. ''I've seen Jewish girls come back from the Bahamas darker than her.''

Donovan hid a smile in the towel. ''So one of her ancestors got friendly with the master.''

''One of her ancestors got friendly with the whole fuckin' Confederate Army,'' Jefferson snapped. He tossed Donovan a terry-cloth robe. ''Put this on. I don't wanna have to look at your ugly body.''

He went prowling around the boat while Donovan dried himself off.

Something was familiar about the robe. Donovan eyed it with vague recognition. He called out, ''Where'd you find this robe?''

''Hanging on the back of the door where she left it for you,'' Jefferson shot back. ''Have you lost your eyesight as well as your mind?''

Donovan searched the robe for the label, and read it. The label bore the name of a men's shop in the Long Island town where his aunt lived. She always gave him a robe or a pair of pajamas at Christmas. It had become something of a joke between them. That one robe must have been among the things he left in Marcie's apartment when they lived together. My God, he thought, she's kept this thing for twelve years.

Jefferson said, ''You know, this ain't a bad joint for a boat. Where's the TV?''

''It doesn't have one.'' Donovan had gone back into the master cabin and was getting dressed.

''How are you gonna exist without a TV?''

''There are other ways to spend an evening.''

''I can just imagine.''

''Besides, who says I'm staying here another night?'' Donovan asked.

Jefferson laughed. "Man, you got a self-destruct button ten miles wide. You'll be stayin' here tonight."

Donovan tied his tie, straightened it, then unbuttoned the collar. In all the years since he made detective and had to wear a suit and tie regularly, Donovan had to have *something* askew. Petty abuses of convention, like wearing socks that didn't match, leaving his collar unbuttoned, keeping a snapping turtle as a pet, or pretending he was sailing in the America's Cup races, nourished him. He daydreamed a lot, sometimes just for the hell of it, and sometimes for good purpose. Donovan had a good thought while in the shower.

"Timmins," he said, pulling on his jacket and joining Jefferson in the main saloon.

"What?"

"Willis Timmins. The numbers guy."

Donovan led the way up on deck and locked the companionway door.

"What about him?" Jefferson asked.

"Have you heard anything about him lately?"

"No. He seems pretty much the same as always. He doesn't cause much trouble. Every two months or so the precinct cops raid one of his places, just like they do Ciccia's couple of shops. With Timmins, the next day the place is open again. Numbers is relatively harmless, Bill, and Timmins isn't greedy."

"Does he or does he not drive a white Caddy?"

"He does not. The chauffeur drives it. He sits in the back with a broad."

"A white Caddy cruised by Riley's just before Ciccia was hit."

"There's a lot of white Cadillacs in this town," Jefferson said. "And I thought you were sure the killer was a bum with a bag."

"I'm sure it was," Donovan said. "Timmins could have been cruising by to watch it happen. God knows he hated Ciccia's guts."

"Enough to take on the Eye-talian boys?"

"Why not? There's a lot of money to be made in sports gambling, and Ciccia controlled it on the West Side."

"I don't know about this. I'm not sure Timmins has the muscle to start a war."

"Well, why don't we find out? While I'm downtown talking to the brass, you pull the file on Timmins. And get a couple of guys to ask around and see if he's been recruiting lately. Up until now Ciccia had all the sports action and a few numbers joints. Timmins had all the other numbers places, but no sports action. Maybe he's a little greedier than you think."

Jefferson nodded. "You get good thoughts when you're taking a shower."

Donovan stopped at the end of the dock, turned, and admired the *West Wind*. "You ought to try sleeping on a boat sometime," he said, "it's good for the soul."

## WALTER BURNS WOULD HAVE BEEN PROUD

Donovan stared at the tabloid newspapers laid out on his desk. "Ciccia would have to get blown away on a slow news day," he said. "There couldn't have been an earthquake or a revolution someplace?"

"That's the breaks," Jefferson replied.

"Couldn't Reagan have pulled a fast shuffle on some banana republic? I mean, what the hell is he *there* for? And I voted for him, too."

"You voted for Reagan?"

"You bet I did. There's no way that any man who even vaguely remembers the war is gonna vote for a guy named Fritz."

"I get the point. I got to admit, I voted for Reagan too."

Donovan picked up a copy of the *Post*. A headline screamed, "Top Cop Noshes While Mobster Knocked Off."

Donovan said, "It *does* have a certain poetic quality to it. And a kind of irony. The other two times I had a chance at page one—

two major arrests—the first one happened on the day Nixon resigned, and the second was when the Russians invaded Afghanistan. I ended up back on the page with the ads for porno theaters."

He laughed bitterly and picked up the *News*. " 'Cop's Meal a Real Blast.' I like that one better. It's punchy and to the point. Walter Burns would have been proud."

"Who's he?"

"Haven't you ever seen *The Front Page?*"

Jefferson hadn't.

"Stay up one night and watch it. But what I don't understand is where the pastrami sandwich came from. This is New York, for God's sake. If they can't tell the difference between pastrami and corned beef in New York, what hope is there for the world? What did the *Times* give me?"

"Three paragraphs buried in the second section," Jefferson said. "Your name wasn't mentioned. Your dinner either."

"A ray of sunshine," Donovan said. "At least somebody knows what's fit to print and what isn't." He tossed the papers into the garbage. "Is there any coffee around here?"

"In a minute. How'd it go with the brass?"

Donovan shrugged. "Nothing much to worry about. I gave them copies of my report. they offered sympathy and help if needed, and the commissioner asked if I wouldn't mind being in a candy store or luncheonette the next time somebody gets blown away before my eyes. Christ, I was only drinking coffee."

"Just be grateful we never had the fireman's pole put in," Jefferson said.

"Actually, I think the brass was kind of happy to see me made a fool of."

"It made my day, too," Jefferson admitted.

"Thanks a lot. Have we gotten anywhere with the composite drawing of the bag lady?" Donovan asked.

"No. We covered both sides of Broadway from Seventy-second to 110th and came up empty as far as storekeepers go. Not one person recalled having seen her.''

"She must be an import that Timmins brought in . . . probably from the Coast.''

"Or a figment of your imagination.''

"Hey, I *saw* that woman. So did Gus. And two or three people at the Bridge Café saw Rigili with a woman.''

"They saw a looker. You and Gus saw a dog.''

"What about the apple? Did Forensics pull any prints off the skin?''

Jefferson shook his head. "Just a whole lot of smudges.''

"Blood type?'' Donovan asked hopefully.

"Type O negative. Not exactly the world's rarest. And it's too early to tell about the genotype. Maybe tomorrow we can gander at the lady's DNA. As for the five-block garbage-can search, it's still in progress. Several bags of stuff are being gone through, but I haven't heard any bells ring yet.''

"Did you get anything on the bullets?'' Donovan asked.

Jefferson stood, cleared his throat, and said, "How about a shot of whiskey to go with your coffee?''

Donovan suddenly looked like a quarterback who is about to be sacked by the New York Giants.

"Oh, no,'' he said.

Jefferson nodded. "You got it. All three slugs could have been made personally by Davy Crockett.''

"I can just see tomorrow's papers.''

"Worry not. The nature of the slugs is being kept under wraps. Forensics doesn't want to look as stupid as you do.''

"Just how much does Forensics know today?'' Donovan asked.

"A little more than yesterday. We got lucky. Because there was a lot more meat on Vinnie Ciccia than there was on Frankie Rigili, one of the slugs was pulled out of the body intact.''

"No shit! So the fat man finally did something good for me.''

"More than intact, the slug is pristine,'' Jefferson went on. "It's definitely a .44, and as far as age goes, it's into triple digits. At least a hundred years old and probably a hundred fifty. Tomorrow, Forensics should get the hard copy from the John Jay College."

"Why do they have to be involved?" Donovan asked.

" 'Cause Forensics ain't equipped for archaeology, Lieutenant. John Jay is."

"Why do I get all the weird ones?" Donovan asked the heavens. "Why can't the oddball cases happen out in Queens or the Bronx?"

"I'm hoping that John Jay can dig up a gun collector who can I.D. the slug. You don't happen to have a name in your Rolodex, do you?"

"Not that I'm aware of, but I'll give the matter some thought," Donovan said. "At least now we know that the bullets had to have been fired from close up at both Ciccia and Rigili. A mid-nineteenth-century pistol can't have been too accurate at long range. But why . . . *why?*"

Jefferson said, "Let's leave the imponderables go for a while and deal with what we have. For one thing, we have all stuff from Bono's apartment that our guys thought might be significant."

He handed Donovan a large manila envelope.

"It's mostly bills and receipts. Tax stuff."

"Don't tell me the bum pays taxes."

"Of course. He's a construction man, and makes twenty-seven thousand dollars a year."

"Which is more than enough to pay two thousand dollars a month in rent," Donovan said.

"Absolutely."

"Who's he work for?"

"Harbison Construction. Their office is on Park and Thirty-second."

"Run that name past the Organized Crime Control Bureau," Donovan said. "Let's see if it rings any bells with them."

Jefferson made a note on his clipboard. "You know, Bono is being released from the hospital and arraigned this afternoon.

Four o'clock at the County Courthouse.''

''I'll try to look over this stuff and have it back in his apartment before he's out on bail,'' an annoyed Donovan said.

Jefferson was sympathetic. ''If I knew that Bono was such a fast healer I would have shot him in a place that's tougher to repair.''

Donovan opened the envelope and dumped the contents onto his desk. ''I have to go through all this junk *and* make a four o'clock arraignment? Get me the coffee, would you? And, hey, what about Timmins?''

''There's nothing new that we can tell at first glance. All I can say is that he still holds court between six and eight P.M. at the Black Diamond Bar on 125th.''

''Okay, after the arraignment I'm going to pay a call on him. I'd ask you to come along, but I know how you feel about black gangsters.''

''You sure you wanna go into that place by yourself?'' Jefferson asked. ''Man, I wouldn't go in there even if I had one of Ciccia's MACs under my belt.''

''Timmins and I go back a long time,'' Donovan said, and began digging into the pile of papers taken from Bono's apartment.

# SIX

The Black Diamond Bar was just west of Broadway on the south side of 125th Street. That crosstown boulevard was, at its western end, the boundary between Morningside Heights and West Harlem. One Hundred and Twenty-fifth Street was the northern perimeter of Donovan's jurisdiction. He didn't often go into Harlem, except on the way to Yankee Stadium or to dine at a black restaurant that Jefferson assured him served the real thing.

The Black Diamond was pretty fancy, with leather-upholstered booths, uniformed waitresses, and a bartender who wore a red vest. The clientele was black and middle-aged, so the music on the jukebox tended towards Billie Holiday, Charlie Parker, Thelonius Monk, Archie Shepp, and B. B. King. That was Donovan's kind of music, though he did occasionally binge on Vivaldi or the Beach Boys.

He liked the Black Diamond. So what if a lot of the customers were numbers operators who worked for Timmins? Numbers guys didn't kill people–at least not while Billie Holiday was singing.

"I presume you know about the recent demise of one of the West Side's leading consumers of pasta," Donovan said.

Timmins sipped a brandy. "I saw the story."

Donovan said, "I wonder what you think about it."

"I think that it's too bad that you got a bum rap because you were eating a corned beef sandwich at the time," Timmins said. "Yeah, I know what you had for dinner. I have friends all over the place, even in Riley's. When you went off the hard stuff a few years ago I knew about it before your liver did."

Donovan smiled.

"I also know that you're too smart to really believe that I had anything to do with the killing. Oh, Ciccia wasn't exactly what you'd call my best friend. I won't send flowers to the funeral."

"Will you suddenly develop an interest in sports?" Donovan asked.

"It depends," Timmins said.

"On what?"

"On who else in Ciccia's, ah, family, develops an interest in sports. All in all, I'm happy with what I'm doing, Lieutenant. When was the last time I gave you any trouble?"

"I don't recall you ever giving *me* any trouble," Donovan replied. "You aggravate the uniforms every so often, but that's not my problem."

"Look at me," Timmins said. "My business harms nobody, and it gives the people something to think about other than their lousy jobs or the weather. And what's it cost them? A buck a day? Two bucks? They get some excitement, I make a living, I give a few people jobs, and none of my bread gets turned around into running hookers or dope like it did with Ciccia. And I don't sell guns, either. Especially not to kids. You *know* that. I'm strictly low-key; a class operation. Do you think I'd do some crazy thing like hire a hit lady to dress up like a bum?"

"So you know about that, too."

Timmins unfolded one of Donovan's composite drawings of the bag lady and laid it on the table. "How smart do you have to be to figure it out? Ciccia gets blown away Saturday, and on Sunday these things are all over the West Side."

"Where were you Saturday evening?" Donovan asked.

Timmins shook his head. "Aw, Lieutenant, you disappoint me. Who was it that tipped you off to that gun sale that was going down on 106th Street? You know how I hate violence."

"Who was it who put a few words in the D.A.'s ear a couple of years ago after you were clumsy enough to be on the premises when one of your joints was raided by the uniforms?"

"So that makes us even."

"Where were you Saturday evening?"

" Shooting pool with some of my friends," Timmins said, inclining his head in the direction of four neatly dressed but very big and tough-looking black men. This quartet had been glaring at Donovan from the moment he walked into the Black Diamond.

"Your 'friends' will back up your story, I suppose."

"It's no story. It's the truth. You want to talk to them?"

"No. Why waste my time? They'll make themselves available if I need statements, I'm sure."

"Definitely."

Donovan got up to go. Timmins stopped him with a hand on his arm. "If I was you, I'd look inside Ciccia's organization. It just may be that one of his little helpers wants to move up in the ranks, and is using me as the scapegoat."

"Who, Bono? He was in the hospital at the time."

"You said 'was.' Is he out now?"

Donovan replied, "I thought you had friends all over the place. He was arraigned a few hours ago and made bail. And if you're thinking about Facci, I doubt he has the balls to knock off his boss. Facci is a candy-ass. He mainlines Maalox."

"I was just trying to be helpful," Timmins said, letting go of Donovan's arm. "Hey, you know what I did the second I heard about Ciccia?" He laughed.

"You sold your stock in the spaghetti company?"

"I went out and played the numbers," Timmins said proudly. "I *never* play the numbers. The odds against winning are too high."

"So what?"

"I had this hunch on a number. That's the only way to play—hunches. So I played one forty-four. Get it? One forty-four."

Donovan said that he got it. "How'd you make out?"

"I lost," Timmins said.

## ALLORE, DI SMETTI CANTARE

Roberto Facci was a small, gaunt man with black eyes that darted around the restaurant, inspecting everyone. While Bono was slick and oily with self-confidence, Facci tingled with suspicion and fear. To Bono, every strange face belonged to a chump. To Facci, every stranger was either his assassin or the police. Ciccia had kept them in line through intimidation; left on their own, with Bono the heir apparent, anything could happen.

Facci kept his fingers from shaking long enough to pick up a bit of sautéed bass, but set down the fork when Bono walked in. He had on a beige suit, the jacket of which was draped loosely over the cast on his left shoulder. He took a seat at the bar and had a manhattan, looking around the interior of l'Attesa to see who was there.

Bono spotted Facci dining alone at the company table, which was a semi-circular booth in a dark and secluded recess of the otherwise packed restaurant. Bono finished his drink and went to join Facci.

Facci said, "How's your shoulder?" His voice was as nervous as his fingers.

"It could be worse. The bullet just chipped off a few bone fragments. I got enough Darvon to get through it okay."

"You must be out of your mind! A few days after getting shot you're out doing the town? I keep telling you that wine, women, and song are gonna kill you."

Bono shrugged, and said: *"Allore, di smetti cantare,* . . . okay, I'll give up singing."

Facci frowned and tapped his fork on the table top.

"What the hell is going on? First you walk into a trap set up by the cops. The next day Vinnie is wasted. Frankie winds up in the river. Who is behind this?"

"You've been on the outside, not me. Suppose you come up with some answers."

"Obviously somebody tipped off the cops to the deal you had going down on 106th. It could have been the 'Ricans, you know, a rival gang. And as for Vinnie's office, I had it checked. There are no bugs in the office or on the phone. The only other one of our guys who knew about the deal was Palucci, and he was killed at the garage."

Bono rubbed his cast. "I want that nigger cop who shot me," he said.

"You know how Vinnie felt about taking on cops," Facci said.

"Yeah, but Vinnie isn't around to tell us what to do anymore, is he?"

"Jesus Christ, we got enough problems without . . ."

"Who was supposed to be working in that garage that night? It was a colored guy, wasn't it?"

"Pete . . . not every black guy on the West Side works for Timmins."

"No, but this one could. You know that Timmins likes to think he knows everything that's going on. Check out the garage attendant for me."

Facci bristled at having been given an order by someone he hadn't come to accept as his new boss, but said nothing.

"Timmins has been wanting our action for years," Bono said. "I think he's making his move now."

"There's no proof he had anything to do with any of what's happened. As a matter of fact, the cops are looking for a bag lady."

"A what?" Bono asked incredulously.

"You know what I mean. A bag lady. Donovan thinks that a pro shooter dressed up like a bag lady shot Vinnie. At least that's what I hear."

Bono sneered. "Haven't I always told you that Donovan isn't playing with a full deck? Did you know that he keeps a pet snapping turtle? A goddam turtle?"

"So did Rocky Balboa," Facci said. "And is it any crazier than you running around, drinking and doing drugs, when you should be home in bed?"

"I'm not doing drugs," Bono said angrily. "I got a pain, so I got a painkiller."

"Whatever you say."

"A bag lady! For Christ's sake, would you stop telling me fairy tales and check out that garage attendant? I *know* that Timmins is trying to move in on us. And call Bensonhurst and see if we can get some more muscle. I don't want any more holes put in me."

Facci had been given a second order, but still kept his anger to himself.

Bono said, "If Timmins wants a war, then I mean to give him a war. A short one."

Facci nodded and poked at his dinner. "I'll take care of it."

"I got to get back to the bar," Bono said. "You watch out for yourself, hear?"

"I have a man outside in the car."

Bono smiled as he got up. "And stop worrying, Bobby. It's too bad about Vinnie, but we'll make out okay. Will you be in the office tomorrow?"

"Sure."

"See you then."

While Facci tried to concentrate on his dinner, Bono worked his way through the crowd and reclaimed his seat at the bar. He ordered another manhattan, and had just picked it up when he noticed the allure of expensive perfume. To his left had appeared the most beautiful woman he had ever seen. She had long, honey-blond hair, a face he had only dreamed of, and was elegantly dressed. Moreover, she was looking at him. Quickly, he checked how he looked in the backbar mirror.

Andrea Jones held a glass of white wine in one hand, and with the other gently touched Bono's cast.

"It's too late in the year for skiing, so you must have fallen off a horse," she said.

## REAL MEN DON'T DO DISHES

"Pignoli nuts are the kernels of pine cones, used widely in Turkish, Balkan, and Italian cooking," Marcie said.

"Is that what they are?" Donovan replied.

"They're more commonly known as pine nuts. You grind them, mix them with basil leaves, olive oil, salt, pepper, garlic, and, in this case, finely chopped spinach. You sauté them for a while in the olive oil, then mix them with cooked pasta and let the whole thing cool. The result is pasta al pesto."

"You cooked this yourself, on a boat?" Donovan asked.

"I bought it at Zabar's."

"And the duck à l'orange?"

She nodded. "That's from Zabar's, too. I got two ducks for $3.99 each. With the pasta al pesto and the wine, we have dinner for two for under twenty dollars. That's not bad for Manhattan."

"That's not bad for anywhere," Donovan said, uncorking the wine and pouring two glasses. It was about eight-thirty in the evening, and night life was just beginning at the marina. There were about 200 boats in all, most of them year-rounders, but a handful were transients. Among the transients, which nearly always were the fancier boats, was a '72 ketch moored a space down from Marcie's boat, in the outermost berth of the southernmost pier. The ketch was fiber glass and had the spanking-new look of a custom-designed ocean racer. Before Marcie brought dinner up on deck, Donovan noticed, on the foredeck, an impeccably distinguished gentleman in a blue blazer talking to a younger man who was wearing new jeans and a white turtleneck. The older man looked like the stereotype of the yacht club commodore, always using white gloves to inspect the brightwork for specks of dust.

From the houseboat moored to the shoreside of the *West Wind* came the sound of opera and the occasional view of a tall, barrel-chested man who had a predilection for going about bare-chested, displaying a chestful of hair that was as white as that on his face and head.

Marcie dished out the duck and the pasta. "Eat," she said, and sat beside Donovan on one of the cockpit benches.

Donovan cut himself a slice of duck. "How'd it go with Arnie the Carpet Maven?" he asked.

"Not too bad," she replied. "We have him on tape making the offer. Now all I have to do is accept delivery and we've got him."

"Did the bastard buy you a nice breakfast?"

"No," she replied, a bit angrily. "He took me to some place in the Garment District that looked like a Howard Johnson's."

"Howard Johnson's makes good food," Donovan said.

"Perhaps, but I was hoping for French, not steak-and-eggs with home fries on the side."

"Hundreds of generations of Donovans have done okay on steak and potatoes."

"Yes, I can see," she said, and gave him a poke in the stomach.

"Do I hear complaints?" he asked.

"So you've been pumping iron. That probably revokes your Irish citizenship."

Donovan said, "I've been thinking of moving to Dublin. I can get a job with the Guarda."

She laughed. "You'll never leave the West Side."

Donovan swallowed a bit of duck and sipped some wine. "I just might surprise you."

Marcie breathed in the soft northwest wind and said, "It's nice out. The air is good. I'm told that when it gets really hot, this river doesn't always smell very nice."

''Lies, just lies. The Hudson is just like the perfume department of Bloomingdale's. How long has that big ketch been there?'' Donovan nodded at the older gent, who was fiddling about the cockpit with a different young man, this one in khaki slacks and a blue polo shirt.

''Three weeks, maybe a month,'' she said. ''Why do you ask?''

''I didn't notice her before.''

''She's hard to see at night. Today was the first time you've spent much time here in the daylight.''

Donovan nodded, and watched as the sun dipped towards the horizon over New Jersey. ''And the guy on the houseboat to starboard? Santa Claus? What's his story?''

''I don't have a clue, other than that he sometimes starts singing *Tosca* in the middle of the night. Wait until you catch the act of Peeping Nikon.''

Donovan asked who she was talking about.

''He's a guy who lives on an old Chris-Craft on pier two. I guess he's a photographer, 'cause he watches me through a telephoto lens whenever he can.''

Donovan felt a surge of jealous anger. ''He watches just you?''

''No, he watches whatever woman happens to be around and in a bathing suit. So far it's been me. I'm the new kid on the block.''

''I sense an ass about to be kicked,'' Donovan said.

Marcie shook her head. ''He's a harmless voyeur. Forget about him.'' She touched Donovan's hand and said, ''I can kick his ass just as hard as you can, darling. Leave the poor bastard alone. You go find your killer bag lady and let me deal with the neighbors.''

''I like the pasta al pesto,'' he said. ''I may be breathing garlic fire for the next week, but I like it.''

''At the very least, it'll keep Jefferson out of your office. Vampires can't stand garlic.''

The meal was consumed. When that had been accomplished, Donovan sipped a cup of espresso. ''I never knew you could do so much on a boat. I thought it was all emergency rations—or Chinese food that was sent out for."

"I try my best," she said.

"You do very well."

Marcie said, "I don't suppose that you want to help me with the dishes?"

Donovan stared wistfully at the lines of the big ketch one berth down from the *West Wind*.

"Right. I didn't think so. Real men don't do dishes." She collected the plates.

Donovan looked up at her, untimely ripped from a far-off musing. "You said something?"

"No," she said with mock haughtiness, "what you heard was the whistling of the wind in the wires that hold up the masts."

"Stays," Donovan said. "They're called 'stays.' "

At the companionway door she turned and said, "I'm going *below*."

## DONOVAN'S CHAIN IS PULLED

"He pulled my chain," Donovan said.

"Who?"

Marcie brought up a cup of espresso for herself and sat next to Donovan. Both had their feet up on the port quarter rail. The sun was below the horizon, and the lights of Manhattan glowed at their backs.

"Willis Timmins."

"Refresh my memory."

"This black numbers guy. He pulled my chain a few hours ago. I can still hear the clinking."

Donovan explained about Timmins's having gone out of his way to tell how he played the number 144 after having heard that Ciccia was dead.

"How did he know the murder weapon was a .44?" she asked. "It wasn't in the papers."

"My point exactly," Donovan said.

"Coincidence?" she offered.

"Coincidence," Donovan said grandly, "is a marvelous way of avoiding the trouble of finding a logical explanation for two or more events that occur simultaneously."

"Plutarch?" she asked.

"Donovan," he replied.

"Nonetheless, a .44 is a common weapon," Marcie said.

"There are dozens of common calibers, from rat-flatteners to elephant guns. Timmins picked the right one, and he smiled when he told me about it. He pulled my chain. I'm pissed off that I let it slide at the time."

Marcie rested her head on Donovan's shoulder. "I think you need a good night's sleep, sailor. You have a big day tomorrow."

"What's tomorrow?"

"Memorial Day. We're attending the parade, and after that the captain is having a party on his yacht."

Donovan offered a quizzical look.

"The old guy in the boat you were admiring before—he's a retired captain in the Royal Navy. His sons and he will be at the parade on Riverside, in uniform of course. So will you."

"Barnes . . ."

"No arguments. I want to see you in your dress uniform with all your medals."

"I don't know where my goddam medals are," Donovan snapped.

"They're probably still in the shoe box in your bedroom closet."

"I hate wearing my dress uniform."

"*I'll* be wearing *mine,*" she said.

Donovan sighed. "Until now only the mayor has convinced me to dress up."

"I think we'll all look lovely together."

Donovan saw that further argument was hopeless. He looked

over at the big ketch, and noticed that she had lowered her colors; precisely at sundown, he presumed. He went back to musing about the case.

"Timmins could have tipped me off to the Duke Ellington Boulevard gun sale by way of getting me to help knock off the Eye-talian competition," Donovan said.

"What?" Marcie asked, spilling a bit of her coffee.

# SEVEN

The neon cattails were the only light in Bono's living room. They cast their cool, pallid glow over all present, with the exception of Andrea Jones, who could look radiant in a mortuary.

She looked especially radiant in the fashionable Calvin Klein floppy suit worn with a tight pastel T-shirt. Her long hair hung everyplace, and shimmered in the glow of the cattails.

Bono was flying higher than even the Darvon and the manhattans could take him. Just out of both a hospital and a jail, he had a gorgeous bit of fiction out of a dream to help him forget the pain in his shoulder.

And she seemed to want it! She had come on to him, not the other way around, as he was accustomed to. She spoke first, mentioning his cast. After that he was in command, his ego told him, directing the conversation, telling all the usual lies about what a big shot he was in the construction business. What the hell, Bono thought, the lies worked on girls from Jersey, they should work on a tourist from Maryland or Virginia, he couldn't recall which.

They sat on the couch, drinking wine and listening to a Sinatra record, until Bono had run out of lies and also was feeling giddy from the alcohol and the Darvon.

When the last record ran out, it was Andrea Jones who got up to switch off the stereo. It automatically receded into a white box.

"Charming," she said, and turned to face him.

"I like to have good things around me, you know what I mean? And I like the color white."

He had taken her switching off the stereo to mean that she was ready for the main event.

"White is a good color," she said, "but I prefer autumn colors—yellows, oranges, and reds. Country colors. Do you ever go out to the country, Peter?"

"Sure. I go visit my folks out in Lake Hopatcong on Christmas and Easter."

"Where is that?"

"In Jersey."

"It must be very nice," she replied, sitting alongside him once again.

She touched his cast. "This must hurt you," she said.

He was brave, and drunk. "Nah. I try not to think about it."

"How did it happen?"

He thought for a second, then laughed and said, "A cop shot me."

"You're kidding, of course," Jones replied.

"Yeah, it was an accident at this building I'm putting up on Park Avenue. You're cool, you know that, real cool. Anyone else would look shocked when I said I got shot, but not you."

"People get shot all the time," she replied. "It's the true national pastime."

He laughed again. "Like I said, you're cool. I like you. Move closer."

"Shouldn't you think of getting a good night's sleep so your shoulder will heal?"

"I'll sleep okay," he said, "after."

"After what?" she asked coyly.

He pulled her to him, and after a fleeting resistance, she submitted. But when she felt his hands begin to prowl her body, she pulled back. "Isn't there someplace more comfortable?" she asked.

Bono stood, a bit shakily, and took her by the hand. "This way," he said, and started with her toward the bedroom.

At the door, Andrea Jones stopped. "I have to use the bathroom."

"Sure thing. Hey, I got a great TV in here. Is there a movie you'd like me to put on?" Bono gave her a leering sort of wink. "You know, something sexy?"

"What do you have?" she asked.

He gave her the basic rundown of where five thousand years of civilization had taken him.

"*The Devil in Miss Jones* sounds appropriate," she said.

"You got it." He turned to arrange for the screening.

She found the bathroom, went inside, and locked the door. Laying her purse on the ledge provided in modern apartments for grooming paraphernalia, she withdrew the old leather case that held the Colt Dragoon. After checking to see that it was loaded, she cocked the hammer and put the case back into her purse.

She picked up a brush and gave a few strokes to her hair; Jones liked to look her best for an execution. The bag lady disguise had been a necessity that embarrassed her. She flushed the toilet, picked up her purse, and walked out of the bathroom and into the bedroom, the Colt hidden in the folds of her suit.

Bono had taken off his shirt and gold chains and was sitting on the side of the bed. All lights were out, and the only illumination was provided by the opening moments of the pornographic movie on the large-screen television.

"Come here," he said, and stretched out his arms, beckoning her.

Jones surveyed the scene with distaste, but no emotion showed on her face—perhaps a slight, wry satisfaction at the upturned corner of her mouth.

She moved the Colt into plain view and aimed it at Bono's chest.

Drunk and drugged, he laughed. "What's this?" he asked.

"The national pastime," she said, and pulled the trigger once. The room shook as the black powder propelled the Civil War slug deep into Bono's chest. He was hurled backwards onto the water bed, which rippled and shook. Jones fired again. Bono's body bounced up and down, and then began to sink as the punctured water bed let go its contents. As the water rose around the body, Andrea Jones put the revolver back into its case.

Before leaving, she pressed the red button that made waves, and closed the apartment door while the body shook hideously in the flickering light of the television.

## A DÉCLASSÉ WAY TO DIE

Donovan was back at the tiller of the old wooden sailbaot he raced when he was a kid and summered at his aunt's house on Long Island. He had gotten a mediocre start in a field of eleven boats, but the wind was in a shifty mood and even as a teen-ager Donovan had an eye for matters shifty.

He played the wind shifts, and, by the time the first mark loomed, was in second place and gaining on the leader, a posh yacht-club type named Tad who was known for showing off his new boat, new clothes, and new Porsche. Donovan distrusted anything new, feeling that ideas and machines, like people, needed a few years to break in. He also disliked guys named Tad, and Porsches, which made Donovan think of Volkswagens that had been stepped on. And he delighted in proving that new boats were not innately faster than old ones.

Donovan rounded the mark and was about to swoop down on the increasingly nervous Tad when the light snapped on in the cabin. He groaned and rolled onto his back.

Marcie wore his bathrobe, and, cuddled up in it, looked like a teddy bear. She sat on the edge of the bed, ran her fingers through his hair, then played with the four-day-old stubble until he reluctantly opened his eyes.

"I am *not* getting out of bed to put out the garbage," he said.

She smiled. "You're growing it back."

"I wasn't aware it had fallen off."

"I mean your mustache! That's what you're doing, isn't it?"

"Did you wake me up to ask that?"

"Answer the question," she said.

"I'm growing it back," he replied.

"Why?"

"I don't know. I just got this impulse. Well, that's not entirely true. I happened to be going through some old stuff a few days ago and ran across a snapshot of us standing by your father's pool. The mustache looked good then. It'll look good now."

Marcie was amazed. "You kept a picture of us for twelve years?"

"You kept my bathrobe," he said, smiling.

"I only kept it to cuddle up in when it's cold," she said, looking a bit embarrassed.

"Whatever you say." He found himself staring at the gentle curve of her thighs.

"I hate you," she said, and kissed him on the lips.

"Does that mean I can go back to sleep?" He started to roll over.

"Sorry, slugger, but I'm afraid that the world needs you again."

He sighed. "What now?"

"To make it short, one Peter Bono, whom I believe you knew, was blown away on his very own water bed. A *very* déclassé way to die, Donovan."

Donovan sat up. "Where'd you hear this?"

"From the poor man's Eddie Murphy, where else? He's pacing the deck this very moment, requesting your presence."

Donovan swung his legs out of bed. "If it doesn't happen when I'm eating, it happens when I'm sleeping. What did Jefferson say?"

"As I recall the quaint way he put it, he wants you to 'haul your honky ass the hell out of the sack.' Donovan, the man is walking insubordination.''

''He's my friend.''

''And that,'' she said, ''excuses a multitude of sins.''

''What time is it?'' Donovan asked, standing.

''Half past midnight.''

Donovan buckled his belt over a wrinkled shirt. ''I had better get back to my apartment for a change of clothes soon. Two days in this suit and it's taking on a life of its own.'' He slipped on his shoulder holster and jacket.

''You had better pick up your dress uniform while you're there,'' Marcie said with a yawn. ''We have a busy day tomorrow.''

''Are you wrapping up the hot-carpet scam?''

''Yes. And then comes the parade and the captain's party.''

Donovan stuffed his wallet and keys into a pocket.

''I don't know if I can make this party.''

''You have to. I already promised to be there . . . and to bring my intended.''

''Your 'intended'? And that's me, I suppose.''

''Certainly.''

''What do you *intend* to do with me?''

''I haven't made up my mind. Ask me again in a few days.''

Donovan patted her on the ass. ''How did I get to be your intended?''

''The captain noticed that you've been staying here. I had to hang some kind of title on you. I could have called you my beau, my fiancé, my periodic flame, or my extended one-night-stand. However, because the captain is British, and the invitations were engraved, 'intended' seemed more proper.''

A roar came down the aft companionway: ''Donovan, you dumb shit, would you get a move on!''

A roar went back up: ''Kiss my ass, you black bastard! I'm moving as fast as I can.''

''Did I hear you call him your friend?'' Marcie asked.

''He's the best I've got,'' Donovan replied.

## SAVING THE TAXPAYERS' MONEY

"Try to think of it as the ultimate out-of-court settlement," Donovan said.

"I'm not sure I understand," the division commander replied.

Donovan gazed at Bono's partially submerged body. "If the man lived, the city would have had to cough up at least a million to try him on the gun charge, taking court costs, jail costs, etc. and so forth, into consideration. Some thoughtful citizen saved us the expense."

The division commander had known Donovan, and his father, for close to forty years, and in that time had come to recognize the wisdom of the platitude, "Like father, like son."

"You're kidding, of course."

"If one of those reporters outside asks me that, I am," Donovan replied.

"Umf. Well, you always were good with the press. I see that you haven't shaved in a few days. Are you going into your 'bloodied but still in there fighting' act already?"

Donovan was known to manipulate the press by altering his appearance to give the impression that he was really slugging it out with the forces of evil. "Actually, I'm growing my mustache back."

The division commander offered a thoughtful expression. "Your dad had a pretty good mustache, as I recall. What did he call it? A soup-strainer."

"Something like that."

"You'll have to call a press conference, Bill. This West Side gang war thing has to be challenged. It *is* a gang war, isn't it?"

"It looks that way."

"And this guy Timmins?"

"He looks like the prime actor."

The division commander regarded Donovan with suspicion. "That makes two times you've added a qualifier to your assessment of the situation. It 'looks' like a gang war. Timmins 'looks' like the bad guy. Am I reading more than I should into what you're saying?''

''It could be,'' Donovan said, with a laugh.

''I have to go. You're as hard to pin down as your father was, rest his soul, and I don't have the strength I used to.''

''I'll keep you posted,'' Donovan said.

''Do. The mayor wants to get into the act. He's been taking a lot of heat for not being tough enough on crime, and the clown is thinking of running for governor again.''

''Keep him out of my way,'' Donovan said. ''Do the West Side a favor and don't send in the clowns.''

The division commander laughed. ''Your old man used to talk like that. One time he told me, 'Hizzoner may run City Hall, but I run the West Side.' I'm glad to see that nothing has changed.''

When the division commander had left, Jefferson walked over. ''Man, brass makes me nervous.''

Donovan said, ''There's brass and there's brass. Connelly and I go back a long time. He knows he can trust me.''

''What's he know that I don't?''

Donovan gave Jefferson a withering glance. ''Tell me what happened.''

''Bono was shot sometime between eleven and eleven-thirty. A neighbor herd two shots.''

''Did the neighbor see anyone?''

''No. The shots were so loud, she went and hid.''

''What about the doorman?''

''No luck there, either. Apparently, Bono came and went via the underground garage, which is automated. There are TV monitors that the doorman can see, but he can't watch them all the time. I can tell you this, though . . . Bono brought a woman home with him.''

''Home? You mean he went out this evening?''

Jefferson nodded, and handed his boss a slightly soggy matchbook. ''I found this in his shirt. Now, none of our guys reported a matchbook from that restaurant when we tossed the joint the other day. Bono went out tonight, for sure.''

Donovan read the name of the restaurant: l'Attesa, the Italian place on 83d and Columbus. ''I ate there once. The scampi stinks.''

''I arranged for the restaurant staff to stay late tonight,'' Jefferson said. ''I thought you'd want to talk to them.''

''Good. What else have we found?''

''Some interesting stuff,'' Jefferson replied. ''There are two wine glasses in the living room, and fingerprints on both of them. In fact, there are prints all over the place. If the lady Bono was entertaining was our shooter, and I don't think there's much doubt of it, she didn't take great pains to hide the fact.''

''Or was in too big a hurry,'' Donovan said. ''Or didn't care.''

''Didn't *care* that we would find her prints at the murder scene?'' Jefferson asked.

''I was just musing.''

''Well, I like them muses, 'cause the lady also left a clear print on the red button that makes waves. We lifted the print before I turned off the machine.''

''*She* turned the machine on? I guess after she shot him. Why create a moving target? So the lady has a sense of humor. And, yes, I can smell the black powder.''

''It's all over what remains of Bono's chest,'' Jefferson said.

''Fascinating. She's going out of her way to draw attention to herself. Now, why would a pro shooter do that?''

''Don't ask me. You're the one who gets paid to think. I just take notes.''

''And wake me up in the middle of really neat dreams.''

''One other thing,'' Jefferson said, consulting his clipboard. ''When the first cops got there, the TV was still on. Bono's ghost was watching *The Devil in Miss Jones.*''

''Was he now? Listen up, Pancho. If you were Peter Bono, a young and good-looking macho stud with a lot of bucks, would you go out on the town a few hours after getting out of the hospital, go to a West Side restaurant, and then come home with a dog?''

''No way.''

''Let's play a game. Let's revise that composite drawing to remove the bag lady disguise.''

''Good idea,'' Jefferson said, making notes.

''Let's give her good looks, which she probably has anyway. We'll have the artist give her long and short hair, blond and brunette. We'll show that around, particularly to the guys who work at l'Attesa and the Bridge Café, and see what happens.''

## MAZZACUAGNO, AT THE VERY LEAST

Donovan scanned the facade of l'Attesa, which was unremarkable save for a batch of credit card stickers.

''I don't recall what caused me to eat here, but the heartburn lies vivid in my memory,'' he said.

Jefferson sniffed the air near his boss. ''You fall in a garlic patch or somethin'?''

''Pasta al pesto. Marcia got some from Zabar's.''

''And you *dined* on her *yacht,* no doubt.''

Donovan nodded. ''It's typical of the West Side that the only place to get good Italian takeout is a Jewish deli.''

''And it's typical of her that she can't cook. Gotta order out.''

Donovan gave Jefferson a slightly-harder-than-playful shove.

''This is the last warning I'm gonna give you,'' Jefferson said. ''Getting takeout from Zabar's was only the beginning. Next it will be a credit card at Bloomingdale's. Then up the Yuppie Corridor to Croton-on-Hudson and a big house with a pool and kids and private schools and . . .''

''Shut up,'' Donovan said.

''Just remember who warned you.''

''What's the situation inside this dump?'' Donovan asked.

''We kept the whole staff under wraps and interviewed them. And Bonaci and Corrigan have got the maître d' out back in the alley and are twisting his linguine a little.''

They went inside, where seven or eight staff members were sitting sullenly, waiting to be allowed to go home.

''How long was Bono here?'' Donovan asked.

''Estimates average out at half an hour. He came in, had two drinks, and left.''

Donovan said, ''There's something wrong. Bono was winged by you the day before yesterday, released from the hospital this afternoon, and a couple of hours later he goes to all the trouble to get dressed in his finest polyester and come all the way across town just to have two drinks at this overcrowded, overpriced dump? What would you have done if you were him?''

''Send out for a bottle of wine and a pizza, what else?''

''Exactly. So we have to figure that Bono came here to meet somebody.''

''The broad who shot him?''

''If he wanted a woman, he could have sent out for that, too. I think he came here to meet one of his buddies and get caught up on the news from the front.''

Jefferson agreed, and said, ''On that score, you might consider the fact that all the waiters and busboys came up with the same story. Bono had two drinks, didn't talk to anybody, and left.''

Donovan smiled. ''Everybody who works in this place, which gets very busy at night, had their eyes on him all the time, right?''

''The maître d' got to them before we did,'' Jefferson said.

Corrigan wedged a police van against the walls so that it blocked the alley behind l'Attesa. Bonaci and he stood guard to ward off any prying eyes that might try to see past the van.

The maître d'hôtel of l'Attesa, a sixtyish man named Corro, stood with his back to the alley wall, sweating profusely. Jefferson had his coat off, shirtsleeves rolled up, and was pacing back and forth in front of the hapless restaurateur. Donovan had found a two-by-four and leaned up against the far wall, every so often using the board to give a stout whack to one of the restaurant's garbage pails. Otherwise he tossed it into the air and caught it by the opposite end, like a long-ball hitter playing with his Louisville Slugger before batting practice.

Jefferson poked Corro in the chest and said, "The lieutenant says you have lousy scampi."

"It's . . . it's the best on the West Side," Corro said uncertainly, shifting his eyes back and forth.

"What *is* scampi, Corro?" Donovan asked.

"Unh . . . sautéed shrimp."

"Did you hear that, Sergeant? Scampi is sautéed shrimp."

"I heard it."

Donovan brought the two-by-four crashing down on a garbage can lid, crushing it. Corro winced.

"It's not sautéed shrimp?" he asked.

"Where are the 'shrimp' caught?" Donovan asked.

"In the ocean." Perspiration stung Corro's eyes, and he wiped them on his cuff.

"What ocean?" Donovan asked, flipping the two-by-four.

Corro panicked. "Ocean? What difference does it make? An ocean is an ocean!"

Donovan turned toward him. "My friend, scampi is made from a large prawn caught in the Adriatic Sea. The word 'scampi' is Venetian for 'prawn.' The body of the animal is pale amber, with a thin shell and no claws. The flesh is tender, with a shrimp-like flavor. Did you hear me? I said 'shrimp-*like*.' "

"I heard you." Corro's perspiration was now drenching his shirtfront.

"A prawn is not a shrimp. It just looks like one. And scampi should be made from Adriatic prawns. Failing that, it should, at the very least, be made from *mazzacuagno,* which are prawns caught in the Bay of Gaeta, off Naples. Are you sure you're Italian?"

Corro nodded frantically.

"Now, in England scampi is often made from prawns caught

in Dublin Bay, which even to an Irishman like myself is sacrilegious. Where do you get the shrimp that you stick in the gooey mess that you call scampi?''

Corro swallowed his future and said, ''They . . . they come frozen from the fish market.''

Donovan hit the garbage can hard enough to make for a home run in Yankee Stadium. ''Frozen?'' he said.

Jefferson took Corro by the lapels and said, ''Listen, m'man, you could be frozen yourself by dawn. If I don't bust you for lyin' to us about Bono, the lieutenant here is gonna nail your ass for makin' scampi out of frozen shrimp!''

''Okay! Okay! What do you want?''

''Who did Bono come here to meet?'' Donovan asked.

Corro looked from side to side as if spiders were crawling up his shoulders. ''You got to keep this quiet.''

''Let's hear it.''

''Facci, he talked to Facci!''

''Roberto Facci, Ciccia's numero tres. I should have guessed,'' Donovan said.

''Facci's numero uno now,'' Jefferson said.

''If you guys say anything about this I'm a dead man,'' Corro said.

''Where can we find Signor Facci?''

''I don't know. He moves around. Anyway, all I do is run the place where he comes to meet his friends.''

''I knew it couldn't be for the food,'' Donovan said idly, tossing the two-by-four down the alley.

''What did Facci and Bono have to say?'' Jefferson asked.

''Come on, officers, I don't know and I don't wanna know. All I can tell you is that they only talked for a couple of minutes and that Facci looked nervous.''

''As well he might,'' Donovan said.

Jefferson let go of Corro's lapels.

''You swear you didn't hear this from me?''

"Tell us about the woman," Donovan said. "He met a woman here, right?"

"Yeah, he met a woman. Right at the bar after talking to Facci."

"I don't suppose you know her name," Jefferson said.

"No, but she was class, real class. Tall . . . blond and dressed like a model."

"We'll get you over to the police artist," Donovan told Corro, who by then was paler even than a scampi.

"Was there anything else about her you can remember?"

"Like what?"

"Like did they seem to know each other?"

"No. From what I saw, he picked her up. I saw them talking, and the next thing they were gone." Corro paused, grabbing for a thought, then said, "Jesus Christ! I think she's the same one!"

"What do you mean 'the same one'?"

"The same woman who got picked up here by Frankie Rigili on Thursday night."

Donovan and Jefferson exchanged astonished stares.

Corro was so excited he was shaking. He knew he had come up with something to get the spiders from crawling up his arms.

"Rigili picked her up on Thursday night, and Bono tonight?" Donovan asked.

"She's a real knockout, Lieutenant, hard not to notice her in this place."

Donovan wanted to get back the two-by-four and hit himself over the head with it. "A Civil War weapon, black powder, and more nerve than an old-time gunslinger," he said. "I wonder if Davy Crockett left any ancestors."

# EIGHT

To the first microphone thrust at him by one of the half dozen reporters milling in the hallway outside the West Side Major Crimes Unit, Donovan said, " 'Take thy beak from out my heart, and take thy form from off my door!' "

"What?" the offending reporter asked.

" 'Quoth the raven, "Nevermore." ' "

The reporter, clearly a novice, asked if he could quote Donovan on that.

"You had better quote Edgar Allan Poe," Donovan snapped. "How much does tuition *cost* at journalism school these days? Why don't you guys buy some used books and read? I have work to do."

He pushed his way through the crowd, ignoring further inquiries, and soon was safe within the confines of his office. It was 3:30 A.M.

Jefferson said, "I don't see how you keep getting away with shit like that."

"All I did was give him a quote he can't use without making himself look like an idiot. Do you believe that guy? 'Can I quote you on that?' " Donovan laughed. "Next time I'll try a bit of

Marc Antony's eulogy of Caesar and see if anyone catches on.''

''And the stuff about scampi. Did you make that up?''

''Nope. I looked up the recipe after the time I had scampi at l'Attesa.''

''You got some memory.'' Jefferson said.

''Think of me as an information dilettante. I know a little bit about lots of things. That's what makes me so good at cocktail parties. I'm the best idle bullshitter you'll ever meet.''

''And the humblest.''

''Also true.''

Jefferson accepted a folder from Bonaci and thumbed through the contents.

''Well?'' Donovan asked.

''The revised composite drawing of the killer bag lady? She don't look so bad without the stage-makeup dirt.''

Donovan inspected the papers, especially the drawing of the suspect that showed her with long blond hair. ''Not bad isn't the word for it. If I sit at the bar at l'Attesa long enough I wonder if she'll come along and pick me up too. The place *is* known as a pickup spot.''

''You *do* think that's what happened, then? Ms. Crockett let herself get picked up by Rigili and Bono and then plugged 'em?''

''That's what I think happened. She 'met' Rigili Thursday and he was bumped off Friday. She 'met' Bono last night and did the job a few hours later. Both Rigili and Bono got dumped in the drink, the only difference being that there's more waves in Bono's water bed than there are in the Hudson.''

''And in between she dressed up like a bag lady so she could break through Ciccia's security,'' Jefferson said. ''His chauffeur has the reputation of being a world-class shot.''

''It kinda looks that way, my friend.''

Jefferson said, ''Timmins is a lot shiftier than I thought, hiring someone like that.''

''I guess he is,'' Donovan said. ''Either that or we got a nut case who likes to pull off costume-party executions of mobsters.''

''It ties her, too.''

''You bet. After this composite drawing . . .''

''. . . the one with long blond hair. We found some on a brush in Bono's throne room. It's down at Forensics now.''

''. . . after that drawing is reconciled with Corro's, have it shown to the waiters at the Bridge Café.''

There was a ruckus at the door. The press, which had been following Donovan around for several hours, was beating at the gates. The nightwatch officer and a few detectives were doing their best to herd them back down the stairs.

''I bet this is how Rome fell,'' Donovan said. ''The barbarians were all newspapermen.''

''What *are* you gonna do about the press?''

''Type up a statement announcing a press conference a half hour from now here at the house. Have some copies run off and thrown down the stairs at them.''

''What are you gonna say at this press conference?''

''The usual platitudes: 'We shall fight on the beaches . . . we shall fight in the fields . . . we shall never surrender.' ''

''Lieutenant, you *know* that the press is all-out for a gang war story. What are you gonna tell 'em about that?''

Donovan tossed up his hands. ''It looks like a gang war to me. What's it look like to you?''

''The same.''

Donovan pounded his fist on the desk. ''Right. Pull the file on Facci and bring it to me. And round up half a dozen guys and bring in my old friend Willis Timmins. Get another half dozen guys from the Twenty-sixth to back you up. He won't put up a fight, but I want to make an impression on the sonofabitch. If this is a gang war, he's behind it, and I don't like the way he pulled my chain the other day.''

''Do you really think he fed you the dope on the sale of MACs to the kids from the Bronx in order to get us to put a dent in Ciccia's machinery?'' Jefferson asked.

"It ain't out of the question."

"Okay, I'll bring the bastard in. What charge?"

"Suspicion of conspiracy in the murders of Peter Bono and Vincent Ciccia. Timmins is a wise-ass. Thinks he knows more than everybody else. Thinks he can out-think everybody else. He's just the type to hire a hit lady to dress up like a bum and blow away Ciccia. You know—hire a bum to kill a bum. It's the sort of thing that Timmins would think funny."

Jefferson smiled and made some notes. "Gotcha. I'll have him in an hour. But you know that he's gonna be hollering for his lawyer."

"So we'll run the old Manhattan Shuffle on him," Donovan said.

Jefferson shook his head. "Lieutenant, the Miranda decision is twenty years old. Timmins has the right to an attorney."

"Sure, but it's our duty to protect a suspect, and that crowd outside the door looks pretty nasty to me. We might have to move Timmins to another precinct for his own safety."

"That crowd is made up of reporters."

"How do you know that? Did you check all their credentials? If an assassin can disguise himself as a bum, dressing up like a newspaperman should be no problem at all."

Jefferson smiled in admiration of his boss.

"Besides," Donovan went on, "I bet that Timmins's lawyer is too young to have heard of the Manhattan Shuffle."

## THE ANNUAL PILGRIMAGE TO THE OLD SOD

Donovan read the file on Roberto Facci, then sent Bonaci and four other detectives to pick up the man at his house in Bensonhurst. Jefferson had left to pick up Timmins. There was little for Donovan to do other than reread the files, which he already knew by heart, and wait for the leaders of the rival gangs to be hauled in.

He looked forward to bringing Timmins and Facci together in the same room and banging their heads together. That was unlikely, at least for an hour, so Donovan sought entertainment elsewhere. He turned command of the Unit back over to the nightwatch officer, and dialed seven digits on the telephone. He said, ''Unlock the back door. I'm coming down the spiral staircase,'' and then hung up on a string of obscenities.

Donovan crossed the squad room and opened the back window that led to the fire escape. He stepped outside. Corrigan yelled, ''Hey Lieutenant, bring me back a six of Bud, would you? I'm off as soon as Bonaci gets back, and everyplace will be closed.''

''Sure,'' Donovan said, and headed down the old, iron stairs. The alley behind the building housing the Unit and Riley's was dark and narrow, and only three police cars could be crammed into it, making for endless petty disagreements over who would have to move whose car so someone else could get out. As Donovan descended the iron steps, he built upon one truism to create wisdom of his own.

Wherever there exists the opportunity for life to arise, it will do so, Donovan knew. Wherever there exists the opportunity for a ruckus to be created, a ruckus will be created, he imagined. Donovan was struck by the symmetry of the notion. He felt that he had discovered a basic law of nature—all things moving inexorably toward chaos, with life merely a comfort station along the path. Donovan was as proud as Newton after he was bonked on the head by that apple. He knocked on Riley's back door.

''We're closed, you dumb fuck,'' George snarled.

The back door creaked open. ''Now you're open,'' Donovan replied. He stepped inside.

''It's after four,'' George protested.

''I'm only looking to kill some time. Are the curtains drawn?''

''Yeah, the place is locked up. Your reputation is safe from the eyes of the press.''

''Knowing that you like to sit alone and watch TV after everyone's gone . . .''

". . . You thought you'd make it impossible. It's not enough for you to ruin my days. You have to show up when I work nights, too. Come on in."

George closed and relocked the back door. Donovan passed through the empty back room and into the bar. One customer lingered, finishing a glass of whiskey. Donovan smiled at an old friend. "Mr. Flanagan, sir."

The Irishman, in his late fifties and of average height, but built to carry the hod and possessed of a formidable brogue, tipped an imaginary hat. "Willie my boy," he said, pronouncing the last two words as "me buy."

Donovan sat next to him. "I haven't seen you around lately," Donovan said.

"I've been packing for the past week."

"Packing? Oh, your annual pilgrimage to the Old Sod."

"I'm leaving next week and won't be back for a month. Is there anything I can be gettin' for you in the old country?"

George said, "You could get him some brains, but there ain't none *there.*"

"That's enough out of you, you bloody Hun," Flanagan snapped.

"A four-leaf clover will do," Donovan said. "I could use some luck."

"Done."

"And I want one picked from a real Irish meadow. None of the packaged ones you can buy at Shannon Airport."

"I shall make a note of it," Flanagan replied, and reached for a pen and a paper napkin.

George opened a bottle of beer and leaned back in his special barstool. On television, a gunfight was raging at the O.K. Corral. "Finish your drink and get outta here," he said to Flanagan.

"I'll leave when I'm good and ready."

Donovan said, "Remember, I can tell the difference between a Midlands clover and one picked at the coast."

"That's right," Flanagan said. "Your people came from the Midlands, did they not?"

"*His* people came from the moon," Kohler muttered. he was ignored.

"My grandmother was from Roscommon. French Park, to be precise."

"I was born in Castlerea," Flanagan said. "There's but a few miles difference. When I was a lad, we used to play football with French Park." He addressed himself to George: "That's soccer to you."

Donovan felt a sense of regret that he had never gotten to visit his relatives in Ireland. They seemed so far away, and he couldn't even leave his desk to spend a week with his aunt on Long Island, as he had long promised.

"Did I mention that my cousin was elected to the Dail last year?" Donovan asked.

"I believe that you did, yes."

Flanagan didn't seem terribly interested in the matter, which was just as well, as Donovan had only the vaguest idea what the Dail was and no idea as to his cousin's importance in that governmental body.

The man finished his drink with a flourish, and said to Donovan, "I'll be leaving you in the hands of this fine gentleman."

"If I don't see you in the next week, have a good trip," Donovan said.

"Thanks, I'll do that."

"Don't come back," George said, and relocked the door.

"You're a pillar of the community, Mr. Kohler," Donovan said when Flanagan was gone.

"Before I sit down, do you want anything to drink? 'Cause one I sit down I ain't gettin' back up again."

"Give me a beer mug filled with Coke."

"That's it?"

"Yeah. I'm gonna be up all night and all day. I have to stay reasonably alert."

George got Donovan his Coke.

"This would have to do with that guinea that got killed over on the East Side?"

Donovan nodded.

"I heard about it from the reporters. When you don't let them into your place, they come into mine."

"You see, I bring in business for you. So don't give me any more shit about my taking up space at the bar and only drinking Coke."

Donovan sipped his drink.

"One guy told me it looks like there's a gang war brewing on the West Side."

"Brewing, hell. It's bottled, refrigerated, and on its way to the stores."

"Who would be crazy enough to take on Ciccia's gang?"

"Can you keep this to yourself?"

"Do I look like Dan Rather to you?"

"Willis Timmins," Donovan said.

"He's crazy enough," George said. "Did you know that I had to eighty-six that bum? He used to come in here with three or four guys who looked like pro wrestlers and try to take over the place. I mean, 'Turn down the TV, turn up the jukebox, make me a Singapore Sling.' I told him, 'Your ass is gonna be in a sling. Get out!' "

"And he took that from you?"

"Well, I got you guys upstairs. All I have to do is bang on the pipe."

So George needed him after all. Donovan realized that what he had just heard was as close to an actual admission that he would ever get, and decided not to press the point.

"So who did Timmins have knocked off tonight?" George asked.

"Timmins is at this point the most likely suspect, no more. Anyway, the dead man is Peter Bono."

"That's the guy you shot on 106th, right?"

“Wrong. Jefferson shot him. Jefferson is out picking up Timmins now. Not that any good will come of it. I'm sure he was dining with the Queen Mother at the time the murder took place.”

“And has ten guys to swear to it,” George added.

“Yeah,” Donovan said, a bit bleakly.

He looked around the room and marveled at how little the joint had changed over the years. The stamped-tin walls and ceiling; the slowly rotating globe advertising Budweiser beer that served as a chandelier and clock; the row of brightly colored signs high above the backbar mirror that advertised prices; the New York Yankees season schedule posted above the cigarette machine; and other signs that were etched in time. There was the sign, posted in the worst of blizzards, offering a screwdriver as a “warm weather special.” There was the sign, pinned up by the owner, that read, “If You Don't Think the Dead Can Come Back to Life, You Ought to See This Place at Closing Time.” And there was Donovan's favorite—a bowl of hard-boiled eggs above which hung a sign reading “Boneless Chicken Dinner, 25¢.”

A strange and bizarre object caught Donovan's eye. The machine was so large that he was amazed at not having seen it sooner. A tall, rectangular box held a TV monitor and a bunch of buttons. Neon lettering read “Space Battles.”

“What's that?” Donovan asked. “Reagan's defense policy?”

“I told you there was a new video game coming in. Try not to let anyone bleed to death on it.”

“How's it work?”

“Put a quarter in and find out.”

Donovan put a quarter in and found out.

As he saw it, Space Battles consisted of a central and presumably evil laser-gun turret that fired on the player's spaceship. The turret was better protected than the guns of Navarone: three concentric rings, two rotating clockwise and one counter-clockwise, had to be breached before the laser could be hit. The player had to use his “fire” button to punch holes in the rings and maneuver his spaceship so that an opportune shot could be made at the laser at the precise moment that the punched holes lined up. At the same time, the laser gun tracked the spaceship and could return fire through the same holes. Three enemy fighter craft pursued the player's vessel.

"Who dreamed this up, the Marquis de Sade?" Donovan asked.

"It's a challenging game. It's so challenging that it took the local press corps for about thirty bucks this evening."

"No machine is going to beat me," Donovan vowed.

There were three controls available for the player to use in handling his spaceship: thrust, directional buttons, and the fire button. Donovan had three chances to get the laser cannon. He began to play.

On his first try, one of the enemy fighters got him before he could maneuver his ship into position for a shot. On the second, he managed to poke two holes in the outer ring before being destroyed. The third attempt went on longer. Donovan managed to poke holes in all the rings, only to be zapped by the laser cannon the instant the holes lined up. The whole exercise had taken less than a minute.

"Shit," he said.

George laughed.

"How many points can you score on this thing?" Donovan asked.

"Ten million. How'd you do?"

"Eight hundred. What's the best the reporters did?"

"Three thousand and change."

"There must be a system," Donovan said.

"Sure. How many guys have lost their shirts in Vegas or Atlantic City with that idea?"

Donovan was adamant. "It's only a computer. Computers work logically. It's just a matter of determining what logic this one uses."

He spent three more quarters and perhaps ten minutes trying to find out. His best score was a little over four thousand points.

Donovan returned to the bar. "At least I beat he press," he said.

"You want a drink now?"

"No. More Coke."

"I never play those fuckin' machines," George said, pouring some soda into Donovan's mug. "They're one-arm bandits, only they have buttons instead of levers."

"No mass of silicon is smarter than I am," Donovan said. Then he sipped his soda in silence until the movie was over. At about five in the morning, a ruckus developed out on the sidewalk. Donovan peered through the slats of Riley's venetian blinds and saw Jefferson, flanked by fifteen or twenty other cops, bringing a handcuffed Willis Timmins into the Unit. A lone TV crew filmed the proceedings.

"What's up?" George asked.

"Jefferson got Timmins. He doesn't look too happy about it."

"Just don't bring him in here," George said. "He's still eighty-six'd."

Donovan bought a six-pack of Budweiser for Corrigan, then went out the back door and up the fire escape.

## EAST SIDE, WEST SIDE, ALL AROUND THE TOWN

Timmins was indeed unhappy, handcuffed as he was to the radiator. It was one of Donovan's favorite techniques for humiliating pompous suspects.

As Donovan walked into the office, Jefferson loitered in the doorway. "Have any problem finding him?" Donovan asked.

"No sweat, Lieutenant. I just drove up to Harlem, turned over a watermelon, and there he was." Jefferson laughed.

People's prejudices were so unpredictable, Donovan thought. George Kohler, a German-American, disliked every ethnic group on the face of the earth, including his own. Jefferson disliked Hispanics and positively hated blacks who committed crimes. Donovan had never met a Palestinian terrorist, but suspected he wouldn't like such a man very much. Otherwise, Donovan judged people on a case-by-case basis. His war with the twentieth century occupied most of his free time anyway.

Donovan sat at his desk, facing Timmins, who was forced by the handcuffs and the radiator to sit crumpled over a rickety chair, looking like somebody's old coat.

''Did you Miranda him?'' Donovan asked Jefferson.

''You bet. You can still see the tread marks on his forehead.''

''Why don't you go and see how we're doing finding Facci,'' Donovan suggested. ''I left a note on your desk with some ideas and phone numbers.''

When Jefferson was gone, Timmins said, ''I want to talk to my lawyer.''

''Don't tell me that Jefferson denied you your obligatory phone call?'' Donovan asked.

''I called my lawyer all right. He'll be here in half an hour.''

Donovan consulted his watch.

Timmins said, ''Can't you let me sit up like a dignified man? What have I ever done to you?''

''You're a suspect in at least two murders, Willie my boy,'' Donovan said. pronouncing the last two words like ''me buy.''

''Murders? I already told you I have an alibi for the Ciccia hit.''

''So it *was* a hit.''

''What else could it have been?''

''I don't know, there could be a homicidal lady swagman wandering around town. I've seen stranger things in my time.''

Timmins looked especially uncomfortable, and Donovan had someone come in and unchain him from the radiator. The man rubbed his wrists, which were still cuff-linked together.

''You got some nerve dragging me in here in the middle of the night. I was with a fine lady when your *oreo* got me out of bed.''

Donovan said, ‘‘I wouldn’t let Jefferson hear you refer to him with that word. Despite the Brooks Brothers suit, he can get a little worked up now and again.’’

‘‘I’m not sayin’ anything else until my lawyer gets here.’’

‘‘Where were you between eleven and one?’’

‘‘What happened then?’’

‘‘Bono got blown away.’’

‘‘Peter Bono, the guy who worked for Ciccia?’’

‘‘No,’’ Donovan said, ‘‘Sonny Bono, the guy who used to be married to Cher.’’

‘‘I don’t know anything about Peter Bono, ’’ Timmins said.

‘‘Bullshit. You’re the one who claims to know everything that happens on the West Side.’’

‘‘So maybe I was exaggerating.’’

‘‘Or lying.’’

‘‘I want to see my lawyer.’’

‘‘In due time,’’ Donovan said, again looking at his watch.

‘‘I suppose that your lady friend gave us a complete statement saying that she was with you all night.’’

Timmins nodded.

‘‘What a surprise! Well, let’s get to the meat of this mess—who did you hire to kill Ciccia, Rigili, and Bono?’’

‘‘Like I said . . .’’

‘‘You’re not talking until your lawyer get here. Right. That’s fine with me. Now, let’s be sensible. You have lots of money. You have a nice territory carved out. You *had* a nice working relationship with the boys from Bensonhurst that divvied up gambling on the West Side. You got numbers and Ciccia got sports. So why do you want to take on Mancuso and company? Is this some kind of death wish, or do you really have the troops for a war?’’

‘‘I want my lawyer,’’ Timmins insisted.

Donovan drummed his fingers on his desk. ‘‘In the past couple of days I’ve heard that in Italian and in Spanish. You want to give it to me in Swahili?’’

"I got rights," Timmins said.

"Who did you hire? And why did you go to all the trouble of dressing her up like a swagman?"

Timmins strained at his handcuffs. "Donovan, have you ever heard of the Sixth Amendment?"

"Yeah, did you ever hear of the First Commandment?"

He checked his watch one more time, then grabbed Timmins by the handcuffs and hauled him to his feet. "Okay, let's go."

"Go? Go where?"

At that point Jefferson burst into the office. "Lieutenant, there's quite a mob outside. They know we got Timmins in here."

Donovan looked out the window and nodded. "We'd better move him to a secure location."

Timmins looked around. "What's going on?"

"I talked to Paul DiGioia at the 19th," Jefferson said. "He'll be more than happy to let us use his facilities for a while."

"That's on the East Side, Willie. The Silk Stocking District. It's where the mayor and the Rockefellers live."

"I have a car ready," Jefferson said. "We better use the spiral staircase."

Donovan shoved Timmins toward the window. "Hey, I know this one," he protested. "You guys aren't pulling this deal on me."

"Aren't we?" Donovan asked.

"You got to tell my lawyer where you're taking me."

"Sure thing," Donovan said, and called across the squad room to the nightwatch officer. "Tell the gentleman's lawyer that we're taking his client to the Nineteenth Precinct on East 67th Street."

The officer waved in acknowledgment.

Donovan and Jefferson escorted Timmins to the back of the building and helped him out onto the fire escape. Once down in the alley, they pushed him into the back of Donovan's car.

"Take us to the 70th in Brooklyn," Donovan said to the driver.

"You can't do this to me," Timmins burst out. I . . ."

"Shut up, asshole," Jefferson snapped.

The car pulled onto 87th Street and turned south on West End Avenue.

"I'm a generous man, Mr. Timmins," Donovan said. "If you talk to me I'll let you go. On the other hand, if I hear something I don't like, I just might let you go in front of the Mancuso family estate. I assume by now that they've been made aware of your arrest. There were a lot of reporters in that mob outside the Unit."

Timmins seethed, but said nothing. The car continued south, toward the Brooklyn-Battery Tunnel. Donovan leaned back and closed his eyes.

"I haven't had a chance to use the Manhattan Shuffle in years," he said. "We should be able to keep two precincts ahead of this bum's lawyer for at least two hours. . . . It's nice to know that some of the old ways still work."

# NINE

Donovan delivered Timmins to his front door just after a red dawn had broken. The red of the dawn was almost as deep as the color of Donovan's eyes. Not counting the hour or so of sleep he had gotten aboard the *West Wind,* he had been awake for more than twenty-four hours.

Moreover, he had learned nothing more from Timmins, despite having taken the man on a tour of police stations ranging from Coney Island to the Bronx. At the end, both Timmins and he were exhausted, too tired even to be mad at one another. Donovan unlocked the man's handcuffs and let Timmins out of the car.

"This kind of tour would have cost you fifty bucks anywhere else," Donovan said.

Timmins simply bobbed his head. "I didn't do it, Lieutenant. As God is my witness, I had nothing to do with it."

"Sorry I dragged you out of the sack," Donovan said.

When Timmins was back in his building and Donovan back on the road, Jefferson said, "He's the coolest mother I've ever seen. I wish that bruises didn't show, 'cause I wanted to do a breakdance on his skull real bad."

"Me too."

"What a waste of time. What do we do now?"

"Go back to the house, what else? I'll let Timmins's lawyer scream at me for a few minutes . . ."

"I picked up some news while you and Timmins were at the City Island station house, Bill. Timmins's lawyer was last seen out by Shea Stadium. It seems that he was caught exceeding the speed limit and driving with a busted tail light while roaring up the expressway on a rumor that Timmins was at the station house in Rego Park."

"It's bad to drive with a busted tail light," Donovan said. "Lawyers should know better."

"While one of the uniforms that pulled him over for speeding was writing out the ticket, the other cop stuck his knee in the tail light. It took an hour to straighten everything out."

Back at the Unit, Donovan was duly yelled at by Timmins's lawyer, but only for ten minutes. He too was worn out. When the counselor was gone, Bonaci and Corrigan came into Donovan's office to report that Facci was nowhere to be found. He told his wife he had to go out of town on business for a few days and gave her the number of a hotel in Chicago. Donovan told Corrigan to check out the hotel, then sent out for coffee and donuts.

There were phone messages. The division commander and the police commissioner wanted to see him. The deputy commissioner for public relations wanted to know if she could be of any help. A TV station was making a fuss over Donovan's having insulted one of its reporters a few hours earlier.

"The ones who don't want a piece of the action want to have me for breakfast," Donovan said. "All of a sudden the captain's party doesn't look so bad."

Jefferson appeared, carrying a cardboard box and a paper bag. He deposited the bag on Donovan's desk. "One coffee, light. Two crullers."

"What's in the box?"

“The flyer I had run off. You know, the new composite sketch of Ms. Crockett.”

Donovan took the lid off his coffee. “Okay, make sure they're shown to everyone you can think of.”

“Will do. Oh, and Corrigan put in a call to that Chicago hotel. Guess what?”

“Facci's not there,” Donovan said.

“You're right, but the sonofabitch made a telephone reservation using his own name and address.”

“Come on.”

“No shit. The guy really phoned in a reservation.”

Donovan's face acquired a sour look. He said, “I hate having my chain pulled, and that's twice in three days.”

“Should I bother to ask the Chicago cops to check out the place?”

“I guess we have to. Facci isn't anywhere near Chicago, but we have to go through the motions.”

Jefferson turned to leave, but Donovan called him back. “Is that warrant on Ciccia's office still good?”

“Sure.”

“I have some time to kill before the parade kicks off. Let me eat and get cleaned up, then we'll go over there.”

“You don't think . . .”

“No, Facci's not there. He's probably gone underground somewhere in Brooklyn or the west fifties. Put out a bulletin on him. Wanted as a material witness.”

When Jefferson was gone, Donovan ate the crullers and drank the coffee.

“On the other hand, maybe Facci *is* in Chicago, figuring that we're too smart to bother looking for him there.” Donovan pondered that for a moment, then said, “Nah.”

He tossed the coffee cup into the garbage, then opened his desk drawer. Donovan took out the picture of Marcia and him and stared at it for a while before slipping it into his jacket pocket.

# TOO FAT TO FIT IN THE CHAIR

"I want the mustache like this," Donovan said, handing the snapshot to the barber.

Rudy Pandozzi ran the three-chair barber shop down Eighty-seventh Street next to the parking garage. Donovan had been getting his hair cut there for as long as he could remember. He loved the place. It smelled of bay rum and shaving cream, and nowhere could be seen a sign reading "hair stylist." Customers could buy combs off a cardboard rack for thirty-nine cents and a bottle of Brylcream for somewhat more. A table was piled high with much-thumbed magazines, mainly *Playboy, Popular Mechanics,* and *Field & Stream.* As a lad, Donovan used to lose himself in *Popular Mechanics* articles about how we all would be living in space colonies by the year 2000, while waiting to get his hair cut.

Now Donovan came to get a good, inexpensive shave from a man who called himself a barber and not a hair stylist, and to smell the bay rum and pick up whatever local gossip escaped him at Riley's. It was also a good excuse to read *Playboy.* Donovan already got the other two magazines at home.

Pandozzi squinted at the snapshot. "This was taken a while ago. She used to be your girl, right? What was her name, Mary something?"

"Marcia Barnes."

"That's it. I cut her hair once. She had the most beautiful hair I ever seen on any girl, black or white. Straight as an arrow, and jet black. Whatever became of her?"

"She's still around." Donovan took back the picture and slipped it into his shirt pocket just before the barber's cloth was tossed over him.

"I always said, with hair like that she's got to have Indian blood."

"It could be," Donovan said. "If your family's been in America long enough, God only knows what kind of relatives you can acquire."

"Me, I'm pure *paisan,*" Pandozzi said. "Look at that nose."

He displayed his profile, dominated by a proud eagle-beak. "Which reminds me, I see we're getting fewer in numbers these days."

"I came here for a shave, not to be reminded of my imperfections. Would you just fix up the mustache so I'll look nice for the Memorial Day parade?"

Pandozzi got a steaming hot towel and covered Donovan's face. Donovan loved the feel of the steam as it seeped into and softened his skin. Ten minutes later he was staring at a perfectly crafted mustache. The fledgling soup-strainer was exactly symmetrical and turned down, stopping just at the corners of his lips.

"Nice job, Rudy. I think it complements my rugged good looks."

"You want another complement on your good looks? I can touch up those gray hairs in your eyebrows."

"No. Them I like."

Donovan returned the hand-mirror to the barber and climbed out of the chair. He handed over six bucks, which included a dollar tip.

"Did I ever tell you about the time Albert Anastasia got shot out of my chair at the Sheraton?"

"Jesus, I've known you for thirty years and nobody has ever believed that story."

"Anastasia got shot thirty years ago. I decided to open a shop in a safer neighborhood." Pandozzi stashed the six bucks in the cash register.

"Speaking of gangsters, did Ciccia ever come in here?" Donovan asked.

"Nah. He was too fat to fit in the chair. Palucci came by every so often, though. In fact, he was in here just two weeks ago. He was telling me how he was looking forward to taking his family up to his country place for the month of June."

Donovan's mustache abruptly grew a full eighth of an inch. *"What?"*

"He's got a cabin by some lake in the Catskills. Just got it last year. He used to take the boys fishing there."

"Took 'the boys' fishing, did he? I don't suppose you know what boys."

"Nope. He never mentioned any names."

"Did he mention the name of the lake?"

Pandozzi thought for a moment, then shrugged. "He said it was a hell of a drive. Almost all the way to . . . what was the name of that soap opera that was on the air ten years ago?"

"I don't get much time for soap operas," Donovan said.

"I mean the funny one that was on late at night. You know. There was this old guy who was a flasher."

Donovan smiled. "Right, the Fernwood Flasher. The show was 'Mary Hartman, Mary Hartman.' "

"That's it," the barber said proudly.

## WHEN WE WERE YOUNG AND BULLETPROOF

Donovan held back a yawn while "Taps" was played. It was the longest time he had gone without yawning in a few days.

As things turned out, he barely made it to the ceremonial end of Manhattan's Memorial Day parade, having found the shoe box in which he kept his medals wasn't in his bedroom closet, as Barnes thought, but in the linen closet outside Clint's room. How the medals got from one place to another was something Donovan wrote off as yet another of the mysteries of living in a huge, old apartment.

But he managed to pull on his dress uniform, pleased that it fit better than ever, and carefully pinned the medals in place. Donovan combed his hair and mustache, tossed Clint a mackerel, then went to join Barnes at the monument.

Donovan lived in a handed-down-through-the-generations apartment on Riverside Drive at Eighty-Ninth Street directly overlooking the monument, so it was a short trip. Only about a thousand veterans marched in the parade, and the number of spectators wasn't much larger, so he had no trouble finding Barnes, the captain, and his party.

Barnes had never worn her dress uniform in Donovan's sight, and he thought she looked splendid—both traditional and amusing. The sight of someone he was accustomed to seeing in cutoff jeans and a t-shirt, or wearing nothing, dressed like the head honcho of a banana republic fascinated him.

''You ought to apply to the Pentagon for emergency military assistance,'' he told her. ''All you have to do is fill out this form saying that you've been invaded by Cuban mercenaries.''

She gave him a wan look. ''It's pointless to ask what you're talking about, but thanks for showing up.''

Marcie was at the end of a line that included the captain and his two crewmen, all of whom were in uniform and very attentively saluting the placing of the ceremonial wreath. The captain sported even more medals than Donovan.

''Showing up was no problem,'' he said to Marcie. ''*Standing* up may prove to be difficult. Do you think that the captain will let me crash on the foredeck?''

''No!'' she snapped. ''If you must, you can put in a token appearance and then go take a nap on the *West Wind*.''

''Sounds good to me.''

''I'll introduce you,'' Marcie said, leading Donovan to where her pier-mates had wandered. They were inspecting the stonework detail of the several-stories-high, columned monument to veterans of the Civil War.

The captain was marvelously dressed in the uniform of Her Majesty's Navy, as were the two young men with him. All three stood tall and proud when Donovan was brought to them.

Marcie beamed as she introduced her intended: ''Captain Ashton, this is the man I told you about, William Donovan.''

Ashton shook Donovan's hand with a firm grip. ''I've heard

much about you. Lieutenant,'' he said, pronouncing the title ''*lef*tenant'' in the British manner. A longtime Anglophile, Donovan was thrilled.

''It's a pleasure, Captain. May I say that your yacht is magnificent.''

''Lieutenant, you may praise my humble boat without end.'' Ashton nodded at the two young men with him. ''These are my sons, William and Kevin.''

The proper exchange of introductions was arranged.

''They are generously acting as my crew on this cruise.''

''Why have you come to America?'' Donovan asked.

''Actually we're making a circumnavigation. We sailed from Southampton—our Southampton, not yours—and came straight here to watch your Independence Day activities, and then we're off to Australia for the America's Cup defense.''

Every bit of Donovan's being throbbed with envy. ''Do you need another hand?'' he asked.

Ashton laughed and said, ''I'd love to have you aboard, if your police department will give you a few months' vacation.''

''Perhaps some other time,'' Donovan said sadly.

''We've paid our respects to your war dead,'' Ashton said. ''Now let's get on with the party. If we are going to remember the dead, let's do it in style.''

He led the way to his yacht, which was named the *Christopher E.* It swarmed with caterers' aides and party guests, and the crowd spilled out onto the dock. A young couple sat on the transom railing of Marcia's boat, smoking a joint. Donovan gave them a dirty look as he passed. They noticed his uniform and quickly flipped the marijuana cigarette into the harbor.

Marcie squeezed Donovan's arm. ''I can remember a time . . .''

''When we both were young and bulletproof. I was really objecting to them borrowing our boat.''

''Our?'' she asked.

The entire community that inhabited the Seventy-ninth Street

Boat Basin seemed to have turned out for the occasion. A string quartet played Renaissance music from the bow of the *Christopher E.* The bearded, hairy chap who lived on the houseboat moored to the other side of the *West Wind* sat in front of them, sipping a glass of wine and humming along. Class act, Donovan thought, everything done delicately and without pretension.

"I have a table reserved for us," Ashton said, leading the group to it. It was set up amidships, just forward of the mizzenmast.

They were served indeed: bits of marinated lamb, cherry tomatoes, assorted vegetables, and even mandarin oranges were served on beds of lightly spiced rice. Marcie had a glass of red Bordeaux. Donovan was offered a bolt of the hard stuff and tried to decline.

"I won't hear of teetotaling on one of your national holidays," Ashton said, waving his hand at a bartender presiding over a silver tray of liquors.

"I've been awake for a long time, and this day is far from over," Donovan explained. "If I even sniff alcohol I'll collapse on the cellist."

"You are going to take a nap, William," Marcie said. "It can't hurt to have one or two drinks. Besides, I want to get a picture of us in our dress uniforms, and you look too uptight."

She brandished an autofocus Nikon.

"Come on, Lieutenant," Ashton said. "The sun is over the yardarm, and a drink will help you relax."

"If you insist . . . a Bloody Mary, please, and light on the spice."

"I'll have a whisky," Ashton said, and his sons ordered the same.

The five of them made small talk while eating, mostly about blue-water sailing and the reasons for America's losing the Cup to Australia in 1983. Not one question came about Donovan's case, which pleased him no end, and he celebrated with a second Bloody Mary.

After a time he found need of the head, and Ashton told him where it was. Donovan went below on his own, leaving Marcie to entertain the others.

The *Christopher E.* was a special boat indeed. While her shell was made of reinforced graphite and fiberglass and very modern, the interior was a museum of ages-old nautical artifacts. There was scrimshaw, brass telescopes and sextants, lithographs of tall ships all bearing the British ensign, a passel of family photographs, a coat of arms, and framed citations signed by assorted First Sea Lords. Quickly, Donovan discovered that during World War II Ashton had commanded a destroyer that operated in the Mediterranean and on North Sea convoy duty.

The head was occupied, and Donovan wandered into what proved to be Ashton's cabin. It was, like the rest of the interior, a museum, and included a captain's desk that looked at least two centuries old. Once used for keeping the log, the desk now held personal correspondence and several small, framed family photos. One of the photos caught Donovan's eye and he picked it up. It was a few years old and showed Ashton, his two sons, and another young man, that one dressed in a Royal Marines uniform. They were standing in front of an English country manor house.

''Lieutenant,'' Ashton said, startling Donovan. The old sailor walked more quietly than even Marcie, who could slip in and out of a room without disturbing the air.

''I'm sorry,'' Donovan said. ''The head was occupied, and I was killing time. I hope you don't think I was snooping.''

''Of course not. How do you like my cabin?''

''Like the rest of the boat, it's wonderful.'' He handed the photo to Ashton, who put it back on the desk.

''This is a terrible confession for someone who is supposed to be an old sea dog,'' Ashton said, ''but I like comfort, especially on circumnavigations.''

''I guess that upwards of a year at sea is rather on the demanding side.''

''The route to Australia is going to be a long haul,'' Ashton agreed. "I'm afraid we'll have time for only three port calls en route—Cape Verde, Rio, and Capetown."

"I wish I could go to Perth for the races," Donovan said. "But it would mean taking at least a month off, and spending a few thousand dollars on air fare and hotels."

"Well, if the department gives you the time and you have the money, you're welcome to stay aboard the *Christopher E.* once you get down under," Ashton said. "In the meantime, the head is now yours."

Donovan slipped inside and closed the door. When he got back on deck, Marcie lined up the whole group, herself included, and conned a guest into taking their pictures. She held Donovan's hand for the photo.

The string quartet had switched to Mozart, and the burly man who lived on the houseboat had disappeared. Donovan went to the *West Wind,* took off his dress uniform, then fell onto the bed and soon was asleep, dreaming of white sails and blue seas.

## YOU GOT FERNS, YOU GOT WOODS

"Why not a Fernwood?" Donovan asked.

"But Lieutenant, that was a name on a TV show," Jefferson protested.

"It's also a name on a road map, in Sullivan County, right up near the Pennsylvania state line. And there's a lake nearby, Silver Lake."

"This is too easy to be true."

"It's better than wasting the time of our counterparts in Chicago."

It was Tuesday, May 27. Donovan had slept through the balance of Memorial Day and the night after, and Marcie, now officially on vacation, didn't disturb him. A cursory search of Ciccia's office revealed nothing, news that certainly didn't warrant interrupting a long-needed slumber. The division commander and the police commissioner wanted to talk to Donovan, but Marcie lied and told them he was out.

He paid for her thoughtfulness the following day. Donovan was subjected to a dayful of indignities that would have humbled a lesser man. The division commander didn't want to get his ass in trouble with the police commissioner because of Donovan. The commissioner didn't want to get *his* ass in trouble with the mayor, who, facing an election campaign, wanted to look as if he were tough on crime. The commissioner's pretty young press aide was so eager to help Donovan with his press problems that he came to wonder is she was unattached romantically, and so inquired around One Police Plaza. It turned out that she was attached, but Donovan's inquiries assured that rumors would be flying around police headquarters for weeks to come. Donovan liked rocking boats, so long as no real harm came of it.

The late afternoon air was crisp and the visibility nearly unlimited. But the roar of the engine and the rotor was overwhelming, especially when contrasted with the absolute silence below. From a thousand feet, Manhattan looked like an architect's model of a city: neat, clean, and quiet.

''I hate choppers,'' Jefferson said.

''This is a Bell JetRanger II. It's one of the most common and safest helicopters in the world.''

''I like aircraft that have wings, like birds. If the engine stops, they can coast to a landing.''

''Most likely on the Garden State Parkway, or, if we luck out, Giants Stadium.''

The NYPD helicopter passed over Manhattan and the Hudson and headed across New Jersey toward its destination, Skytop Airport. That was in Fremont township, just south of Route 93, and about five miles from Silver Lake.

The chopper cruised over the Jersey Palisades and the high-rise buildings that Donovan had watched grow, looking from the windows of his fifteenth floor apartment. Ever since they were completed, they made the western horizon resemble a crosscut saw.

"I think that one five-hundred-pound blockbuster per building would do nicely, don't you?" he asked idly.

"What?"

"Never mind. How far is it to Skytop?"

"About half an hour at present speed," the pilot said over his shoulder. "Of course, once we get out of the TCA and don't have to worry about picking our way through traffic, we'll be able to speed up."

Jefferson began to ask a question.

"*T*erminal *C*ontrol *A*rea," Donovan said. "It's an air traffic control method around major airports."

Jefferson shook his head in admiration of his boss's knowledge.

"I thought you flew a chopper in 'Nam," Donovan said.

"No. I did just about everything else, though. Mainly, choppers were the things that dropped us off in places that were dangerous to our health. That's why I don't like 'em."

"We're only going to the Catskills. Think of this as a vacation. Do you know how much people pay for a day in the Catskills?"

Jefferson said, "A nice piece of change. But then, they get Paul Anka or Sammy Davis and I get you."

"What about the local cops?"

"The town police will meet us at the airport. They got a warrant on the house. The last I heard from them was that an '82 Buick registered to Facci was parked behind it."

"If Facci really is in that house," Donovan said, "then he ain't exactly as cunning as John Dillinger."

Jefferson agreed. "I've seen better jobs of going into hiding."

"Yeah," Donovan said. "Curious."

Jefferson asked what was curious.

"Rudy the barber told me that Palucci was planning on taking the whole month of June off so he could vacation in that house with his wife and kids. And Facci . . . between the bullshit in Chicago and the house on the lake he might as well have sent us a telegram where he was going."

"How do you read him?"

Donovan said, "Either Facci is a lot smarter than we think, or he's confused . . . confused and scared."

Jefferson watched the New Jersey countryside go by until the rows of development houses began to give way to larger estates surrounded by trees and fields.

"We'll talk to Facci and see what he says," Donovan said. "But I'll give you ten to one he says pretty much the same thing as Timmins."

Jefferson was exasperated. "*Somebody's* got to know what's going on," he said.

"Why?" Donovan asked, and launched into an exposition of his theory that all things moved inexorably from order toward disorder, and that after a certain point attempts at logical explanations were pointless. This was the theory that Donovan hit upon while going down the fire escape from the Unit to Riley's, and despite his fear of helicopters, Jefferson fell asleep during the telling of it.

# TEN

Silver Lake was a typical glacial lake, about a mile across and formed when the glaciers of the last ice age retreated some ten to fifteen thousand years ago, leaving behind gigantic ice cubes that, once melted, formed round, deep lakes that eventually became fed by streams and aquifers. They were to be found throughout the mid-to-northern latitudes of North America.

Donovan and Jefferson were picked up at Skytop Airport by Detective Sergeant Howard Eakans of the Sullivan County P.D. He seemed like a decent-enough fellow, with the calm demeanor that suggested he wasn't one of those country cops who resented big-city detectives. During the twenty-minute drive along back roads to Silver Lake, Eakans filled in Donovan and Jefferson on the steps he had taken. Eight of his men were emplaced around the Palucci cottage—four to maintain roadblocks on Lakeside Road, and an equal number in sniper positions.

"We have some pretty decent marksmen in this county," Eakans said.

"I guess there must be a lot of good hunting out here," Jefferson said.

"I guess there is," Eakans replied. "Personally, I don't approve of hunting. Most of my men work out on the rifle and pistol range three times a week.''

Jefferson was chastised, and Donovan tried to hide a smile. He said, ''Howard, has there been any action at the cottage?''

''Not a thing. We've been watching since eleven this morning, and no one has come or gone. Not only that, no one has been seen in the place. All the shades are drawn.''

''That means if Facci is in there, he's alone. There's no way you can keep a half a dozen guys from peeking out a window now and then, let alone going for a stroll.''

The SCPD car passed two motels, a liquor store, a bait shop, and a run-down grocery store.

''How isolated is the cottage?'' Donovan asked.

''There's a mile of woods on either side,'' Eakans said. ''Palucci's cottage is one of the first of a new development planned for the lake.''

''I'm sure Palucci paid cash. I love these guys who tell the IRS they make twenty thousand dollars a year then go out and plunk down fifty grand cash on a summer house.''

''Sixty-seven five,'' Eakans said. ''I checked it out before you landed.''

''You got the roads blocked, what about escape by sea?'' Jefferson asked.

''The only boat on the property is a small sailboat. If that worries you I have a twenty-three-foot Mako with a ninety-horsepower Merc standing by.''

Donovan was impressed. ''You guys don't fuck around, do you?''

Eakans smiled, and said, ''It gets kind of boring out here, Lieutenant. After a while you get sick of drunk drivers and family disputes. When something like this comes up, we try to do our best.''

Donovan nodded appreciatively.

''Tell me, just how dangerous is this Facci?''

''Not very, at least not in person. He's too high on the ladder to be much of a gunslinger. Besides, I got this feeling he's running scared and is sitting in that cottage, half-panicked, trying to figure out what to do.''

''But he *is* important? I mean, in the New York mobs.''

''No doubt. And someone in that position should be in Bensonhurst huddling with his *caporegime* on on Park Avenue in consultation with his lawyer, not holed up in a country cottage that was ridiculously easy for us to find.''

''Meaning?''

''Meaning that I intend to walk right up to the front door and ask him what the fuck he's doing,'' Donovan said.

''Sergeant, don't bother trying to tell Lieutenant Donovan he might get his ass shot off. Lieutenant Donovan's on a roll, and he don't listen to nobody but the spirits when he's on a roll.''

At Donovan's request, Eakans pulled his car right up in front of the cottage. When there was no response from the house, the three of them walked up onto the porch. All around, hidden behind white oaks and pitch pines, were SCPD snipers.

Jefferson stood to one side of the door. ''You sure you want to do this?'' he asked, in a loud stage whisper.

''Yeah, if he's armed he's probably so scared he'd shoot his foot off. Let me handle it.'' He rapped on the door with the barrel of his Clint Eastwood Special. Eakans stood behind, carrying a double-barreled 12-gauge Remington.

After half a minute's silence, they could hear footsteps inside.

''Who's there?''

''Bill Donovan, Facci. Open up.''

Ten seconds went by. ''You alone?''

''Of course not. I'm a sailor at heart. I get lost in the woods real easy.''

''Okay, okay. Am I safe?''

''From me, yes,'' Donovan said.

The lock turned in the door, and the door swung open.

Donovan went in first, his gun in front of him just in case. He had guessed wrong in the past, and had the scars to prove it. He didn't want to guess wrong again.

Facci looked as if he had been sacked out on the couch, but not asleep. Days without sleep were evident on his already haggard face. Donovan motioned for Jefferson and Eakans to search the house, and it was quickly done.

''I'm alone,'' Facci said.

''Guns?''

''One shotgun under the couch. It's licensed.''

Jefferson retrieved it.

The coffee table was littered with wine bottles and cigarette butts. The country cottage that Palucci had so carefully laid out for family vacations looked as if it had just suffered from a long bachelor party. Facci produced the license for the shotgun, which Eakans went off to check.

Facci had been shaking when Donovan first saw him, but after a minute calmed down enough to talk.

''How'd you find me?'' he asked.

Donovan laughed. ''Are you telling me that you didn't lead me here?''

''What?''

''That Chicago business was pretty superficial.''

''To you, maybe. But not everyone's as smart as you.''

Facci's cigarette shook ashes onto the carpet. Donovan put an arm around his shoulder and led him out the back door. Facci balked at the exit.

''There could be guys out there with guns,'' he said.

''There are. Mine. Right now, you're the safest man in the world.''

''Where are we going?''

''I want us to talk alone.'' Donovan led the way toward a fourteen-foot catamaran perched on the sandy beach.

''Aren't you going to read me my rights? Let me call my lawyer?''

''You're not under arrest for anything,'' Donovan said. ''And as for calling your lawyer, do you trust him? At this point, who do you trust?''

''I don't know, Lieutenant. I wish I did.'' Facci took a long drag on his cigarette and tossed it into the lake.

Donovan looked over at the boat. ''I hate Hobie Cats,' he said. ''I wish they had stayed in California where they belong.''

Facci looked confused.

''Look at that sail,'' Donovan went on. ''It must have eight different colors in it. It's called a 'Tequila Sunrise' sail. No real sailor would race a boat that has a sail named after a dumb drink. For one thing, dark colors absorb the sun's heat, thereby screwing up the aerodynamics. For another, there's the question of taste.''

''Lieutenant . . . ?''

Donovan took off his jacket, shoes, and socks, and rolled up his pants. ''Let's take her out for a spin.''

Facci said, ''Hey, hold on a second! I can't swim, and the rumor is that this lake is bottomless.''

''Every glacial lake is rumored to be bottomless. Mothers keep their kids from straying into deep water by dispensing ridiculous tales about being sucked into submarine caverns and reappearing, quite dead, just outside Pittsburgh. Take off your shoes and socks and get on the boat.''

''I don't know about this.''

''Facci, it's all ready to go. The sail is even on the boom, which lends credence to the notion that Palucci was planning to bring his family here.''

Facci said, ''Dom *was* planning to take the month off. His oldest kid sails the boat.''

Donovan raised the single sail and fastened the halyard. He pushed the boat into the water and stood, ankle deep in the lake, holding the starboard hull.

''Come on, Facci, it's only a light breeze.''

Facci shook his head but did as he was told. Soon he was

sitting cross-legged on the nylon trampoline that connected the twin hulls. Donovan gave the boat a shove out onto the lake and hopped aboard.

"Do I have to do anything?" Facci asked, once again nearly in a panic.

"Nah. I can run it all from back here. I have one line to pull and a tiller to steer the thing." He steered out toward the center of the lake, moving swiftly but not fast enough to cause the windward hull to lift out of the water.

"How much sailing have you done on these catamarans?" Facci asked.

"None," Donovan replied.

"*What!*"

"Think nothing of it. One boat's like another. This one just has an extra hull and a sail that resembles an antipasto. You're safe with me at the helm."

To illustrate the point, Donovan hauled in on the mainsheet. The added wind pressure caused the windward hull to lift two feet out of the water. Donovan felt like the California kids in the orange juice commercials.

Facci screamed and dived for a handhold.

"Come to think of it," Donovan said, "there's a glacial lake near where I used to spend summers on Long Island. That one is rumored to be bottomless, too."

"Donovan!"

The lieutenant let the hull slip back into the water and the boat ease to a halt. They floated quietly in the middle of the lake while Facci regained his senses. Finally, he sat next to Donovan, but still held tightly to the hull.

Donovan said, "Okay, I've heard Timmins's side of this thing. Let's hear yours."

Jefferson was perplexed. It was a feeling he got often when Donovan was around. "Let me see if I got this straight," he said.

''Timmins told you he's a saint and you believed him. Facci fed you the same line and you believed him, too.

Donovan swirled the last of his coffee around in the bottom of the cup. ''I don't think there's a gang war on.''

''Bill . . . Rigili, Ciccia, and Bono are dead, all knocked off by the same person. So the hit man is a lady. Not every pro shooter has to look like Charles Bronson.''

''On that boat, in the middle of a fairly routine frog pond, Facci was a man scared out of his wits.''

''I would be too, sailin' with you. Did you really win races when you were a kid?''

''A few. That pewter dish I keep my keys and pocket change in was for the local championship. I did make a try for the North Americans, but capsized a couple hundred yards from the finish line while running third. I figured that was God's way of telling me that yachting really is a summer game for the idle rich, and while I was idle enough, I was hardly rich. So, back to the West Side. Once I got out of the academy and started working I never got the chance to spend summers by the sea. I hardly go to the country anymore.''

''I wouldn't mind spending a few days at the beach,'' Jefferson said wistfully.

''Facci was *scared,* and not just of drowning. I don't think he was lying to me. He said he didn't know what was going on. There were no plans for a war. He didn't think that Timmins had the manpower, and as far as Facci knew both Ciccia and Timmins were happy with the status quo.''

''Timmins still could have hired that broad,'' Jefferson said. ''Like you said, it's the sort of thing he would do.''

''And face a massive retaliatory strike from the boys in Bensonhurst? I don't think so.''

''I still don't know whether Timmins is raising an army,'' Jefferson said. ''Some word may have come in while you and me were tourin' the Catskills. I'm going upstairs to find out. You comin'?''

Donovan shook his head. "I've worked enough for one day. I just want to sit here for another couple of minutes, then go back to my apartment."

Jefferson got off his barstool. "Don't tell me you're not spending the night at the Floating Palace?"

"See if there were any messages from me while you're upstairs," Donovan said.

George came over and parked his beer next to Donovan's coffee cup. "You got any money on the game tonight?" he asked.

"What game?"

"Roundball. The NBA playoffs, remember? The game starts in an hour. I've got the Lakers and the points."

It didn't surprise Donovan that Ciccia's gambling operation was still working. It was like all mindless bodies—the head and right arm might be cut off, but the creature lived on.

"I'm not interested in pro basketball," Donovan said.

"The Lakers are coming back strong. Tonight's game could be decisive. If you're not gonna bet on the game, you could at least get in the pool."

"You've got a pool going on the NBA playoffs, too? Isn't the baseball pool enough?"

"Bill . . . there's only one box left. If somebody doesn't buy it in the next hour, Morty will. And you know he always wins."

Morty was the owner of Riley's, but was seldom on the premises and not considered one of the boys. Yet his knack for picking the winning box in various sports pools was uncanny, and, to the regulars, unfair to the highest degree.

"Why do I always get stuck saving you guys from the boss?" Donovan complained. "I've been in more pools than Johnny Weissmuller, and I ain't won nothin' yet. Okay, how much?"

"Ten bucks."

Donovan put the money on the bar, waited for the posterboard to be brought to him, and signed his name in the last box.

Kohler was delighted. "Okay, I can pick the numbers after I

finish my beer. You might get lucky tonight.''

''Sure,'' Donovan said, and crossed the room to feed some quarters into the space battles game. After fifteen minutes, he was out three dollars but had pushed his score up to over ten thousand points.

He retook his seat. 'I make it to be some basic, very static logic program. The defense is tough and inflexible. All I have to do is figure a way around it.''

''You better figure your way around this,'' Jefferson said, the door swinging shut behind him. He was bearing his clipboard, which when Donovan was tired looked like the torturer's rack. ''I got word from my source on 125th that Timmins is starting to hire guns. You still think that Facci and him are sweethearts?''

''I'm busy saving this bar from Morty.''

''As for your other messages, you got four calls from Sergeant Barnes inquiring as to what you would like for dinner. She wants to celebrate the start of her vacation. You better get yourself some caffeine tablets, baby. Your day is far from over.''

''My God.''

''I see some *hard* boogie'n in your future.''

''Shut up and go away.''

''I'll go, but you better be bright-eyed and bushy-tailed in the morning. Like it or not, you got a gang war on your hands.''

''Scram,'' Donovan said.

George had finished the random picking of numbers for the pool. Donovan got three and eight. If the last digits of the final score were Celtics three and Lakers eight, Donovan would win.

''One more thing,'' Jefferson said. ''We got a phone call from Eakans. Facci failed to take your advice and stay in that cottage with maybe six or seven cops to protect him.''

''What did he do?''

''As soon as we cleared out, he bolted for parts unknown. It didn't take him long to lose the tail Eakans had on him. Now Facci's gone, and God knows what he has in mind.''

Donovan got off the barstool and headed for the door. "I'm going home to change my clothes, feed Clint, and pack."

"Pack?" Jefferson asked.

"Yeah. I just decided to spend the summer yachting with my intended."

## RED SKY AT NIGHT, SAILOR'S DELIGHT

His canvas L. L. Bean bag weighed down with clothes and other items, Donovan picked his way slowly through Riverside Park. He walked down the path circling the Soldiers' and Sailors' Monument and onto the lower level of the park, where joggers jogged and couples walked hand-in-hand. It was beginning to cloud over, and the temperature was falling into the fifties. A stiff breeze had come up from the southwest. A freight train rumbled along the subterranean tracks, shaking the ground beneath Donovan's feet.

He paused to rest at the stone overlook that gave such a fine view of the marina. To the south of the marina, a rotting half-sunken dock supported the remains of a rowboat. Seagulls roosted everywhere. To the west, a red sun was setting. Donovan liked to think that the color was caused by dust from the eruption of El Chichon volcano in Mexico, but realized that the more likely culprit was New Jersey's thriving chemical industry.

Down the stone overlook a few yards, a thin man in a seersucker suit was taking photos of the sunset, using a long telephoto lens. Donovan picked up his bag, and, feeling a bit like a swagman himself, went down the steps to the marina. He was a quarter of the way out onto the southernmost dock when Marcie leaped off the transom of the *West Wind* and ran to embrace him.

"I bought us tons of Chinese food . . . and wine, good wine. Let's eat in tonight. We can celebrate my vacation right here."

She stuck her hand in the back pocket of his pants and steered him down the dock to the boat. Neither of them was aware that the man who had been photographing the red sunset had begun taking pictures of them.

It was windy and rather chilly on deck, so they ate in the main saloon, sharing platters of braised bean curd with Chinese mushrooms, and shredded beef with bamboo shoots. They split a bottle of Mouton-Baron-Philippe and listened to a program of Vivaldi on the radio.

When all the food wrappers and boxes were thrown out and the dishes piled safely in the galley sink, Donovan leaned back on the L-shaped couch and Marcie rested her head on his shoulder.

"How do you feel?" she asked, running a fingertip over his mustache.

"Good. I feel good. I've always wanted to run away to sea." He swept an arm around the wooden warmth of the boat's interior.

"Do you really mean it? Are you going to stay with me?"

Marcie switched positions so that she was lying with her head in his lap, looking up at him.

"I *am* your intended, am I not?" he replied. "Think how disappointed the captain would be if his neighbor's intended suddenly jumped ship."

"Donovan, I . . . well, twelve years ago I made the mistake of letting you get away. But I had an excuse: I was only twenty-four at the time. I've since learned not to make the same mistake twice."

Donovan ran his fingers through her hair. "There's one thing about you that hasn't changed. When you see something you want, you go right for it."

"We've been dancing around each other for twelve damned years. Well, my love, the band just stopped playing."

Locking her fingers behind his neck, she pulled his head to hers. They kissed long and passionately, touching each other, pressed tightly together, and when they pulled apart both were out of breath.

He laughed and gasped at the same time. " 'You fight for love and glory,' indeed," he said.

They kissed again, and this time when their lips parted she stood, and with a grunt lifted his Bean bag and handed it to him. "Why don't you put your stuff away. I'll lock the companionway door . . . I have a present for you, something I've been wanting to give you all day."

He went into the cabin and started unpacking. The large port-side clothes locker had taped to it a note reading "in here." On a whim, Donovan switched on his Sony Watchman and tuned in the eleven o'clock news just in time for the sports. Donovan could never be very far from the latest news bulletin, and this particular one he had a stake in. He listened to the scores, then shook his head in disbelief.

A hand snaked over his shoulder and switched off the Watchman. "I should have known you'd manage to sneak a television in here," Marcie said.

Donovan was overwhelmed. "The Celtics beat the Lakers 113 to 108."

"B.F.D."

"Yeah, Barnes, it *is* a Big Fuckin' Deal. I have numbers three and eight in the pool at Riley's. I just won four hundred bucks. How do you want to spend it?"

"On something practical," she said, "like dinner at Lutèce."

"You're on. Where's my present?"

She stood back, wrapped in Donovan's robe and striking a model's pose. "See . . . I told you, I cuddle up in this when it's cold."

"It *is* chilly tonight," he agreed.

She shrugged, and the robe dropped to the cabin floor. When she switched off the cabin lights, her body gleamed in the harbor lights streaming in the windows.

"You'll catch cold," he said.

She hooked her fingers around his belt. "Make me warm," she said.

## SOLDIERS, SAILORS

The man in the seersucker suit opened the passenger's-side door of a gray BMW that was parked by the Soldiers and Sailors Monument. He slipped inside, holding a camera case in his lap. The car pulled out into traffic and headed south down Riverside Drive.

"Did you get them?" asked the driver, a carefully groomed man wearing a blue sports jacket and gray slacks.

"Both. Half a roll of them walking down the dock and getting into the boat."

You're certain it was Donovan?"

"It was him—new mustache and all. The girl was unmistakable; definitely Marcia Barnes."

"So they're back together," the driver said.

"It certainly looks that way," his partner replied.

The driver made a hard turn onto Seventy-sixth Street, and the tires squealed. "They could be a problem for us," he said.

"Donovan alone is a problem."

# Eleven

Despite having gotten a scant five hours' sleep, Donovan awoke ready to take on two battalions of Huns with one arm tied behind his back.

His life—his personal life, at least—seemed to make sense for the first time in years. While he was on a boat, he was no longer at sea; maybe the relationship between two such strong personalities as Marcia Barnes and him *needed* twelve years to age. At any rate, the time had come and he meant to stay with her, be it on the boat, in his apartment, or, if it came to that, in her apartment on the East Side. All doubts had been washed out by the rising of the sun.

It had warmed up considerably by daybreak, and Marcie had, in her sleep, kicked off the covers. To look great in the morning was an achievement at any age. To look great in the morning after spending the night in unspeakable pleasures and getting only five hours' sleep was a miracle.

Her lips were half-open and curved sensuously even as she slept. Her hair lay in ringlets across her shoulders. Donovan toyed with it, lightly so as not to wake her. There wasn't a wrinkle on her light bronze skin, and her breasts and thighs were as firm as they were twelve years earlier. She too had been making regular trips to the gym.

Donovan slid down the bed and brushed a fingertip gently across her stomach, looking for the scar that he knew must be there. The last time they worked on a case together she was wounded by a bullet, but no trace of it remained. There was not so much as a blemish. He looked closer, and heard a yawn and her voice: "If you find anything you like, I have a Memorial Day sale still going on."

He slid back up and kissed her. "I like everything."

She said, "God, what did we *do* last night?"

"Everything."

"And I thought I dreamt it!" She hugged him, pressing his cheek against her breast.

"Last night you were grade-A, government-inspected dynamite," Donovan said.

"*We* were. We always have been. You and I were meant to be. Do you believe me now?"

He believed her.

"What were you looking for down there?"

"The scar. Remember! The one that was going to ruin your life by keeping you from wearing a two-piece bathing suit."

"Oh, *that*. I had plastic surgery done to remove it a year and a half ago. Got the department to pay for it, too. The doctor did a nice job, wouldn't you say?"

"Incredible."

Donovan kissed her breast, then rolled onto his back. There was the sound of a tugboat chugging up the Hudson, and the occasional lapping of waves against the hull of the *West Wind*.

"What are you going to do on your vacation?" he asked.

"Absolutely *everything* I never get around to doing. I'm going to every museum, every art gallery, every Broadway show, every movie, and every restaurant with more than one star."

''Ambitious.''

''And you are going to come along and pay for it all with the money you won last night.''

''Why am I not surprised?'' Donovan asked.

She whispered in his ear. ''Because I'm beautiful, brilliant, a marvelous conversationalist . . .''

''. . . Modest . . .''

''And dynamite in bed. And I'm in love with you, William Donovan. Now it can be told.''

He smiled, and she said, ''Make love to me again.''

''Christ, I'm still sore from last night. And I have to get to work. There are two battalions of Huns to be fought.''

''They can wait. You can make it a luncheon engagement.'' She reached down his body, but he slipped out of bed.

''Donovan!'' she cried out, as he went into the head.

He had his old shaving mug lathered and his face brushed with Krank's when Marcie pushed her way in. She was still without clothes, as was he.

''You had better take a shower and start dressing if you're going to make it to every museum, every art gallery, every . . .''

''Dammit, I'm on vacation! I'll do things at my own pace.''

She wrapped her arms around him from behind. He said, ''Hold still! I've been working on this mustache for five days now, and I don't want to slip and slice off half of it.''

He shaved around his mustache, then began on his sideburns. Marcie worked her fingers through his chest hair.

''Knock it off.''

''Poor baby. So terribly put-upon.'' She kissed the back of his neck.

Donovan paused in his shaving to admire his new face. ''I think I look a bit like Ted Turner, don't you?''

She elevated her eyes. ''Two years ago it was Harrison Ford. Before him, Christopher George. And we mustn't forget Clint Eastwood.''

''Lies, just lies,'' Donovan said.

"And before *him,* Gregory Peck," she insisted.

"Rumor and innuendo."

"Donovan, why do you have this pathological need to imagine that you look like celebrities?"

Marcie slapped his behind. "You are *not* a normal person," she said.

"I'd bore you if I was."

He draped the towel over her head and stepped into the shower.

## ARNOLD SCHWARZENEGGER DIDN'T GET HIS START THIS WAY

"I'm sure of it," Donovan said to himself, as he took time out from pumping iron to stretch his arms. It had been quite a few days since he had made a pre-work stop at the gym that was neighbor to the Unit, and in that time the place had grown in the number of color-coordinated leotards, leg warmers, and headbands.

Donovan had long feared the day when he would show up for a workout only to be told that he would have to get a manicure first. The day didn't seem far off; indeed, the "gym" had become a "health spa" within the past year, and the membership fee had doubled. That part of it didn't bother Donovan, who invoked neighbor's rights and got his workouts for free, the gym owner being Morty Rinzler, the same guy who owned Riley's.

After he finished with the weights he lay down on an exercise mat to do his situps. The night on the river had given him a burst of adrenalin that wouldn't quit, and besides, if he didn't keep his stomach flat he would hear about it from Barnes.

Donovan did two sets of forty situps and was lying on his back, resting, perspiration clouding his eyes, when he noticed a woman working out on the same mat. She was facing him, and doing leg-lifts. Donovan rubbed his eyes on his wristband and stared directly into her eyes, as she stared back.

For a moment, Donovan looked at the ceiling then turned toward her. She was about six feet away, and, unlike many other women in the room, was dressed plainly. She wore regular gray gym shorts and an old, white polo shirt that bore the name of a hunt club in faded letters.

"This is Wednesday, isn't it?" he asked.

"I think so."

"There's a new rule in this place," Donovan said. "On Wednesdays you have to wear mauve."

She scanned his gym clothes, which were blue and clearly marked with the letters "NYPD."

She stopped exercising and sat up. "Then I guess we both have to leave."

He said, "My name's Bill Donovan. I work next door. Can I buy you breakfast?"

"Why not?" she said, and got to her feet.

He did the same. She stepped up to him, close enough for him to notice that she hadn't worked up a sweat. They shook hands.

"Andrea Jones," she said. "I'll take a shower and meet you in ten minutes."

Donovan watched her walk off to the women's locker room, then went to take a shower of his own.

When he was done and had toweled himself dry, he stepped up to the mirror to comb his hair. The mirror had a glaze of mist from the hot shower. Donovan stared into the mist for a very long time, thinking. Then he pressed his thumb against the mirror and made a check-mark in the mist. He combed his hair and went to his locker to get dressed.

Outside on the sidewalk, Jones looked anything but plain. She wore what Donovan could only described as a designer camouflage suit, made for the woman who can look good in anything, and she was quite eye-catching. Her long hair blew softly in the morning breeze.

"There's nothing very fancy in the way of breakfast places around here," Donovan said.

"No matter. I'm not hungry. Would you like to go for a walk?"

"Sure."

She headed down Eighty-seventh Street toward the river, and Donovan took a quick-step to catch up with her.

"I've seen you before," he said.

"I don't think so. I don't live in New York, and while I come here often on business, I usually don't stay more than a week."

"Casual visitors aren't likely to come to a walkup gym on the Upper West Side."

"I like to walk, and I happened to walk here," she said. "The gym looked interesting. Are you really a policeman?"

"The last time I looked at my paycheck I was," Donovan replied.

"Is this your 'beat'?"

"It has been for some time."

They crossed West End Avenue and continued toward Riverside Drive.

"Then you could tell me if this is a good place to live. I'm thinking of taking a flat in New York."

"It's good enough," Donovan said. "It's safe, but not cheap. And I thought you only come here on business."

"I own a farm for racehorses down in Virginia," she said. "I have an entry in the Rogers Stakes at Belmont this weekend. As I said, I'm in New York often, and I'm tired of staying at hotels."

"Where are you staying now?"

"At the Plaza."

"I guess you can afford an apartment on the West Side," he said. "Me, I'm lucky. I inherited a rent-controlled one on Riverside. It's a huge old monster with low rent. You know, 'Six Rms Riv Vu,' except I have nine rooms."

"Nine rooms? Those are quite some digs."

"The landlord has been trying to get me out for years so he can triple the rent. But he can't run any of the usual landlord games on me, because of the line of work I'm in."

She stopped at the corner of Eighty-seventh and Riverside, not far from the entrance to his building. "May I see your place?" she asked.

"You're awfully sure of yourself, asking a total stranger to take you to his apartment."

"You're a policeman," she replied, adjusting her large, suede shoulder bag. "I think I can trust you."

"Come on up to my parlor," Donovan said, and led her there.

## PURPLE HAZE

"It's odd that you can't see the fog so well from the river's edge," Jones said, looking out Donovan's fifteenth-story living room window and across the Hudson.

"That's not just fog," Donovan replied. "It's a mixture of fog from the river and chemical waste from New Jersey. In the morning, just after dawn, it ranges from a cool blue to a purple haze. Just before dusk, the color turns orange, then red. In an odd sort of way it's quite beautiful."

She said, "I can't imagine chemical waste being beautiful."

"This is New York City. We have to take our beauty where we find it."

"I guess I'll always be a country girl. I like to see colors in the fields and trees."

Clint splashed in the bathtub, and Jones turned in the direction of the sound.

"That's my turtle," Donovan said. "He can always tell when there's somebody in the apartment."

"That was a rather loud splash for a turtle."

"Clint is rather large."

She gave Donovan a queer look. "May I see him?"

"Sure. This way." Donovan took her to the guest bathroom, and switched on the light. Clint looked up at them through squinty eyes, and swished his tail from side to side.

Andrea Jones laughed. "You keep a snapping turtle in your bathtub?"

"I have two other bathtubs," Donovan said, "and Clint would have been left to die if I hadn't taken him in." He sighed. "Actually, the time for us to part company is near. He's getting to be too much for me. One day soon I'll drive him to the country and let him go in some nice pond."

"You're remarkable," she said. "I can't imagine anyone in Manhattan going out of his way to save a snapping turtle."

"Maybe you should spend more time here. We're not as hard-bitten as we're made out to be."

He went back to the living room window, opened it wide and sat on the sill, facing sideways. When she walked up to him, he said, "If you have good eyes, you can watch the haze turn from blue to purple."

"I'm not sure that I want to. However, you do have a sensational flat, Lieutenant."

She stepped close enough for her hair to brush his cheek, and slipped her hand into her shoulder bag. At the same time, Donovan slipped his hand inside his jacket and wrapped his fingers around the handgrip of his magnum.

Her lips curled into a wry smile. She pulled a brush out of her bag and gave several strokes to her hair, letting the strands blow in the wind from the window.

Donovan reached up suddenly, and uninvitedly, and ran his fingers through her hair. She jerked away, as if stung, and jammed the brush back into her bag.

"You said I could trust you," she said sharply.

It was Donovan's turn to offer a wry smile. "No I didn't. You made that assumption."

He could feel the anger in her; anger, yet indecision. He nodded out the window. "See . . . purple haze."

"I had better be going," she said.

"Let me walk you back to Broadway."

"I can find my way there," she said, and walked to the door.

"Good luck at Belmont this weekend," he said. "What's the name of your horse, by the way?"

"Gamesman," she said.

Donovan stayed seated on the windowsill until Jones was out of the building and onto the sidewalk. He watched as she crossed Riverside Drive and turned south to walk down the park mall.

Donovan held up the strands he had stolen from her mane of hair and inspected them. Then he went back into the guest bathroom. Clint looked up at him.

"Now, what do you think that was all about?" Donovan asked, and sat on the edge of the tub.

Clint opened his razor-sharp jaws.

"Yeah," Donovan said, "me too."

## "ALL HANDS TO BATTLE STATIONS!"

"This is not a drill," Donovan announced, stalking into the West Side Major Crimes Unit.

Jefferson was amazed. He followed the lieutenant into his office and said, "I asked for bright-eyed and bushy-tailed, but I never expected the Charge of the Light Brigade. What happened, did Sergeant Barnes and you score some coke last night?"

"I got a good workout, both mentally and physically," Donovan said, sitting behind his desk and turning on the lamp.

"Across the hall?"

"Here, there, and everywhere. Get me some coffee and a cruller, would you?"

Jefferson stuck his head out into the squad room and sent someone out for the lieutenant's breakfast.

"What have you got for me?" Donovan asked.

Jefferson's clipboard was piled high with papers. He plucked the top one and laid it in front of Donovan. It was the newest version of the composite drawing.

"Not bad," Donovan said. "Now, all you have to do is make

the hair longer and thicker and the mouth wider. The eyebrows could be thicker, too. Oh, and give the hair a part on the left and make it swept back. She likes to brush it back off her forehead.''

Jefferson gave his boss a quizzical look. ''Anything else?''

''She's about five-seven and has a slight southern accent. She comes from Virginia.''

Jefferson pulled up a chair and sat down. ''You didn't score coke last night. It was mescaline, right?''

''And check out the Riverton Hunt Club. It's probably in Virginia. Don't let them know that we're asking round. I just want to confirm that the place exists.''

''Mescaline can give you real strange dreams. That's what I hear, anyway.''

*''What else?''* Donovan asked. ''Did we get a report from Forensics on the prints in Bono's apartment?''

Jefferson returned to his clipboard. ''Apart from you and me, there's no recognizable prints except for Bono's and some girl's. We picked up prints from her all over the place. And we lucked out in another way. Take a look at this.''

He handed over an evidence bag that contained several strands of honey-blond hair. Donovan held them up in front of the light.

''She brushed her hair with Bono's brush,'' Jefferson said. ''You were right . . . Ms. Crockett ain't exactly tryin' to keep her involvement secret. Forensics say the hair belongs to a female Cauc, adult but fairly young.''

Donovan produced another plastic bag, and held it up to compare the hairs in it with the ones taken from Bono's apartment. They looked identical.

He gave both bags to Jefferson, whose look of astonishment was growing by the second. ''Have Forensics compare these two samples. Have the print guys dust the inside front door knob at my place.'' He tossed Jefferson his apartment keys. ''If the hairs and the prints match, and they will, our shooter is named Andrea Jones.''

Jefferson held the two evidence bags as if they contained TNT.

''Next you're gonna tell me you had breakfast with her.''

Donovan shook his head. ''I asked, but she wasn't hungry.''

''She said she was staying at the Plaza, and I have no doubt that she did,'' Donovan went on. ''I would guess that she checked out within the last twenty-four hours. Ask anyway.''

Bonaci came in with Donovan's breakfast, and he pulled off the lid of the steaming-hot coffee container. The cruller smelled sweet and wonderful. ''I was gonna take her to the donut shop, but it wasn't exactly her style. Anyway, she wasn't after me for food, only information.''

Jefferson reassembled the papers on the clipboard, and gave his boss a good, hard frown. ''Let's hear it,'' he said. ''Start at the beginning, and stop when you come to the end.''

Donovan recounted the tale of how he had been picked up by Andrea Jones at the gym and how she had invited herself up to his apartment. For the first time in as long as Donovan had known him, Jefferson was silent for a full ten minutes.

Donovan concluded, ''She was there to find out how much I know. I'm pretty sure I gave the impression I know nothing. I want her to underestimate me. The phony pass I made at her was partly for that reason, not just to collect a hair sample. With any luck, she's thinking that I'm just a dumb, horny cop.''

''The notices you been gettin' in the press will help in that regard,'' Jefferson said, his old self back in gear.

''Right. Praise the Lord and pass the pastrami. Remind me to write thank-you notes to the *News* and *Post* when this is over.''

Jefferson said, ''I know this is gonna make me sound really dumb, but did it ever occur to you that she might have been there to blow you away?''

''The thought crossed my mind,'' Donovan said. ''And I assure you that if her hand had come outta that bag holding anything more ominous than a brush, my cleaning lady would be real pissed off.''

''She could have just shoved you out the window.''

"Nah. She couldn't see it, but I had my foot behind the radiator."

"Why *did* you sit in the window?"

"To see if she'd try to push me out, why else? Certainly not for the view. All you can see that early in the morning is the goddam pollution from Jersey."

"She didn't try, which means . . ."

"She had concluded that I wasn't onto her," Donovan said, adding, "I hope."

He finished his cruller, wiped his lips, and tossed the paper napkin into the circular file.

"I wish you had an excuse to bring her in," Jefferson said.

"No way. Not until I find out what's going on here, and it's shaping up to be a whole lot more complicated than I thought."

Jefferson protested. "Lieutenant, she's feeding us practically everything. She's almost begging to be caught. Like in the movies—'stop me before I kill again.' "

"It's not one of those," Donovan said. "It may be that she's a pro shooter working for Timmins, but . . ."

"Hey, no 'maybe's,' please. She's working for Timmins. Let's leave it simple."

Donovan was skeptical. "I still think that we're missing something."

"Yeah, you missed being thrown out a fifteen-story window. So she's fancy and a bit of a showboater. Dutch Shultz was pretty colorful, too. I really think you need a nursemaid. Christ! Taking a pro shooter home to meet your goddam turtle!"

"He didn't like her, either."

"So where are we gonna find this Andrea Jones, assuming the hair and prints match?"

"Not at the Plaza," Donovan said. "I bet she made reservations at three or four top hotels. Send some guys around with the composite drawing revised as per my instructions. Start with the Sherry-Netherland; if she's following the pattern she seems to be in, it would be like her to register at the hotel across the street from the Plaza. You know, 'hide in plain sight.' Dammit, Pancho, there's a whole lot more to this! For one thing, she knew that I'm a lieutenant without my telling her, for whatever you want to make of that."

*"Please,"* Jefferson pleaded. "Let's catch her, then sort everything out."

"Okay, have the picture shown to our friends at l'Attesa, the Bridge Café, and to Gus Keane. And make a couple for me. I want to shove them under a couple of noses.

"Plug the fingerprints and everything else into the NCIC computer and see if anything shakes there. Also, find out if we have a contact in Virginia, either the state cops or the state D.A. I want the book on her, but without her knowing it."

"Got it," Jefferson said.

"I'll take care of the horse racing angle myself," Donovan said. "If there is a racehorse owner named Andrea Jones who had a nag in the Rogers Stakes this weekend, Irving will know."

"You don't mean Nakima?"

"He gets off for lunch at eleven and goes straight to Riley's. That will give us four hours to talk."

"Nakima takes four-hour lunches?" Jefferson asked.

"He works for the City of New York," Donovan explained.

# TWELVE

"What's that you're drinkin'?" asked Ahmad Jordan, a young and very tough black man who Timmins had brought in from Chicago to run the war for the West Side.

"A White Cadillac," Timmins replied, twirling a swizzle stick in the concoction.

"What is it?"

"Scotch and milk,"

"You got to be jivin' me."

"This is a classic Harlem drink. It was made famous by Adam Clayton Powell back in the fifties."

"Who's he?" Jordan asked.

"He's the guy that Adam Clayton Powell Boulevard was named after."

"Oh," Jordan replied.

Timmins said, "Powell was a very powerful Harlem congressman about thirty years ago. He drank White Cadillacs because of his ulcer . . . like the one I'm gettin." Timmins laughed. "For a while, he was so powerful that people used to joke that 'N-double-A-C-P' stood for 'Never Antagonize Adam Clayton Powell.' "

‘‘We’ll take care of your ulcer for you,’’ Jordon said, indicating the thirty or forty black men who crowded the Black Diamond.

‘‘Let’s hear the plan.’’

‘‘First, we take out one of Ciccia’s—I guess I should say Mancuso’s—numbers joints, just to let them know we’re moving in. Then we take over the other numbers joints—burn ’em out if we can’t buy ’em out—and then move on the sports operation. The important thing is we gotta move fast, and get ’em before they know what hit ’em.’’

‘‘What abut Facci?’’ Timmins asked.

‘‘The last word on him is that he’s taken to the hills; scared of his own people even. I got to tell you, Timmins, using that white chick was one sharp move. She’s got everyone fooled.’’

‘‘Ain’t it the truth,’’ Timmins said.

‘‘We’re moving on the first numbers joint in a day or two. Right at peak operation’ time, when the tracks are about to open. After that, we’ll send our ‘salesmen’ to Mancuso’s other operations. Things are gonna get hot out on the streets. And if any cops get in the way . . .’’

‘‘No cops get hurt,’’ Timmins snapped. ‘Especially not Donovan.’’

Jordan looked miffed. ‘‘I keep hearin’ about this guy, and I ain’t seen nothing yet to make me scared.’’

‘‘Ahmad, my friend, Attica and Sing Sing are full of guys who bought Donovan’s laid-back act. Stay away from him, and if that’s not possible, *never* underestimate him.’’

Timmins sipped his White Cadillac, and the whiskey burned away at his ulcer. He winced.

‘‘You take care of your body, Timmins,’’ Jordan said, ‘‘and let me take care of business.’’

‘‘Just get it over with quick,’’ Timmins said. ‘‘This is the best chance I’ve had in thirty years, and I don’t want to blow it.’’

## THE THIRD BATTLE OF BULL RUN

"That's where the farm is, Bill," Nakima said, peering through aging eyes at a page in a thick tome. "It's in Riverton, right on the Shenandoah and slightly north of Front Royal, which is where the Confederate Museum is."

"I won't suggest that Jefferson take his vacation there," Donovan mused. "Tell me more."

Nakima said, "It's not the most famous horse farm in America, but you'd have to include it in the top twenty. Like I said, they had one Triple Crown winner and a whole bunch of Belmonts, Kentucky Derby, and other major winners. At the moment, Jones Farms' big horse is Gamesman, which is five to one to win the Rogers Stakes this weekend and has a shot at the Triple Crown."

"Is there any history on the farm?"

"Let's see," Nakima said, running a finger down the page. "The farm was a plantation before and after the Civil War. It was founded by Andrew Pierce Jones, who . . . what's that say, my eyes ain't too good."

"Who distinguished himself," Donovan said.

"That's it. He 'distinguished himself' by fighting on the Confederate side in the second battle of Bull Run. The farm passed down from generation to generation, becoming a horse farm round the turn of the century.

"The current owner is listed as Andrea Pierce Jones. There are no other owners or relations." Nakima rubbed his eyes and sighed. "I guess that's why she wants to get out of the business. I mean, there's no one to pass the farm on to."

"What do you mean 'wants to get out of the business'?" Donovan asked.

"Didn't I mention it? The story was in today's *Racing Form*. She's put Gamesman and the ranch up for sale. It doesn't make any sense, selling the horse now."

"Why doesn't it?"

''The horse could get twenty-five grand in stud fees now. If it does as well as it's predicted to do this season, it'll get seventy-five grand, which I think is what Secretariat gets.''

''Not bad for a one-afternoon stand,'' Donovan said.

''Not bad, I'll say. So why's she selling it now? The only reason I can think of is that she has a bad debt or something and *has* to sell the horse and the farm now.''

''Or no longer means to stay in the country,'' Donovan said.

''I don't understand.''

''I'm beginning to think I do.''

Nakima said, ''I don't know what all this is about, Bill, I just play the horses and the numbers. Which reminds me, I got a line on a number today. You want part of it?''

''Single action?''

''No. The whole works. I got a feeling that today the New York number is gonna come up five-four-one.''

''The address of your building: 541 West 113.''

''Yeah. Today is the thirtieth anniversary of my moving into the neighborhood.''

''Go for it.'' Donovan said. In an expansive mood, he gave Nakima ten bucks.

''It's also the forty-third anniversary of my joining the Jap Air Force.''

Donovan hid a grumble. The sixtyish, white-haired Japanese was notorious around Riley's for his preposterous claim that he was the only kamikaze pilot to have flown twenty-nine missions. This claim he repeated every December 7, when one or another TV station reran the movie *Tora! Tora! Tora!*, about the attack on Pearl Harbor. During the staged attacks Irving would stand at the bar, pointing at Japanese fighter planes on the TV and shouting, ''That's me! That's me!''

''Like I told you, the first word I learned in flight school was 'abort,' '' Nakima said.

Donovan knew that Irving never flew anything more dangerous than a paper airplane, but as was so often the case, Donovan preferred to allow the man his preposterous yarn. It did not harm; nobody believed it, yet it amused many.

"If it's the forty-third anniversary of your joining the kamikazes you ought to play zero-four-three," Donovan said.

"Good idea," Nakima said, and fished another sawbuck from his wallet.

From his usual seat near the door, George hollered, "Anybody who wants to spend money *in here* can just raise his hand."

He was ignored.

Nakima said to Donovan, "Did I ever tell you how my uncle, Admiral Yamamoto, planned the attack on Pearl Harbor?"

"At least a thousand times."

"It worked, didn't it?"

"Right. Now tell me how he planned the attack on Midway."

Nakima brushed off Donovan's sarcasm. "He couldn't have known that you guys had broken the code. If it wasn't for that lucky stroke, we'd all be eating with chopsticks now."

"Uh huh," Donovan said, without terrific interest.

Nakima put away his horse book, and his notes on the day's races. "The numbers joint opens in an hour, and I feel lucky today," he said.

"Let's hope you are," Donovan said, and slapped twenty on the bar, nearly giving George a heart attack. Donovan indicated Nakima, George, and himself, and said, *"Ici, ni, san."*

"The NYPD buys a round?" George asked.

"The NYPD may just have gotten a hot tip from a horse."

They were served, and drank, and George even accepted a free beer, the first anyone could remember (he didn't like to owe favors).

Irving said, "To tell the truth, we only did it for the sake."

"Did what?" Donovan asked.

"Went on suicide missions," Nakima said. "We got a free snootful of sake before we went out on a kamikaze mission. Twenty-nine snootfuls. And if you guys hadn't dropped you-know-what on you-know-where I could have made fifty missions."

Donovan was about to say, "Sure, sure," but quite abruptly

Nakima's words struck a bell. Donovan's mind churned for several moments and he said, "Kamikaze missions," talking to his image in the backbar mirror. "If you go on one, and have no heirs, you would sell your property ahead of time, right?"

"Right," Nakima agreed.

"Who's going on a suicide mission?" George asked.

"The woman who's been running around killing people, who else?" Donovan explained having met Andrea Jones, but only after extracting a pledge of silence from his longtime confidants.

Donovan said, "I think that she'd prefer to stay alive. I think that she's egomaniacal enough to assume she's gonna get away with it. But I also think that for some reason she has nothing to lose, and isn't afraid of death."

"It don't make sense," George said. "If she's a professional killer, why would she go so far out of her way to sign her name to the crimes?"

"I'm still not sure she's professional. She may be a talented amateur. But in any event, she's proud of the crimes."

"Proud?"

"Sure. Look how fancy she's made them. She wants the world to know that Rigili, Ciccia, and Bono were killed for a very special reason."

"*What* reason?" George asked.

Donovan mused a moment, then said, "It's not for money. It's not for fun. And it's not to enhance her career: she's already planned her departure by selling the horse and the farm. There's only one motive I can think of—vengeance."

"For want?" Nakima asked.

"That, my friend, is the sixty-four-thousand-dollar question. Why would a well-off horse breeder from Virginia want to bump off a couple of New York hoods? And do it with a gun her great-great-grandfather might have used in the Civil War?"

"Family honor," the Japanese man said, "if it is vengeance, and she is from an old family, that could make sense."

"It would be imperative," Donovan said.

"Then this has nothing to do with a gang war?" George asked.

"Oh, it may *start* one," Donovan said. "But any gang war would be incidental, or a clever smokescreen."

"The papers are saying that the blacks and the Italians are gonna be fightin' it out for the West Side," Nakima said.

"The papers also had Dewey beating Truman. If there's a gang war, I'll try to make it a short one. But the Andrea Jones killings have nothing to do with the mob. I'll bet on it."

"How much?" Nakima fumbled for a pencil and the wadded-up list of bets that occupied one whole pocket.

## THAT OLD GANG OF MINE

Ocean Parkway was one of the grand Brooklyn boulevards designed in the mid-1900s after the plan of Paris. It was meant to be one of a series of spokes radiating out from Grand Army Plaza in downtown Brooklyn to, in this case, the vacation beaches along Coney Island.

It had two tree-lined malls with benches, and a trail for jogging and biking, and on each side houses ranged from the single-family expensive to the two-family extravagant. A few palatial homes, some in the old Italian community of Bensonhurst, were still occupied by old-line Mafiosi, those who had chosen to stay in Brooklyn rather than migrate to the suburbs as had so many of their children.

Carmine ("Papa") Mancuso chose to stay, his stone-and-marbel palace guarded by a high stone fence, modern electronic security devices, and old-fashioned security devices, which were somber-looking men with guns.

On a pleasant day late in May he sat in the backyard garden, surrounded by flowers, watching the ripples in his swimming pool and nibbling idly at grapes. He also shared espresso with Roberto Facci, who had summoned up courage previously undiscovered and had returned to the family. He had told Mancuso all he knew about the whole affair, including his conversation with Donovan. To Facci's relief, Mancuso was understanding, even comforting.

"At first I didn't know who to trust," Facci said. "Even Bill Donovan . . . you know, the cop . . . didn't know what was going on. But I had someone talk to Corro, the manager of l'Attesa, and found out that Bono and Rigili were both picked up by the same woman and killed later. I also found out that the garage attendant on 106th Street was a colored guy who owes money to Timmins. This is something that Bono suspected."

"So Rigili and Bono let themselves get sweet-talked into their graves, eh? Idiots! And Timmins, this bum who didn't dare come south of 125th until now, is the one who tipped off Donovan to the gun deal. Our people walked right into a trap."

"I also hear that Timmins has been hiring guns," Facci said.

Mancuso swore in Sicilian. "This Timmins, he kills my people and now he wants to take over my business on the West Side? Can you handle him?"

Facci said, "I need men, a lot of men; and a good right-hand man I can trust—someone with experience in a fight. You know me . . . I'm a manager, and a good one, but I'm no general."

"You're man enough to admit your weaknesses," Mancuso said. "I like that. Suppose I get you Jake Tambora from Atlantic City? He's getting fat and lazy in the casinos. A good fight will add years to his life."

Facci was impressed. Tambora was known as the mob's top street commander. If the Mafia had a Patton, he would be it.

"We'll need a new place to set up," he said. "Vinnie's old office is no longer usable. How about the warehouse on Manhattan Avenue? We haven't used that for years."

Mancuso patted Facci on the arm, and said, "We have suffered some losses, but within a few days you will have the men to take back what is ours."

"What about the woman? The pro that Timmins hired?"

“Have a guard with you at all times,” Mancuso said. “Aside from that”—he laughed—“keep your head down and your pants up.”

## IF THERE'S ARTIFICIAL INTELLIGENCE . . .

“There must be artificial stupidity,” Donovan said.

“It's only a glitch in the computer hookup, Lieutenant,” Jefferson said, profoundly embarrassed that his beloved microchips were fouling up.

“I know that the National Crime Information Center was set up to speed the dissemination of info about bad guys around the country,” Donovan said, “and I expected that the resultant bureaucracy would cause things to take longer than they used to. Remember when it took us two weeks to run prints on a stolen-car suspect with an Oklahoma license?”

Jefferson remembered.

“But this one is simple. All I want to know is if her prints are on file in Virginia. We know she used a gun, which means that she has to practice someplace, and that means she has to have a license. She also has to have a driver's license. And if she owns a horse farm and raises thoroughbreds, she has to be registered with at least half a dozen agencies. Dammit, Pancho, her fuckin' prints are on file someplace!”

“The NCIC computer has never heard of her. Neither has the FBI computer. Nor the Virginia state cops computer.”

“Bullshit! Nakima told me that her farm is well-known. It even has a Triple Crown winner to its credit. And this morning she was wearing a polo shirt from a hunt club. Don't tell me that that her prints aren't on file. In New York you have to be fingerprinted to walk down the damn street.”

Angered, Donovan grabbed the phone book and flipped through

it, looking for the national area-code map. He found it, then dialed 1–703–555–1212.

"Information. What city, please?"

"Riverton. I'd like the number of the Riverton Hunt Club."

A tape recording came on. "The number is 555–4328. If you need further assistance, hold on and an operator will answer."

Donovan held on, and he got the same operator as before. "Do you have a listing for an Andrea Jones, or a Jones Farms? Maybe Jones Stables?"

The operator said, "I have a listing for a Jones Farms in Riverton. The number is 555–0027."

Donovan thanked the operator, then handed the notes he had made to Jefferson. He dialed the Riverton Hunt club, and asked for the club secretary. When the man came on the line, Donovan asked if Andrea Jones was on the grounds.

"No sir. She's in New York for the races this weekend," was the reply. "Is there any message?"

Donovan thought for a second, then said, "Yes, my name is Bill Donovan. Please tell Miss Jones that she left something important in my apartment, and that she can call me at my office."

After some brief pleasantries, he hung up. "Well, the hotshot computers in Washington and Virginia may not have heard of Miss Jones, but the phone company has. Did you notice her number, by the way? She has the twenty-seventh oldest phone in Riverton. Her family has been around awhile."

Jefferson was impressed. "How'd you know what area code to call?"

"Seven-oh-three is the code for northern Virginia, which is horse country."

"I'll find out what's wrong with the feds' computers," Jefferson said. "In the meantime, we got some business to clean up." He began flipping through the papers on his clipboard.

"Let's see, Che Guevara is in the hands of Bronx Juvenile, where the cops are fighting with the social workers over who has custody of the little bum. At any rate, Bronx Street Crime has managed to convince the Melrose Avenue Flames to restrict their activities to sniffin' glue. I don't think we have to worry about any retaliatory strikes from punk kids in pin-striped cars.''

''One less player in any game improves the odds,'' Donovan said.

''The Harbison Construction Company did, as you suspected, ring some bells with the Organized Crime Control Bureau. Seems it's owned by a brother-in-law of Papa Mancuso's eldest kid.''

Donovan began humming the theme from ''All in the Family.''

Jefferson continued, ''The garbage-can search turned up some interesting stuff. Beneath the steps of a brownstone over on West End, Bonaci found a brown wig the inside of which contained hairs that seem to match Miss Jones's. There was also a Handi-Wipe with a lotta theatrical makeup on it, and a whole bunch of bag-lady-type clothes. There was also a pillowcase with a hole in it and what looks like black powder burns.''

''What about Forensics? When do we find out if the hairs I pulled from her head match the ones on Bono's brush? When do we find out if the prints from my place match the ones left at Bono's?''

''You and me got an appointment with Forensics in a while. I've been told that all will be revealed. They even found an expert on Civil War guns.''

''Finally we're getting some action around here.''

''It's been less than a week, Lieutenant.''

Donovan looked content. ''I sense motion,'' he said.

''Things *are* beginning to pick up,'' Jefferson said. ''But tell me this—why did you leave that message at the Riverton Hunt Club?''

''I changed my mind abut keeping a low profile,'' Donovan said. ''We haven't had much luck finding her, so I thought I'd invite her to find us.''

Jefferson was genuinely concerned. ''Bill . . . she's a known killer, and you practically challenged her to a duel.''

''That's exactly what I did,'' Donovan agreed.

# THIRTEEN

The commissioner's conference room had a splendid view of the Brooklyn Bridge. That was about all Donovan could say for the room as he pondered the bridge and the café beneath it.

Others in the room were busy with charts, blackboards, manpower, and press coverage. The New York City Police Commissioner was presiding over a gaggle of law enforcement power brokers and politicians: the Manhattan and Brooklyn District Attorneys; the heads of the local and federal organized crime strike forces; the United States Attorney for the Southern District of New York; the head of the New York FBi bureau; and the NYPD's Division Five commander, Donovan's immediate superior. Donovan felt that if J. Edgar Hoover could resurrect himself, he would be there too.

Donovan had been consulted just twice—once to give a rundown of the case, and again to provide somewhat censored details of his interrogations of Timmins and Facci. The rest of the time Donovan was ignored, which was fine with him. Plans were being made for a massive, two-pronged assault on the forces of Mancuso and Timmins. The loudest mouth among the planners belonged to the U.S. Attorney, who had made the front pages a few weeks earlier by dressing up like a Hell's Angel to show how easy it was to buy "crack," the latest drug craze to hit town.

The plan called for dawn raids Friday on Mancuso's and Timmins's headquarters. The raids would be simultaneous and include hundreds of men, twenty of which would be provided by the West Side Major Crimes Unit. During a twenty-minute break, Donovan got a cup of coffee and gazed out over the region surrounding the Brooklyn Bridge. The division commander sat next to him.

"Friday should be quite a show," he said.

"Enjoy it," Donovan replied tersely.

The division commander gave Donovan a long, hard look, and recognized an attitude he had grown to know over the years. "You're not going to be there, right?"

"Not a chance! I'll give you twenty bodies, but not mine and not Jefferson's. We have work to do."

"What do you call this?"

"A sideshow for the TV cameras. I hope you bust a lot of hoods, but I guarantee that none of 'em will know what's really going on."

"And you do?"

"I have a few suspicions," Donovan said.

"How will I explain this to the commissioner?"

"The way you always do: 'you know Donovan, when he gets an idea in his head. . . .' "

"Besides," Donovan added, "there's enough guys looking to get their pictures in the paper as things stand. My absence won't be noted."

The commander acknowledged that Donovan had a point.

"Look at the Bridge Café and the region around it," Donovan said, pointing with his coffee-stirrer. "On the night Rigili bought the ranch, the ferry landing was teeming with people. Yet nobody saw the killer get away."

"Meaning?"

"There was help, probably from a private car waiting in a side street. I mean to find that car, and who was driving it."

Two hours later, Donovan parked his car in front of the Unit, and, it being lunchtime, went into the Chinese restaurant for lunch. He ordered sweet-and-sour pork and two egg rolls to go. When they were cooked, he took them up to his office.

He patted Jefferson on the shoulder as he went. The sergeant followed Donovan into the office. "How'd it go downtown?"

"Great. The circus is coming to town at dawn Friday. Inform Bonaci that he and nineteen other guys just volunteered to be in on a two-pronged assault on Timmins and Mancuso."

"What about you and me?"

"We don't like the circus. Want an egg roll?"

"No thanks. Remember, this afternoon you and me got to go to John Jay to get the final word on Andrea Jones's gun."

"Okay, any news from the front?"

"Yeah, the hair and fingerprint samples match. Miss Jones is our shooter. I wish we could find her. She ain't at any major midtown hotel."

"Damn! I swore she would hide in plain sight," Donovan said.

Jefferson consulted his clipboard. "You had two visitors, both of whom said they would be back. The first was your old friend, Halftrack."

"What did *he* want?"

"I don't know. He threw a rock at the window like he always does when he wants to get your attention. Then he hollered up that he wants to talk to you."

Halftrack was known up and down Broadway, usually for being a mammoth pain in the ass. Partially paralyzed from the waist down following a run-in with a loan shark, he lived on the streets and got about by using a metal walker, from which hung all his worldly possessions. When he walked, he looked and sounded like a small armored vehicle.

He could be heard three blocks off, giving innkeepers—the favorite target of Halftrack's ceaseless strings of insults—enough time to lock the door. Halftrack practiced a form of extortion. He would block the door to a pub and insult the customers until the bartender gave him money or a beer so he would go away.

"Who was my other visitor?" Donovan asked.

"You 'intended' dropped by."

"What for? She's on vacation."

"She was bored, I guess. Why don't you ask her—she's *your* lady."

"Between the clowns downtown, Halftrack, and Marcia's need to be kept amused, I don't know when I'll get any work done," Donovan said. "Help Bonaci pick out nineteen volunteers for Friday's circus, would you? And, hey! Have we still got problems getting info on Jones from the federal computer?"

Jefferson nodded. "It's the same as yesterday: nada, nyet, nothing. Never heard of her."

"Dammit, I'm gonna find out what's going on here," Donovan said angrily, picking up the phone.

He started to dial a number, then hesitated and hung up. He thought out loud: "Andrea Jones has at least one partner. Her ability to disappear is uncanny. She knows my rank and where I live . . . practically led me there . . . and my phone is unlisted. She knew that l'Attesa, which looks to all the world like a crowded singles bar, was really the hangout for Ciccia and his boys. And she knows when and where I work out. Coincidence?"

"No way, Jay."

"Do we have a debugging guy that we can count on? One who works for *us* and knows how to keep his mouth shut?"

"You don't think . . ."

"Get him over here on the double. And when you make the call, use the pay phone in the luncheonette two blocks down."

## MORE BUGS THAN THE MUSEUM OF NATURAL HISTORY

"They're all over the place, Lieutenant," said the NYPD debugger, Bergman. "Every phone in the Unit has a bug in it, including yours. The pay phone at Riley's is bugged too, as you suspected. And so is your apartment."

"How do they work?" Donovan asked.

"There are individual receivers in each phone, all tied into transmitters in the basement junction boxes."

"What about the phone in the *West Wind?*"

"It's clean . . . too new to be gotten to, and also too much in the open. You want me to pull the bugs.?"

"No. Not now, anyway. Can you tell me where they came from?"

"That's easy enough to say," Bergman replied. "All evidence points south, to Washington."

*"What?"*

"The transmitters in the junction boxes operate on a military-reserved frequency. Even the FBI can't get on it. The CIA and especially the NSA use that frequency on occasion. And there's another thing . . ."

"Getting into a police station and tapping every phone ain't exactly amateur night," Donovan said. "Okay, thanks, Bergman. Not a word to anyone."

Bergman said, "I don't want to be a part of this anyway, whatever it is."

Donovan and Jefferson went down to the *West Wind,* where Marcia was sunning herself on the afterdeck. "I need to use your phone," Donovan said, and they went below.

Jefferson and Barnes watched in wonder as Donovan punched up a phone call to Maclean, Virginia.

When the operator answered the phone, Donovan asked for a Jim Tollison. After a moment the man got on the line.

Donovan said, "Okay, Jim, what the fuck is going on?"

"Who's this?" Tollison asked.

"Bill Donovan, and I want to know which of you guys has my office and home phones tapped. Is it your agency, the NSA, or the Pentagon, and why? I also want to know why I'm being denied access to the NCIC computer every time I ask for information on a certain suspect who just happens to live within driving distance of you."

"Bill, is the line we're talking on secure?"

"On this end it is."

"Okay, calm down. Are your phones really tapped?"

"Yeah, and the transmitters for the bugs work on a military-reserved frequency. All you guys use that frequency now and again."

"I don't know anything about a current investigation that involves you."

"Would you tell me if you did?"

"Bill, I still owe you for saving my ass on the Bolivian-import screwup," Tollison said.

"I'm working on a series of homicides apparently done by one Andrea Jones, owner of Jones Farms in Riverton. The killings have all been of West Side Mafiosi, and there's a twist—she uses an antique handgun complete with black powder and Civil War-era bullets, and makes no attempt to conceal her identity. In fact, she flaunts it. The department here thinks she's a pro hit man with a peculiar way of doing things. I think it's a whole lot more complicated."

Tollison made a whistling noise. "A female shooter with an antique gun! Any apparent motive other than what your department thinks?"

"Nothing obvious," Donovan said.

Tollison reflected for a moment, then said, "Okay, Bill, I'll make some discreet inquiries. How can I reach you?"

Donovan gave him the phone number of the *West Wind,* and hung up.

"This is getting really weird," Jefferson said. "I hate games where I don't know all the players.''

''There's one thing we got to do,'' Donovan said. ''We got to keep this among the three of us. For everyone else, we go along with the gang war scenario.''

''Who's this 'we' you're talking about?'' Marcia said. ''I'm on vacation.''

''You just got put back on active duty.''

''Donovan, this is going to cost you,'' she said.

''We have an hour to kill before going to John Jay College,'' Jefferson said, ignoring her.

''I could use a drink,'' Donovan said.

''You have a choice between papaya juice and Perrier,'' Marcia said.

''I'll take ice water.''

''Me too,'' Jefferson agreed.

They got their drinks and went up onto the bow to catch the light breeze. Captain Ashton was seated in his usual spot on the afterdeck of the *Christopher E.*, and Donovan and he exchanged toasts. Barnes joined them, carrying papaya juice. ''It's very healthy,'' she said.

''So's water,'' Donovan replied.

''Man, this place is dead on a weekday,'' Jefferson said.

''Those who aren't at work are sleeping off hangovers.''

''Lieutenant,'' Ashton called, ''why don't you come over and have one with me? Why don't you all come over?''

''I don't feel very sociable today,'' Jefferson said quietly. ''And Barnes is underdressed.''

Donovan said, ''Well, *I* am in the mood for a nice chat about the eternal sea. If you need me, just run a signal flag up the halyard.'' He went over to the *Christopher E.*, pausing just long enough to request permission to go aboard.

''Have a seat, Lieutenant,'' Ashton said, and Donovan plunked down in a canvas deck chair. ''Is that real whisky you're drinking?''

''Water, I'm on duty.''

“What a pity. It’s too wonderful a day to be on duty. Are you on any particular case?”

Donovan shook his head. “Just the normal stuff—fighting for truth, justice, and the American way.”

“Surely you’re joking,” Ashton said, with a laugh.

“Half and half. Basically, I believe that good people should live forever. I’m occasionally called upon to defend that belief.”

“What about bad people? Should they live forever, or be dispatched as expeditiously as possible?”

“It depends on how bad they’ve been,” Donovan said. “Anyway, it’s not my job to make those decisions. I just catch ’em and let the courts do what they will.”

“Hmmf,” Ashton replied, then said, “I suppose that *is* the way of civilization. I do occasionally miss the days when you could hang them at will.”

“Personally I favor tossing ’em overboard in shark-infested waters,” Donovan said.

He looked around the yacht, then asked, “Where are your sons?”

“Out chasing women, I think. They’re entitled after so many months at sea.”

“I wondered about that,” Donovan said.

“About chasing women?”

“No, about how you managed to get two active-duty military men eight or nine months’ leave. It’s hardly standard procedure.”

Ashton smiled and said, “The privileges of rank and having an old family. I, how do you say it, pulled some strings.”

Donovan nodded, and was about to say something when Marcia called him. He got up from the chair. “Thanks for asking me over, Captain, and please say hello to Kevin and William for me.”

When he got back to the *West Wind,* Donovan found Marcia pointing across the harbor. He saw a small, thinnish man on an old cabin cruiser. The man carried a camera with a long telephoto lens, and was looking at them.

''That's him,'' Marcie said. ''That's Peeping Nikon, the guy who takes pictures of me.''

Donovan finished his glass of water without comment, but he was unmistakably pissed off.

''The guy's harmless,'' Marcie said.

''Maybe, but I feel the need for someone to beat up on, and he's the most likely candidate,'' Donovan said.

Donovan and Jefferson trudged all the way around the harbor, and were surprised to find Peeping Nikon standing in the stern of his boat, waiting for them.

''Hi,'' the fellow said cheerfully. ''I was hoping I could lure you over.''

''Hoping?'' Donovan asked, his need for an ass to kick suddenly deflated.

''Yes. I'm afraid that this is terribly important. Could you do me a favor?''

Donovan nodded.

''Come into the cabin as quickly as you can. I don't want them to see us.''

''Who them?''

''I don't know. Please hurry.''

Donovan and Jefferson followed the man into his cabin, which was literally a photo gallery, with every available spot covered by enlargements. There were a few shots of women in bathing suits, including one of Marcia. But for the most part the pictures showed life at the boat basin in all its many forms—jetties, seagulls, sunsets, Sunday afternoon parties, swirls of tidal pools, and a solarized print of three fish who happened to die in an artistic formation.

The man who Barnes had called a voyeur was in fact a very good photographer. And the acrid smell of acetic acid told Donovan that, in an adjacent cabin, there was a darkroom.

The man said, ''My name's Bob Zimmer. I've been saving this for you and your lady.''

He gave Donovan an eleven-by-fourteen print of Marcia and him lounging peacefully on the foredeck of the *West Wind.* The print, and the moment it captured, were wonderful.

More than a little amazed, Donovan accepted the gift, saying, "Can I give you anything for this?"

"No. But you can have a look at these."

He tossed a handful of eight-by-tens onto the dining table.

"What's this?" Donovan asked.

"I'm working on a book about the boat basin. I have a grant from the National Endowment for the Humanities to do it. Anyway, I make it my business to photograph nearly everything that happens around here."

"And?"

"I don't know if you're aware of it—Lieutenant, isn't it?—but you have somebody following you."

Donovan and Jefferson looked sharply at Zimmer.

"Two guys, actually, driving a gray BMW. One of them has photographed you on several occasions. As you can see, I have closeups of the man who takes the pictures, the car, and the license plate. I'd have the other guy, but he never gets out of the car."

Donovan looked in stunned silence as the blowups flipped through his fingers, each more ominous than the last. He saw the man who had seemed to be harmlessly photographing the sunset when he actually was taking pictures of Donovan and Marcia. He saw the man shooting them from the walkway that ran along the river's edge, and he saw the man photographing Donovan sitting by the window in his office. There also were shots of the man getting into the BMW, and of the car driving off.

"You did all this?"

"Film is cheap and I do my own developing. Also, things that are out of the ordinary catch my eye. These guys caught my eye."

"You ought to be a cop. Did either of them see you?"

"They may have seen me around, but they never saw me taking their picture. I shoot from the waist when I don't want people to know they're being photographed.''

Donovan went through the photos several times, sharing them with Jefferson.

''Who *are* these guys?'' Jefferson asked.

''I'll try to find that out. Can I have the negatives, too?''

The photographer quickly produced several contact sheets with accompanying negatives. ''They're all yours. Make good use of them. I don't like people playing games with my neighbors.''

''Thanks, Zimmer,'' Donovan said. ''I owe you one.''

Jefferson gave Zimmer five. ''He means it, m'man. The lieutenant never goes back on his word.''

When they were alone on the pier, Jefferson nudged Donovan, who had the photos and negatives hidden in a copy of the *News,* and said, ''Hey, Bill, maybe you feel okay about bein' denied information, bein' wiretapped, and bein' followed around by some heavy hitters, presumably from Washington, but I'm just a dumb cop who wants to stay alive.''

''I don't feel okay *at all,*'' Donovan said, his face a snapshot of controlled fury.

# FOURTEEN

Donovan, Barnes, and Jefferson sat around the main cabin of the *West Wind,* waiting for the phone to ring.

Donovan hefted the old and formidable weapon that he had borrowed from the John Jay College of Criminal Justice's antique-firearms expert. It was identical to the one Andrea Jones used, the experts said: a .44-caliber Colt Dragoon revolver first made in 1847 and used extensively by both sides in the Civil War. Though heavy and graceless throughout its breech and barrel, it bore on the wooden handgrip a heart-shaped decoration.

Even to Donovan, whose elbow was beginning to feel the pain of carrying—and, on the firing range, using—his contemporary Smith & Wesson magnum, the Dragoon seemed to weigh a ton. Andrea Jones must need two hands to use it accurately, he thought: two hands toughened by reining in countless thoroughbreds.

The seriousness of the matter at hand had burdened the trio to the point where no one wanted to speak. Everything that could be said, even the simplest observation about the weather, made them feel worse. They had placed unspoken hope on the expected call from Jim Tollison, Donovan's friend who worked for "the

Company.'' Perhaps a logical explanation, maybe even an apology, was in the offing.

Jefferson replaced Barnes's phone with a speaker phone so that all could hear, and that added to their uneasiness. When the call finally came, Donovan quietly put down the old Colt and picked up the receiver.

''Hello.''

''Bill?''

The voice belonged to Tollison, and Donovan indicated that to the others.

''Well, old pal,'' Tollison said, ''I poked around as best I could and came up dry. There's no sign of conspiracy.''

''I'm relieved,'' Donovan said.

''I ran my own computer check and found out that the National Crime Information Center was having transmission trouble when you called it up. There *is* an Andrea Jones, and she does live where you said. As for a criminal record, I can't find anything, unless you count a speeding ticket she got in Norfolk in 1983. I think if you try calling up the system it'll work this time.''

Nobody smiled.

''What about the bugs in my office and home?'' Donovan asked.

''They're not ours,'' Tollison said, ''and I can't find anyone who knows anything about them. I accessed all relevant agencies and came up with nothing. Not military intelligence, not NSA, not us, and not FBI.''

Donovan said, ''Okay, Jim, it must be a local problem. I've got a little infighting amongst the local bad guys. Maybe one of them got a hold of some military surveillance equipment.''

''That's a possibility.''

Jefferson pointed to the photos taken by Zimmer, but Donovan shrugged him off.

''Thanks, Jim,'' Donovan said. ''I appreciate your sticking your neck out.''

''No sweat. This makes us even for the Colombian screwup.''

They said goodbye and Donovan hung up.

"Now, what do you make of that?" Barnes asked.

Donovan went to the galley, got three beers, and distributed them. He offered a toast: "To Jim Tollison, the last honest man in Washington, D.C."

"Bill, the guy lied right in your face," Jefferson protested.

"No he didn't. He told me as much as he could, the main thing being that we *are* being watched by the Feds, to the extent that the guilty parties were uptight enough to listen in on Jim's call to me."

"What?" Jefferson asked.

"Weren't you paying attention? The favor that Jim owed me for involved drug-smuggling from Bolivia, not Colombia. Also, Jim knows that any guy who calls me 'pal' risks getting a knuckle sandwich. He knew he had to give me something, so he gave me some useless information that I already had, and just to make sure I knew where I stood he made that little slip."

"That 'slip' could have been accidental," Barnes said.

"Never. Jim nearly got his head blown off. He'll remember that operation for the rest of his life. But if anyone at the Company who was listening in caught it, he can claim a slip of the tongue and get away with it."

"He did seem a bit too cheerful," Marcia said.

"And the Company had the trivial info on Jones put back on line," Jefferson said. "But why didn't you tell Tollison about the pictures we got from Zimmer? About the BMW?"

"For much the same reason I didn't tell them we found a bug in the pay phone at Riley's," Donovan said, "If they're gonna play games with me, I'm gonna play games with them. I want a phone that I know they're listening to so I can feed them phony information. I didn't mention the pictures or the car because I didn't want to telegraph my next move."

"Which is?" Marcia asked.

"I'm goin' after those bastards," Donovan said.

"I don't know about this," Jefferson said.

Donovan picked up the Colt Dragoon and aimed it out the cabin window, as if sighting in on an imaginary target. ''What's our job?'' he asked.

''To enforce the law,'' Barnes replied.

''And covert operations by American intelligence agencies within the United States—especially on my turf—are against the law,'' Donovan said.

Jefferson nodded in reluctant acceptance of the inevitable.

Marcia said, ''I never did want to live forever anyway.''

Donovan had a slug of beer. ''Ready the bow guns, son,'' he told Jefferson. ''We're going to war.''

And before long, Donovan's office was turned into a war room. Every bit of available wall space was filled with taped-up notices, photos, and memoranda. Bergman, the NYPD debugging expert, had rendered Donovan's phone safe and was rapidly doing the same to the phones in the outer office. Barnes was down at the New York Public Library's main branch on Forty-second Street awaiting Donovan's call.

Jefferson had spent the better part of an hour making sure that his computer was working correctly. When he came into Donovan's office bearing a printout, there was no look of surprise on the sergeant's face.

''The NCIC computer gave us exactly what Tollison said it would.''

Donovan gave the printout a quick scan, then stuck it on the wall next to one of the photos of the BMW.

''Is there any way we can run that car's plate without it going over the computer line?'' Donovan asked.

''Sure,'' Jefferson said. ''I can call Albany. I've done it before—when the computer was down *for real.''*

''Do it, using this phone,'' Donovan said. ''It's safe now.''

''What do you expect to find?''

''That the car is registered to a company that's owned by another company . . .''

''. . . that's owned by another company we can't trace,'' Jefferson said.

“Exactly. But we have to make the effort,” Donovan said.

“Why don't we also put out a bulletin on 'em?”

“I want to know who they are first, if that's possible. Another thing: you remember that outfit that was in here two weeks ago fixing the computers?”

“They weren't fixing the computers,” Jefferson said. “They were installing modems to connect all the computers to the phones.”

“Yeah, so Corrigan and Tieman can play checkers without having to walk across the room,” Donovan said.

“They were certain you had no idea about that,” Jefferson said with a smile.

“They also had no idea—none of us did—that the installers were also putting bugs in the phones. There's no way Timmins or the Mancuso bunch could have done it. Hey, wait a second!”

“What?”

“Two weeks ago was a week before Rigili got hit. You know what that means?”

Jefferson whistled softly. “It means that whoever is backing Andrea Jones started work way before she did.”

Donovan said, “All roads continue to point to Washington. But why? *Why?*”

“What's so important about these half-pint hoods we got around here that heavy hitters from D.C. are interested in knockin' them off?” Jefferson asked.

“Get the name of the company that did the installing and run a check on them. *That* check you can run in the open, since Washington will expect it. But I bet you don't get any further than you will with the license plate on that BMW.”

While he was waiting for Jefferson to come back, Donovan went over the printout from the NCIC computer. There was something there, something important, but he couldn't see it. He could *feel* it, a smoking pistol or a least another fingerprint, but it escaped his eyes.

Jefferson returned. "Kaiser Communication Systems, Inc., West Twenty-eighth Street."

Donovan nodded, and dialed a number at the Public Library. Marcie answered on the first ring. "We have a start," Donovan said, and gave her the name and address of the company. "Try *Standard & Poor's Register, Directors and Executives,* going back five years. If the company is really incorporated, they should be listed."

"Who are they?"

Donovan explained who he thought they were and what he was sure they had done, then added, "I'll give you a shout if and when we come up with a company name to hang on the BMW."

"I bet both the BMW and the computer company can be traced back to the same firm," Barnes said.

"No doubt," Donovan said, "but not by you or me."

"We'll see about that."

"Just watch your ass, kid."

Marcie said, "Darling, I don't have to watch my ass. There are plenty of guys down here doing it for me."

"Talk to you later," Donovan growled.

## AT LAST, A GOOD USE FOR NAPALM

A rock came up and hit Donovan's window right after he hung up the phone. "Speaking of asses," he said, and went to the window.

Halftrack was standing on the curb, looking up at him. The man's collection of clanking memorabilia had been augmented by an aluminum frying pan, a plastic monkey, and a pair of fuzzy dice.

Donovan opened the window. "Whaddya want?" he shouted.

"I got something for you," the man shouted back.

"I got something for you too, but the department doesn't like me to display it in public."

"Come on down."

Donovan put on his jacket and went on down.

Halftrack smelled nearly as bad as he looked, so Donovan stood upwind. "Let's hear it," he said.

"Did you bring money with you?"

"You answer my question and I'll answer yours," Donovan said.

"Over a beer," Halftrack replied.

"You *know* that George won't let you in there."

Donovan's warning was dismissed. "Ah, he's a decent man at heart. He'll let me in this time."

Donovan said, "It's your funeral," and went ahead into Riley's.

True to the warning, George jumped up the second he saw Halftrack approaching. "Donovan, you're *not* bringing *that* in here!"

"It followed me. Besides, he says you're a decent man at heart."

Halftrack was in the door, and George bellowed, "Get outta here, you miserable fuck!"

"I told you," Donovan said.

George yanked open the backbar drawer in which he kept the *Guinness Book of World Records* and other argument-settlers.

Halftrack stopped in his tracks. "Lieutenant! He's gonna pour lighter fluid on me and set me on fire! He's always said that's what he's gonna do."

"I'll do no such thing," George said, smiling evilly as he withdrew a baseball-sized lump of gelatinous material that was wrapped in celophane. He held it as if to lob the thing at Halftrack.

"What's that?" Donovan asked.

"Napalm. I finally found a good use for it."

"Can I get a word out of the gentleman before you vaporize him?"

''Make it a quick one.''

''And a beer,'' Halftrack added.

Muttering under his breath, George got a glass of beer for Halftrack and a Coke for Donovan. Then he set the lump of material down behind the bar. ''Remember, I can nail you at fifty paces with this stuff.''

Halftrack swallowed half the beer in one gulp. ''You know the old warehouse on Manhattan Avenue and 108th?''

''The place that used to be a commercial storage joint?'' Donovan asked.

''That's the place.''

''What about it? It's been closed for years.''

''It just reopened,'' Halftrack said. ''And there's lotsa activity—cars and trucks coming and going, loading and unloading, most of it at night.''

''Any familiar faces?''

''You bring money with you?''

Donovan produced a twenty and waved it.

''Facci. And a lot of friends.'' Halftrack snatched the twenty.

''You sure it was Facci?''

''I'm sure. That's why I called you this morning.''

Donovan felt his spine grow cold. ''What do you mean you called me?''

''I left a message on your home answering machine. Didn't you get it?''

''I haven't been home all day. Did you give the location of the warehouse?''

''I said what I just said,'' Halftrack replied.

''Call my office!'' Donovan yelled to George. ''Tell Jefferson about the warehouse!''

''But I already told *you,''* Halftrack said.

''You already told half the world,'' Donovan replied, knocking over a barstool as he dashed for his car.

# DEATH GAMES

Manhattan Avenue, being in that part of the city known as Manhattan Valley, was about as far north as one could go on the Upper West Side before entering Harlem or Morningside Heights. It had not yet been invaded by condos and chi-chi ice cream shops. The people still spoke a mix of Caribbean dialects and locked their windows at night.

On the last night of his life, Roberto Facci forgot to lock the windows.

The thought of intrusion never occurred to him. He had built himself a fortress in the old warehouse, with two dozen men on the ground floor and a burly guard at his side in the third-floor office. There was a good, soft couch in the office, a television, a phone, and a desk—all a man needed to get back at Willis Timmins and his gang to the north.

Facci was watching the startup of a Mets night game when Andrea Jones and two men climbed down onto the warehouse roof from an adjacent building. All three wore black ski jumpsuits and dark knitted caps. Jones had her hair pinned up and tucked beneath her cap; her companions, both of whom had rubbed their faces with charcoal, had swiftly and silently dispatched the man Facci had left guarding the roof.

In the early evening darkness, Jones and her men tossed three lines over the side of the roof. The ropes dangled to the deserted side-street pavement, unnoticed by Facci and his guard. Their window was dirty, and anyway the Mets were winning.

The two men went down the ropes first, bypassing the unused fourth floor and swinging out just far enough from the wall so that their return momentum carried them smashing straight through the windows of Facci's fortress.

One man fired from the hip with a machine pistol, blowing the guard across the room and against the wall. The other knocked a startled Facci to the couch with an elbow-punch.

Jones swung through the wide-open window and whipped the

Colt Dragoon out of a holster strapped to her thigh. She held it in both hands and aimed it at Facci, who was just regaining what remained of his wits.

Her companions moved swiftly out of the office and onto a metal balcony that looked down on a swarm of caught-off-guard Mafiosi, some of whom were sleeping on cots or old mattresses. The men in black hurled four grenades—two gas, two anti-personnel—then emptied a round each into the few of Facci's boys who had managed to find their own guns. Not a shot was fired back, and before retreating into the office, one of Jones's men tossed an incendiary grenade over the side of the balcony.

A low and fiery *whump* was heard as they closed the door.

Andrea Jones tossed her cap aside, then let down her hair so it could flow free.

Facci stared into the barrel of the massive old pistol. "You!" he stammered. "Why?"

She made no reply.

"There's got to be a reason and it can't be Timmins."

Still she kept quiet, which only drove Facci madder.

"What do you want? I'll do anything! What do you want me to do?"

"I want you to die," Jones said, and pulled the trigger.

Her two men were already halfway out the window. "It's done, Andrea," one said. "Let's not stand here admiring it."

"There's still one more," she replied, then holstered her pistol and joined them in sliding down the ropes.

They hit the pavement just as a massive explosion rocked the building. The grenades had set off Facci's store of ammunition, as they were planned to do. Lights began to go on up and down the block.

The three pile. into the gray BMW and raced off.

By the time Donovan got there, the military-precision operation was history. It was over in less than ninety seconds. The BMW had made the turn onto Central Park West and was out of sight.

Cautiously, very cautiously, people were edging out of their buildings. The fire in the warehouse was already brighter than the street lights, and ammunition continued to go off at random. Donovan shoved his shield in the face of a Puerto Rican teenager who had the nerve to run up. "You speak English and Spanish?" Donovan asked.

"Yeah."

"Tell these people to get out of their houses and away from the warehouse. Tell them to keep their heads down. You too, kid. Move!"

The kid ran down the block, shouting warnings in both languages.

A stray bullet whizzed by Donovan's head, and he ducked down behind his car. A man came running out of the warehouse, all in flames. He faltered for a second or two, then fell to the sidewalk.

Donovan looked at the front of the building, then moved so he could see the side that faced 108th Street. The ropes caught his eye. Keeping low, he ran over to them. With his back to the brick wall of the building he was safe, at least for the time being.

He used a pocket knife to cut four-foot samples of each rope. Rolling up the ropes, he slung them over his neck and shoulder. He stepped out onto 108th Street and looked up. In the growing light from the fire, Donovan could see where the ropes had been draped over the side of the roof.

Then there was a flash of light and the sides of the building blew out, bricks and flames shooting in all directions. The shock wave caught Donovan and tossed him over the hood of a parked car, just before the building collapsed.

# FIFTEEN

Fire trucks from four stations poured water onto the remains of Facci's fortress. It was one of those moments that happened two or three times a year: a monumental event involving hundreds of people, many of them dead, others just looking that way.

Lights flashed and radio messages intermingled with sirens and bullhorns until the background noise resembled Coney Island on the Fourth of July. Donovan sat in the back of an Emergency Medical Services van, his shirt off, having assorted cuts and bruises patched. A bandage covered the gash on his forehead caused when he was thrown over the hood of the car.

Jefferson and several other members of the Unit had been on the scene for half an hour, sifting through the rubble for what little evidence they could find, while the EMS technicians patched up the boss. Temporarily disaffected with computers, Jefferson wielded his clipboard.

"Ain't much chance of finding evidence under that pile of bricks," he said.

Donovan swung his legs off the back of the van and onto the pavement as a technician helped him with his shirt. Everything from the waist up seemed to hurt, and the pain in his knees made him want to have a couple of jolts of hooch and sleep for a week.

"You can bet Facci's under there and his nerves have stopped shaking," Donovan said.

"Maybe, but it'll take a week's worth of bulldozers to dig him out. Man, this must have been some explosion. I'm sorry I missed out on it."

"Me too," Donovan said. "Sorry, but there ain't no instant replay in the football game of life. Where's the brass?"

"Come and gone. You managed to hide behind those bandages long enough for them to pose for the cameras and then split. The oxygen mask was a nice touch."

"I've used it before," Donovan said. "They don't expect long explanations from a guy wearing an oxygen mask."

He pulled out the lengths of rope from where he had hid them and tossed them to Jefferson for preservation in a sterile evidence bag.

"I want Forensics to give these the works," Donovan said. "I especially want the ropes checked for foreign substances, like residue from military boots. This had to have been done by military-trained guys."

"From the way you described it, it sure don't look like any amateur operation. And we *know* they got the location of the warehouse from the tap on your phone."

Donovan got to his feet and tucked his shirt in his pants.

"Anyway, the brass is concentrating on Timmins," Jefferson said. "They've assumed he's behind this mess . . ."

Donovan gave a bitter laugh.

". . . and have moved up their raids to 4:00 A.M. But why didn't you let me tell them about the taps and the rest of the Washington connection?"

"Because they would do the obvious thing and call up the bureau chiefs on open lines," Donovan said. "No, let our local hotshots roust Timmins and spoil Papa Mancuso's slumber. At least it will keep them out of our hair for a day."

Across the street, several TV crews were sighting in on Donovan. He asked, "How come they're not chasing the brass?"

"You're a hero again, Lieutenant. Word got out how you cleared the block and saved lives."

"Shit, that 'Rican kid had more to do with it than me. Where is he, by the way?"

"Giving a statement to Vega. It seems he was making out with his muchacha on a stoop when it all came down. He saw the perps get into . . . yeah, you got it . . . a BMW, and drive off. One of them was a woman."

"Andrea Jones. Man, when I get my hands on that car I'm gonna drive it to the South Bronx and leave it with the keys inside. Within twenty minutes it'll be spread across chop-shops all over the city."

"What now?" Jefferson asked.

"I don't know about you, but *I* am gonna get stinkin' drunk," Donovan said.

Jefferson lowered his clipboard.

"All right, not stinkin', just a little gamey. I owe it to myself."

Donovan pulled on his shoulder holster and jacket, again with the help of EMS technicians.

There was a commotion nearby, and Marcia Barnes was vaulting a police barricade and running toward them. Jefferson said, "I called her after I knew you were okay. I didn't want her pickin' up any false news off the radio."

She wrapped her arms around Donovan, and he squalled, "Hey, take it easy! My body is achin' and wracked with pain."

"Donovan, are you all right?"

"I'm still walking," he replied. "But ask me again in two hours."

"The boss is gonna fall off the wagon with a rumble that'll measure seven on the Richter Scale," Jefferson explained. "And I don't blame him."

"William, is that necessary?"

"Yes! I haven't done it in years and I won't be talked out of it. Besides, I need to think, and I do it pretty good when I'm at Riley's."

"I'm coming with you."

“Me too,” Jefferson said. “You may need help. Drunken sailors are always a pain in the ass.”

The fire trucks were making no apparent headway against the fire. Donovan’s car was buried beneath a heap of bricks, so the trio walked south down Manhattan Avenue to where Jefferson’s car was parked. Several uniformed officers kept the press from doing more than taking Donovan’s picture.

He got into the back seat with Marcia by his side. “Home, James,” he said, and Jefferson started the car.

## A BAD CASE OF CLINT EASTWOOD ELBOW

“It’s starting to hurt again,” Donovan said, his voice a bit wobbly.

“What is?” Marcia asked.

“My left knee. My right elbow. My soul.”

“Quel dommage,” Marcia replied, and sipped her brandy.

Donovan rubbed his right elbow. “Seriously, babe. Between the warehouse blowing up on me and the general ache in my elbow from firing my magnum, I’m a mass of injuries. If this was baseball I’d be on the twenty-five-day disabled list. *Doctor!*”

“Working,” Keane said, and got Donovan another scotch.

“Why don’t you just go back to your .38?” Jefferson said.

“I’ll think about it.”

It was three in the morning, or thereabouts. Donovan, Jefferson, and Marcia were the last customers in the bar. Flanagan—Donovan’s Irish friend who delighted in breaking George’s balls till the wee hours of the morning—had just left to get a good night’s sleep prior to his annual trip to the Old Sod.

In the time that he was at Riley’s that night, Donovan had largely succeeded in his attempt to blot out the memory of the day’s disaster. True, one or another part of him ached to remind him, but Keane dutifully applied the medication.

There was nothing on television, and Jefferson had worn out

the jukebox. The only noise in the joint was the tinkle of ice in the glasses, and, to Donovan's increasing annoyance, the periodic beep from the video game to remind customers that it was available to take their money.

Donovan took a belt of hooch and cast an evil eye at the machine that had robbed him of so many quarters in the previous week. "What do you think Internal Affairs will make of my blowing that thing straight through the wall and into the Chinese restaurant?" he asked Jefferson.

Jefferson, having kept pace with the boss in the medication department, was unusually agreeable. "About the same as if we all do it. Gentlemen and lady, draw your weapons!"

"There's no such need for violence," Keane said hastily. "I will convince the machine to mend its ways."

"How you gonna do that?" Jefferson asked.

"Unplug it."

"That's not like you, Gus," Donovan said. "Simple solutions aren't your style. Can't you talk sense into it?"

The machine beeped again, and followed up with the sound of a laser burst, as if challenging them.

"Dammit," Donovan said, and scooped some quarters off the bar. "I'm gonna send that thing back to the planet from which it came." He went to the Space Battles game and stuck a quarter in the slot.

Ten quarters and another scotch later, Donovan had gotten his score above fifty thousand points, but nowhere near that ten-million limit of the machine. He returned to the bar and leaned against it, glaring at the video game. Marcia rested her hand on his arm. "Let's go home," she said.

"Not until I beat that thing."

"Bill, it's unbeatable," Jefferson said.

Donovan felt the small hairs rising on the back of his neck. "Nothing beats me," he said, and plucked another quarter from the bar. It was his last one.

Like an old-time gunfighter, he hitched up his pants, strode to the machine, and jammed the quarter into the slot. Lights flashed and computer-generated music heralded the arrival of another victim.

As he was about to begin the game, Donovan paused, abruptly and pointedly. He looked at the machine, then at the ceiling, then at Keane.

"That night you started my car when it was cold and raining, what did you really do?"

Keane shrugged. "I willed it to see reason," he said.

"C'mon, Gus, let's hear it."

Keane was adamant. "That's it, Bill. I'm no mechanic, but I know a little bit about engines and tried everything I could think of that was logical. When that didn't work I did the illogical. I talked to your car. It listened."

"It started," Donovan admitted.

"You see, it's really simple," Keane went on. "When reason fails, be unreasonable. You just might catch the enemy off guard."

Donovan was smitten by the sensibility of it all. He thought of Hannibal using elephants to cross the Alps and outflank the Romans. He thought of Lord Nelson attacking Napoleon's vanguard to win the battle of Trafalgar. He thought of Lemmy Caution killing the Orwellian computer with poetry in Godard's film *Alphaville*.

When reason fails, be unreasonable, he thought.

So instead of using the left-and-right control buttons to maneuver his spaceship locigally, as the machine expected, Donovan simply put one finger on the "thrust" button and used another to keep poking the "fire" button. Donovan's spaceship raced across the computer monitor, undirected, firing its laser at random.

"What you doin', man?" Jefferson asked.

"Killing the computer with poetry," Donovan said.

Laser bolts went off one edge of the screen and appeared on the opposite side, some of them hitting the target from behind. Most of the time Donovan's shots, all fired at random, missed the evil target. But about one out of ten hit the mark, and the enemy defenses could never know from what direction they were coming. Moreover, Donovan's ship was moving too fast for the enemy to fire back and simply ran over its fighter cover. The points began to pile up on Donovan's counter.

Keane's face took on a beatific glow—he had made a convert. "A round on the house!" he exclaimed, and began reaching for bottles.

"Be quiet," Marcia said, fascinated with what Donovan was doing, "you'll distract him."

"It doesn't matter," Keane said. "Distraction can only add to his game plan."

"What?"

"Random behavior!" Donovan shouted over his shoulder as the target was hit with a brace of laser bolts, adding a bonus hundred thousand points to his score. "This thing is programmed to deal with people who take it seriously. People who are predictable. It can't handle random behavior."

"Or irrational drunks," Jefferson said.

"Same thing."

"By firing at random and refusing to steer his spaceship he's fucking up the machine's programming," Keane said.

"The geniuses in Silicon Valley didn't factor in folks who don't play by the rules," Donovan said.

"A thought to live by," Keane replied.

Donovan completed his silicon slaughter in less than twenty minutes. At about four-thirty in the morning Space Battles went belly-up, its laser turret exploding in a brilliant series of special effects. Donovan's score was ten million. The machine hesitated a second—as if unwilling to admit defeat—then the target disappeared and was replaced by a list of the initials of the ten persons who had scored highest on the machine.

The first five sets of initials were WMD—William Michael Donovan—all recorded from his previous bouts with the beaten video game. Then a new slot appeared at the top of the list to make room for the all-time winner.

"Put your initials on," Marcia coaxed.

Donovan punched some buttons, and a new set of initials appeared atop the list. The initials read NSA.

"What's that?" Keane asked.

"The initials of the last machine that thought it could beat me," Donovan said.

Jefferson took a drink. "It stands for the National Security Agency," he said solemnly.

Donovan returned to the bar and got his drink. Keane, not wanting to get involved with the one American intelligence agency that was so secret even its charter, signed over three decades earlier by Harry Truman, was still top secret, turned on the radio.

They listened to the weather, the sports news, and then a bulletin: a two-pronged attack by a combined task force of federal, state, and local law enforcement agencies had just concluded a pre-dawn sweep of the headquarters of the Mancuso and Timmins crime families, who were believed to be on the verge of making the West Side ankle-deep in blood.

Jefferson hefted his drink and offered a toast: "The war is over. The brass has solved our problems for us."

"Hear, hear!" Barnes said.

As they clinked glasses, Donovan said, "I guess we all can sleep easily now."

## DEATH GAMES (2)

Andrea Jones never looked better, not at weddings, not even at Churchill Downs. She wore black—a dress this time, and an elegant one—with a single string of pearls about her neck. The Colt Dragoon was in a soft suede handbag, its chambers loaded.

The street earth was soft beneath her feet as she walked up through the park and got into the back of the BMW. The two men in the front seat made perfunctory hellos and then drove off, heading up West Ninetieth Street and making a right on West

End Avenue. Within a few seconds the car parked by a hydrant and she got out.

"I won't be long," she said to her companions, one of whom nodded.

"Are you quite certain you don't want us to come along with you?" the other asked.

"Yes. This one I must do alone."

She walked around the corner and onto Eighty-ninth Street, heading toward Broadway.

It was nearly dawn and the street was deserted. An occasional cab could be seen on Broadway, and behind her on West End, the only sign of life was the steam rising from a manhole cover and lingering momentarily in the crisp air.

Andrea Jones walked up the steps to a brownstone, and, using a ring of keys fished from her handbag, opened the front door. The building was narrow, and the staircase an open one that zig-zagged up six floors. She looked up the stairwell, and could see the early morning light dimly through a dirty skylight atop the stairs. She opened the elevator door—it was an old-fashioned sort with a sliding metal gate that left the occupants visible from the outside—and rode up six flights.

There were four apartments each on floors one through five, but only one on the sixth floor. It was the owner's apartment, and while all the others were quiet, from within it came the sound of a man walking about. Andrea Jones listened at the door for several minutes, until she heard the man inside walk toward the front of the apartment. Then she slipped a key into the lock and silently let herself inside.

Once in the apartment, she took the pistol from her handbag and let the door swing shut with a bang. The footsteps at the front of the apartment stopped.

She began down the long hallway, past the living room and bedrooms, barely noting the photographs of Irish landscapes that decorated the hall. She moved like a cat, the gun held in both hands in front of her.

There was the sound of metal—the bolt being pulled on an automatic—coming from the front room, the den. Jones paused a second, then started again. She passed a photo of an Irish meadow, crisscrossed by stone fences, that held in a small flock of sheep.

She stepped on a board that creaked, and halted.

There was the sound of motion in the den.

Jones's finger tightened on the trigger. She took a step forward, and then there was another sound in the den and the figure of a man appeared in the doorway. He swung the automatic in her direction but his reflexes, once as fine as the guerilla fighter he had been, were older and slower than hers. Andrea Jones fired a shot that hit the man in the chest, just beneath the shoulder, and spun him to the floor. His gun was lost beneath his desk.

She moved quickly into the den, clearly the area for a fast departure. Suitcases and a trunk were in the final stages of being packed.

The man lay on his back on the floor, clutching his wound. Jones turned up the lights so he could get a good look at her. He said nothing, but the fury was easily read on his face.

He started to speak but she waved him silent. "You have *nothing* to say that would make a difference," she said quietly. "I've been waiting three years for this moment: to kill you, you most of all."

She pulled the trigger twice, hitting the man in the face and obliterating it. Then she put away the pistol and left the apartment, locking it behind her.

The noise had wakened some neighbors. A young man peered out of his fifth-floor apartment. As she went by on the open elevator, Jones looked at him and said, "Your landlord is no gentleman."

Then she laughed, and kept on laughing until she was out of the building and into the BMW.

# SIXTEEN

Donovan woke up with a hangover not quite the size of Mount Everest, but close enough. Marcia was nowhere to be seen, and to make things worse, a Puccini opera was raging on the houseboat next door. Donovan got out of bed, slipped on his NYPD T-shirt and a pair of shorts, and left the *West Wind*.

Not only was Puccini raging, but the owner of the houseboat was singing along. He wasn't bad, but any noise was too loud for Donovan at that particular moment. He called out, but couldn't make himself heard over the sound of the music, so he stepped on board and banged on the cabin door.

The music and singing stopped, and in a moment the door opened. Donovan's neighbor was shirtless as always, and seemed more massive in person than from a distance. Donovan was not impressed by a man's size; he liked a man who knew when to keep quiet.

"I don't mean to spoil your morning," Donovan said, "but do you think you could turn down the volume? I have a headache you wouldn't believe."

"It's afternoon," the man said.

Donovan glanced at the sun, and saw that the fellow was right.

''It's nearly two o'clock in the afternoon,'' the man continued. ''But I didn't expect you to wake up with the robins anyway, having noticed the time you got home.''

''We got home at five in the morning.''

''I'm a light sleeper, and I have very good ears. The name's Jack D'Amato, by the way.''

''Bill Donovan.'' They shook hands.

''Want a little hair of the dog? It looks like you need it.''

''I could use something,'' Donovan admitted.

''Come below,'' D'Amato said, and led the way.

The houseboat was decorated with posters for classical music concerts and operas. Two of them were for performances of John D'Amato, tenor, at Carnegie Recital Hall.

D'Amato fixed a blenderful of Bloody Marys, got two glasses, and led Donovan up to the foredeck, where they sat in canvas captain's chairs.

''Sorry about the music,'' D'Amato said. ''When your lady took off, I assumed you were awake.''

''How long ago did she leave?''

''About two hours. I imagine she went shopping, because she was only dressed in jeans and a T-shirt.''

''Zabar's,'' Donovan said; ''she has a homing device in her forehead that leads her to it.''

D'Amato laughed. ''Yeah, I know what you mean. I used to be married to a woman who had the same attraction to Bloomingdale's. She spent me out of a nice condo and a promising career before I left her.''

''What do you do now, aside from sing?'' Donovan asked.

''I give voice lessons and teach basic piano. I have a small studio in midtown that I share with two other guys. I get by.''

''You also make a mean Bloody Mary,'' Donovan said, admiring the way the celery stick projected manfully from the glass.

''Thanks. You can give some credit to Bloomingdale's. The blender was about all I got out of the divorce settlement.''

Donovan said, ''Man, I really tied one on last night. I haven't done anything like it in years; don't think I will again.''

''Never make promises you can't keep,'' D'Amato said.

Donovan flexed his arms, which still hurt, but not like the night before. He felt for the patch on his forehead and peeled it off. It was about to fall off anyway.

''Bad day yesterday?''

''You could say that.''

''I think I heard about it on the news—the warehouse on Manhattan Avenue?''

''That's it,'' Donovan said.

''I understand you're a hero,'' the man said, without any hint of sarcasm.

''I keep hearing that. I can tell you this: it may sound good on the radio, but it hurts like hell in the morning.''

''I know what you mean,'' D'Amato said. ''In 'Nam I got my share of bullet creases and bamboo spike wounds.''

''Regular army?'' Donovan asked.

''Special Forces. I was the best tenor in the whole damn Green Berets. And you?''

''I went straight from high school into the NYPD,'' Donovan said. ''Being a cop is something of a family tradition.''

''You didn't miss anything,'' D'Amato said. ''Here's my best momento of the war.'' He showed Donovan a fading tattoo of a dragon on his right bicep. ''Madam Ki's Tattoo Emporium and Whorehouse, Saigon, 1968. That's what I came home with. At least my uncle came back from World War II with a Nazi helmet and a Luger.''

Donovan finished his drink and let D'Amato refill the glass. He looked up the dock and into the park, trying to spot Marcia. ''Where the hell is she?'' he asked.

''The lines must be long at Zabar's.''

Donovan said, ''Damn! I just thought about it. I'm expected to work today.''

''No you're not. She called in sick for you this morning. Considering what you went through yesterday, I think that's reasonable."

"Marcia told you she called in sick for me?" Donovan asked.

"No. I heard her. It was about nine this morning."

"What do you mean you 'heard her'?"

"On the telephone, of course."

Donovan's eyebrows arched toward the mid-afternoon sky.

"Come below," D'Amato said.

He led Donovan back down into the cabin, but forward this time. The bow storage locker, originally designed to hold life jackets, bumpers, lines, and other nautical gear, had been converted into a pantry. There were cans, jars, and boxes of just about every basic food item a person could want.

D'Amato pointed at a spot near the bow where the fiberglass hull could be seen between mason jars of sugar and flour. "Stick your head in there and listen carefully."

Donovan did as he was told. After his ears adjusted to a half-minute of silence, he could pick up a panoply of sounds: the high-pitched whine of an outboard engine; the lower-pitched thrumming of an inboard engine; waves; and, just perceptibly, the sound of a man talking to a woman.

"Living on a fiberglass boat is like living inside a guitar," D'Amato explained. "I can hear conversations from every boat on this pier, at least at night or early in the morning. When it's really quiet I can hear conversations from my bed. Of course, I have perfect pitch and can hear a lot of things you probably can't."

Donovan got back up. "I must remember to keep a radio on when Marcia and I are at home at night," he said, a bit sheepishly.

"You do. You listen to WBGO, the jazz station in Newark. I listen to it, too."

Donovan's face turned red, and D'Amato saw it. "Hey, don't worry. The sound of lovemaking is too low-pitched. Unless you guys get out of hand, you're safe. Besides, I'm not nosy. I only notice things that are out of the ordinary.''

''Glad to hear it,'' Donovan said, going back up to the foredeck.

He had just sat back down when he saw Barnes coming down the pier, but without a shopping bag. He waved her aboard D'Amato's boat and gave her a hug when she joined them.

''Where were you?'' he asked.

''With Jefferson,'' she said grimly. ''Patrick J. Flanagan—your friend from Riley's—he took three slugs from Andrea Jones's gun. The Mex said it happened about five this morning.''

## THE OLD SOD AND MIDLANDS MEADOWS

The evidence team was gone, and Donovan was left free to roam about Flanagan's apartment.

There was no doubt that it was Andrea Jones who killed him; even a preliminary glance at the den and the body revealed that to Forensics. And there was the usual ample supple of fingerprints left behind by the killer.

The chalked outline on the floor reminded Donovan of the little man he had come to know, but not to know, over the decades. Donovan reflected on that: Flanagan was a familiar presence; they had many talks, discussions, arguments; they had bantered idly about the Old Sod and Midlands meadows and clover. But Donovan really knew little of the man, other than that he was a good conversationalist. And his business—Flanagan was thought to be semi-retired as the owner of a small freight-forwarding business with offices in the Bronx—even that much was uncertain to Donovan. It was an unspoken rule that Riley's regulars could talk sports or they could talk the day's news, but talk of business was left behind, at the desk, on the beat, or in the shed with the jackhammer. There might be logic in Jones's killing of Ciccia's bunch, but Flanagan?

Jefferson had made an inventory of the man's most accessible papers and came to Donovan, who had slumped into Flanagan's easy chair and was deep in thought.

''There's nothing unusual that I can find, Lieutenant,'' Jefferson said. ''Flanagan was booked on the 11:00 A.M. out of Kennedy. That's a non-stop to Shannon. He was almost finished packing when he got it.''

''Anything unusual in the bags?''

''Nope, unless you count a bevnap from Riley's with the words 'clover for Donovan' written on it.''

''I'll guess I'll have to pick my own clover from now on,'' Donovan sighed. ''Did you find any indication that he was having anything shipped other than bags?''

Jefferson riffled through some papers. ''Flanagan had a pocket diary, but most of it is filled with personal stuff—addresses and phone numbers in Ireland and the like.''

Donovan shook his head. ''There has to be more. Flanagan didn't die in surprise. The man had a goddam pistol in his hand, and a nine-millimeter automatic at that. Was the gun licensed?''

''No.''

''Get a warrant on his office in the Bronx.'' Donovan said. ''And let me see that diary.''

Jefferson tossed his boss the diary, then went to Flanagan's desk to use the phone.

''Not that phone,'' Donovan said. ''Use one in the Unit.''

''You don't think . . .''

''Of course I do. Get Bergman over here to be sure, but I have no doubt that this phone is tapped, too. The NSA is famous for that sort of thing.''

Marcia sat on the arm of the chair and looked over Donovan's shoulder as he went through the diary. ''Flanagan sure has lots of relatives,'' he said. ''I'm surprised that he didn't just move to Ireland permanently.''

He flipped through some more pages.

''He had a lot of business contacts, too, both here and in Ireland.''

"And Canada," Marcia said, poking a finger at an entry.

"Yeah, IAS Freight Handling, 122 Rue St. Laurent, Quebec. Why does that name sound familiar?"

"I don't know, but they put a ship at sea, the . . . what does that say?"

"The *Mistress Caroline,* sailed May 27—Tuesday—bound for St. John's, Newfoundland, and then Sligo, Ireland. That's not far from Flanagan's ancestral home."

"What was he going to do, meet the ship in Ireland?" Marcia asked. "That doesn't make sense if he was on vacation."

"*If* he was on vacation."

"I don't get it. You said he goes to Ireland every year."

"I never said it was on vacation."

"But . . ."

"I *assumed* it was on vacation," Donovan went on. "What else was I to think? But now that the man's dead, murdered by the same woman who wiped out Ciccia and his gang . . ."

Donovan lapsed into silence, a thinking kind of silence, one that Marcia respected. Donovan often lapsed into thought, but never for so long or with such intensity.

"Do me a favor, would you?" he said finally.

"What?"

"Run down to Riley's and wait by the pay phone. I'll call you . . ." He consulted his watch. "In fifteen minutes. Play along with what I say."

"Do I have to go into that place alone?"

"You're the one who can do anything," Donovan said, quoting her oft-repeated appraisal of herself.

She got off the arm of the chair. "I'm going to have a Remy Martin, and I'm going to put it on your tab," she said.

"I'll join you in half an hour."

Donovan flipped through the rest of the diary and some other of Flanagan's papers while waiting for her to get to Riley's. At the appointed time, he made the call.

When Gus answered the phone, he called out her name, playing perfectly the role she had given him. She took the phone and said hello.

"Barnes?" Donovan asked.

"No, it's Hulk Hogan."

"I'm stuck at the crime scene for a little while longer. I'm afraid you'll have to hang in there and wait for me."

She said, "No problem, Donovan. I have half the Columbia football team here to entertain me."

"Well, they have to win at *something,*" he said.

"How's it going?" she asked.

"As well as can be expected. Flanagan appears to have surprised a burglar and tried to shoot him with an unlicensed pistol. The burglar won."

"Any leads on the perp?"

"Other than that he used a .44, no. Forensics came up dry. No usable prints. No physical evidence. It looks like we have a simple homicide for once."

"I'm glad for that, but sorry because he was your friend."

"I didn't really know him as well as I thought," Donovan said.

"Don't be long."

"I won't. Hey, what do you say we go away for a couple of days? Now that Mancuso and Timmins are wrapped up, there's not much for us to do."

"I'll try to think of a place," Marcia said.

"Somewhere in the woods," Donovan replied, and hung up.

When he was off the phone and alone, Donovan aimed his comments in the direction of the nation's capital and said, "Did you copy that, you bastards?"

## TAKE ME HOME, COUNTRY ROADS

For the first time in a while, Donovan was cooperative with the reporters, even friendly. Knowing they were hungry for something new and sensational and wanted to know if Flanagan was it, he want on at length abut how preliminary evidence pointed to a gone-wrong showdown between an honest civilian and a burglar. Donovan also vowed to catch the burglar. That much of his story was true.

He was followed into the bar by some members of the press, and after giving Marcia a brief hug, he grabbed Gus Keane and led him into the back room, where the beer and ice was kept. "You have to do me a favor," Donovan said. "The press gets lots of tips from you and George, right?"

"Sure, but nothing that will hurt you guys upstairs."

"This time I want you to feed them a line. You heard about Flanagan?"

Gus had heard.

"Well, he was killed while trying to fight off a burglar. Case closed. And if anyone gets more inquisitive, accent the downplaying of the story by letting it slip that Marcia and me are taking off for the weekend. We're going to a place I rented in the Berkshires."

"Got it. Should I tell George when he comes in at six?"

"Tell him. I owe you both."

"Forget it, Bill," Keane said.

Donovan said, "Let me help you carry out a couple bags of ice. That will give us a reason to be back here."

After Donovan left the ice behind the bar, he paused for a few moments to have a beer with an influential columnist from one of the tabloids, who fancied himself as being the one writer able to capture the spirit of the common man in New York.

After that conversation was over, Donovan took Barnes and went upstairs to the unit. Jefferson was waiting in the office, sitting on the radiator between two piles of information.

"The warrant of Flanagan's office will be here by ten in the morning," Jefferson said.

"Good. You can relay the results of your search to us at my aunt's house on Long Island. You have the number."

"You're going to the Island?"

"Yeah, I was hurt real bad yesterday. Barnes was good enough to call me in sick this morning, and my doctor thinks a weekend in the country will be good rest. By the way, Washington thinks that we're going to the Berkshires. The three of us—and only the three of us—will know that Marcia and I will be on the Island instead."

"Okay."

"Give us two shotguns, twelve-gauge, pump action. Have them put in the back of my car when nobody's looking."

"Is traffic really that bad on the expressway?" Jefferson asked.

"Worse by the minute," Donovan said.

"Anything else you need?"

Donovan said, "I'll make a list and leave it on your computer. I assume all the bugs are pulled by now?"

"Yeah, except for the one on Riley's phone."

"Leave it in. I plan to use it."

"Thank God Riley's phone and ours run off separate junction boxes," Jefferson said, adding that he hadn't heard yet about the condition of Flanagan's phone.

"It makes no difference. The message got through. And speaking of messages, run those photos that Peeping Nikon took through the federal computer. Let's get 'em looking behind *their* backs."

"It won't do any good," Jefferson said.

"We won't get a reply, but it will do good."

"Questions answered and unanswered. Dead ends that really aren't. A lotta stuff I thought about during the past week that I need to have checked out. Get as many men as you need to help you. There will be some library research and a lot of legwork."

"While you're out in the country with your feet up," Jefferson said.

" 'Tis time for Clint and me to part company," Donovan said. "I mean to let him go in my aunt's pond. Hauling a snapping turtle around is work enough."

"Are you sure there isn't anything else?"

"No. I figured out what was wrong with that printout on the wall, the one we got from the NCIC computer."

"What's wrong with it?" Jefferson asked. "It says the same thing that Tollison told you."

"No it doesn't," Donovan said. "Read it closely."

Jefferson got the printout from the wall and scrutinized it for a full minute. "You got me," he admitted.

"The printout says that Andrea Jones's sole brush with the law before this week was a speeding ticket she got in Virginia," Donovan said. "Tollison told me she got the ticket in *Norfolk,* Virginia."

"Is that important?" Marcia asked.

"It's important enough for someone to delete the 'Norfolk' from the NCIC report," Jefferson said. "What's in Norfolk, anyway?"

"For one thing, the largest American naval base on the East Coast," Donovan said.

"Why does the military keep creeping into this?" she asked.

"Good question. It's among the things I plan to think about in the country, and it's also on Jefferson's list of items to check out."

"Thanks," Jefferson replied. "But before you make out this list, your presence is requested at One Police Plaza."

"What for?" Donovan asked. "Is the brass after me again?"

"Nope, It's your old friend, Willis Timmins. After he got caught in the sweep this morning he developed a sudden urge to talk. But he'll only talk to you; he says you're the only cop he trusts."

"It's nice to be liked," the lieutenant said.

## DOES THE NAME "ANDREA JONES" GRAB YOU?

Timmins was in an interrogation room, sitting at a Formica conference table and flanked by his attorney and an assistant district attorney. A uniformed sergeant stood guard.

When Donovan and Jefferson walked in, Timmins smiled and shook the lieutenant's hand. He went to do the same with Jefferson, but the sergeant stayed away in clear disdain.

The introductions were made, but Timmins was eager to get on with it. "I want to cut a deal," he said.

The lawyer, a young man, said, "My client is prepared to give certain information in exchange for a reduction in the charges against him."

"Which are?" Donovan asked.

The A.D.A. handed Donovan a piece of paper. He scanned it and said, "You told me you were content with your current holdings."

"What can I say? Most of the charges are bullshit, and everyone here knows it. Look, can Donovan and me talk alone?"

"That's not advisable, Mr. Timmins," the lawyer said.

"We go back a long time. Besides, he can't run the Manhattan Shuffle on me as long as I'm here."

"What's the Manhattan Shuffle?" the lawyer asked.

"What did I tell you?" Donovan said to Jefferson.

"I can't guarantee a deal of any kind if I'm not here," the lawyer insisted.

"Neither can I," said the A.D.A.

"What is this, a damn Bar Association convention?" Donovan asked. "Would all you guys clear out and let us talk?"

"Mr. Timmins . . ." the lawyer pleaded.

"Get lost," Timmins said. "If Donovan doesn't like the info I got, there's no deal. I trust him to be honest."

There ensued a five-minute conversation between the lawyer and the A.D.A., the result of which was reluctant approval of the plan. Donovan and Timmins were left alone, and after the door closed Timmins shook his head.

"Man, don't you miss the old days when cops were cops and robbers were robbers and everyone knew where they stood?" he said.

"All the time," Donovan agreed.

"How's Marcia? You sure got lucky with her. If I had seen her first . . ."

"She's not your type. Now, so I can get home to her, would you please tell me why you dragged me all the way downtown?"

"I got something for you that'll make you want the A.D.A. to drop all charges."

"Let's hear it," Donovan said.

"Okay. This'll make your day, Bill. I got a friend who's heavily into real estate."

"You know a slumlord," Donovan translated.

"What's in a word? Anyway, one of the man's properties is this four-star hotel on West Fifty-eighth Street."

"He owns a fleabag."

"A whole dogful," Timmins said. "But this particular one comes to mind because of its elite clientele."

"Welfare families and winos," Donovan said.

"Mostly, but there's this one lady who moved in a little over a week ago. She's a white chick, real class. She paid my friend a lot of change to keep his mouth shut about her staying there."

"But your friend . . ."

". . . Who's into real estate owes me a favor, y'see . . ."

"You hold some paper on him."

"See what I mean?" Timmins said. "You and me understand each other. There's no need for lawyers and all that. We *do* understand each other?"

"More than you could possibly imagine."

"How does the name 'Andrea Pierce Jones' grab you?" Timmins asked.

# SEVENTEEN

"The opera ain't over till the fat lady sings," Donovan said.

"Yogi Berra, right?" Barnes asked.

"Nope. Dick Motta when he was coach of the Washington Bullets during the 1977–78 season."

"Does this have some relevance to our current situation?" she asked.

"Yeah, the fat lady's about to hum one."

They were in the front seat of Donovan's car, which was parked with the motor idling at the corner of Fifty-eighth Street and West End Avenue. West Side Major Crimes Unit men were staked out at every conceivable point around the Oxford Hotel, the rundown joint on West Fifty-eighth Street that Andrea Jones had called home during her stay in New York.

Donovan consulted his watch. "It's nearly 1:00 A.M.," he said to Marcie. "Time to make the call."

He got out of his car and went into an all-night luncheonette to use the pay phone. He put a quarter in the slot and dialed the number of Riley's. After two rings, Jefferson answered the phone.

Donovan said, "I just got done going over the hotel reports.

The most likely candidate is a woman matching Andrea Jones's description who's been staying at the Oxford Hotel on West Fifty-eighth for a week or so."

"I can be there in twenty minutes," Jefferson said.

"It'll take me half an hour," Donovan replied. "Get some men together and I'll meet you at the hotel at one-thirty. Better come loaded for bear, Thomas. I think this is the real one."

"Gotcha," Jefferson said, and hung up.

Donovan returned to the car. "I'll bet you a buck the BMW gets here in under fifteen minutes," he said.

"You're on."

They each put a dollar bill in the ash tray, then sat back to wait. After a minute, Barnes cocked her shotgun.

Donovan shifted his sight from his watch to the hotel, which was in the middle of the block and dimly lit. He tried his binoculars on the front door, but could see no better than the previous ten times he tried.

"Think she's inside?" Barnes asked.

"Even if she isn't, she has to come back for her stuff or to destroy evidence," Donovan said. "Her sponsors in Washington will want to make sure that she doesn't leave anything behind that could lead to them."

It was just twelve minutes after Donovan made his call that the BMW came down West End and made the turn onto Fifty-eighth Street, the tires squealing.

"I see two men and a woman," Barnes said.

"It looks like her."

Donovan flicked on the radio, brought the microphone to his lips, and said, "It's going down! Let's take 'em on the street! Go! Go!" He started after the BMW, his own tires squealing as he left the curb.

At the same time, two other unmarked cars started racing down the street from the opposite direction. A fourth Unit car moved into position behind Donovan.

The driver of the BMW got to the front of the Oxford, realized he had been had, then floored the accelerator, heading straight for the Unit cars approaching from Amsterdam Avenue. A split second before a collision, he made a 180-degree turn, causing the two police cars to split to avoid him. One of them knocked over a fire hydrant, sending a stream of water four floors into the night before smashing into the steps of a brownstone.

The other Unit car skipped onto and off the sidewalk, then just clipped the rear end of the BMW before it could pull away, headed, this time, for Donovan.

Barnes leaned out the passenger's-side window and fired two shotgun blasts. One hit the BMW in the right-side windshield, shattering it; the other took out the left side headlights. "The tires!" Donovan shouted. "Get the tires!"

The Unit car that was backing up Donovan did a ninety-degree and screeched to a halt, blocking half the road. But before the drivers could get out, the BMW, accelerating flat-out, clipped the front end of the police car, shoving it to one side.

Donovan slammed the steering wheel and swore, then made his own turn and raced after the BMW, which had turned south on West End Avenue and was heading toward the on-ramp for the West Side Highway.

"I shoulda let them stop the car by the hotel and get out," he said.

"It's not your fault," Barnes said. "They could have been listening in to our radio."

"Get on the radio anyway," he yelled. "Seal off all exits to the highway from here to Ninety-sixth. Make it a general alert. Everything's in the open now."

She made the call as Donovan kept pace with the foreign car, twisting and turning and finally making the entrance ramp to the highway, only a few hundred years behind the BMW.

The only way to go on the elevated highway was north, the southbound lanes having been closed years before, starting at Fifty-seventh Street. A long-ago accident, capping decades of neglect, had effectively turned the West Side Highway south of about

Fiftieth Street into a sealed-off no-man's-land used during the day by cyclists, joggers, and skateboarders, and at night by homeless people. They slept there in a four-lane refugee camp of impromptu shelters made from cardboard boxes, wooden crates, plastic garbage bags, and any other available materials.

The shelters were put up on the sides of the former highway, the center of which was pockmarked with holes large enough for a man, or a truck, to fall three stories to the street below.

When the BMW got onto the highway it hesitated, then abruptly turned south.

"What are they *doing?*" Barnes asked.

"They were listening to our radio and know there's no way out to the north," Donovan explained.

"Do they know what's to the south?" Barnes asked.

"No. They're from out of town."

As Donovan's company Dodge reached the top of the ramp, the BMW smashed through a wooden barricade and headed into the darkness of the no-man's-land. There were no street lamps on that part of the road, and the BMW's remaining headlight was knocked out when the car went through the barricade. Only an occasional cooking fire outside an impromptu shelter offered light.

Donovan switched on the red flasher that Barnes had stuck on the roof, and turned up the volume on the siren as high as it would go. Far behind them, other Unit cars and several marked cars had joined in the chase.

Marcia leaned out the window and got off three more shots. One missed entirely as Donovan swerved to miss a ten-foot-wide hole, and another hit the trunk of the BMW, popping it. The trunk shot upwards, making the driver's view to the rear as bad as his view to the front. Barnes's third shotgun blast got the left rear tire and then the BMW was entirely out of control.

It swerved right, scraping the concrete wall, sending up a shower of sparks, and wiping out an elaborately constructed cardboard shelter while its owner dived over his campfire and out of the way.

Donovan pounded his fist on the wheel again, then made an emergency left-hand swerve to miss another hole. The BMW crossed the highway, moving as fast as it could on three good tires. Barnes leaned over to get the other shotgun from the back seat, and as she did so, Donovan put the pedal to the metal and rammed the BMW from behind. Marcia was sent flying.

The BMW lurched forward, skidded to the right, and, as several homeless people watched in stunned silence, sailed out over a thirty-foot hole in the pavement. The momentum kept the car in the air seemingly for an hour; in fact, it took but a second to cross the hole, and, falling, impale itself on the rusting steel beams that projected from the other side. Two beams smashed through the windshield and out the back window.

Donovan saw a flash of long, golden hair, and blood.

He stood on the brakes. The Dodge squealed to a halt, its front bumper just over the side of the hole. Donovan and Barnes scrambled out of the car and started toward the BMW, but then the car blew up in an explosion that sent fragments of glass and metal flying in all directions. Donovan grabbed Marcia and tucked her head against his chest, protecting her with his arms as a brief but searing wave of heat passed over them.

When Barnes looked up, the fire inside the BMW was so bright that no one could look at it for long. Donovan thought of walking to the car, then figured it was hopeless. Let Forensics deal with the cremated bodies, he thought. The all-too-familiar sound of sirens was far off, but closing. Donovan took Marcia by the hand, interlacing his fingers with hers, and together they walked to the concrete wall that overlooked the Hudson River.

To the north, the lights of the *Intrepid* Air and Space Museum were on, and the flight deck of the magnificent carrier was loaded with fighter planes of all eras. Immediately below them, an open-air rock concert was going on atop a pier, the audience apparently unaware of the happenings above. Someone named Lou Reed was singing a song entitled "A Walk on the Wild Side," a sensuous jazz ballad.

Donovan shook his head at the hideous irony. *Only in New York.* He kissed Marcia on her forehead. "Want to take a walk?" he asked.

She nodded, and with their arms around each other's waists, they walked up the ravaged highway, past the homeless shelters and the campfires, past the broken minds and wasted bodies, toward the tidal wave of sirens and flashing lights that was sweeping down from the north.

## IT AIN'T OVER TILL IT'S OVER

"*That* was what Yogi Berra said," Donovan told Marcia.

"So what?" she replied. "It's over."

"No it ain't."

"Are you jivin' me?" Jefferson asked from his perch on Donovan's office radiator. "Andrea Jones is dead, incinerated along with her two buddies."

"Maybe, but I want to know why all this happened."

"Bill, Timmins hired Jones to wipe out the Eye-talian competition, then when he got caught in the sweep he gave her up in an effort to save his ass."

"That doesn't explain Flanagan's death," Donovan said. "He was killed by the dragoon, and Jones's fingerprints were all over the place. We even have an eyewitness who saw her on the lift."

"The what?" Jefferson asked.

"The elevator. Sorry."

Marcia said, "My, aren't we getting posh?"

"It happens to people who live in sensational flats," Donovan said.

Once again he was asked to elucidate.

"When Jones was in my apartment, she said I had 'a sensational flat.' "

"You do."

''True, but how many Americans would say that they're thinking of *taking a flat*? Americans 'get apartments.' They don't 'take flats.' What Americans call an 'apartment' a 'flat'?''

''Americans who have spent time in England,'' Marcia said.

''Or who have spent a lot of time with Englishmen. There's no evidence of that in Jones's history. Unless . . . Jefferson, as part of the research I asked you to do, would you look up the records of ship movements in and out of Norfolk, Virginia? See if a British warship didn't make a port call there, especially in 1983.''

''I don't understand,'' Jefferson said.

''Don't you remember when I said the NCIC printout on Jones didn't fit with what Tollison told me over the phone?'' Donovan said. ''The printout only said she got a speeding ticket. Tollison told me she got the ticket in *Norfolk*.''

''One other thing. That company in Quebec that was noted in Flanagan's diary? IAS Freight Handling? The initials IAS also stand for 'Irish Assistance Society,' of which Flanagan was a leading member.''

''They're the bunch that the FBI suspects of supplying arms to the IRA in Northern Ireland,'' Marcia said. ''But it's never been proved.''

''And who did we know who sold arms?'' Donovan asked.

''The late Signor Ciccia and his crew,'' Jefferson said, a gleam in his eye.

''Therein lies the connection between Flanagan and Ciccia,'' Donovan said. ''But Andrea Jones? Her involvement requires more thought, thought I plan to do in the country.''

''I'll get right on the research,'' Jefferson said, his interest in the case rekindled.

''Before you do that, call the Coast Guard and tell them we have circumstantial evidence that the *Mistress Caroline* is ferrying illegal arms to the IRA,'' Donovan said. ''The Coast Guard can alert their Canadian counterparts and have the ship searched when it reaches Newfoundland.''

"Done," Jefferson said.

"Well said," Donovan replied.

He cleaned up the papers on his desk and finished keyboarding the list of things he wanted Jefferson to do. Then he pressed the buttons that sent the list to the memory bank of Jefferson's computer.

"I feel ridiculous," Donovan said. "But it *is* faster."

"As long as there aren't any bugs in it," Marcia said. "After the last episode I worry about people listening in on my thoughts."

"That's only Gus Keane practicing," Donovan said. "Don't worry about electronic bugs—Bergman has swept this place clean and I'm having him send in a team once a month to make sure it stays that way."

Donovan switched off his desk lamp, and the office was lit only by the lights of Broadway.

"What now?" Marcia asked.

"Back to the *West Wind* to pack, what else? I want to get an early start for Long Island tomorrow, and we have to drop by my place to pick up Clint."

"Did you get a new car?"

"Sure. The department has no end of Dodges and Plymouths to give to its officers. Why can't they give us a goddam BMW, or at least a '57 Chevy with all the trimmings?"

They stopped at Woolworth's to buy a large plastic laundry tub. Donovan wanted an especially heavy-duty one, Clint being especially heavy-duty. He had spent nearly his entire life in the bathtub in Donovan's guest bathroom, and his reaction to a change of scenery was uncertain enough for Donovan to buy a sturdy container.

He thought of calling in Gus Keane to convince Clint that he would be much happier in a frog pond than in a porcelain bathtub; then it occurred to Donovan that he was the only one Clint would listen to.

Donovan was wrong. Clint would have none of it. He hunkered down at one end of the bathtub and flashed his jaws at anyone who came near. He also refused to listen to Donovan, who went on for half an hour describing the joys of pond life to an unsympathetic, city-bred turtle. Finally, Donovan gave up and resorted to force, using the same technique needed to get Clint out of the tub for its monthly scrubbing. Donovan used a forked stick to hold Clint's head away while cautiously hoisting him by the back of the shell and easing him into the laundry tub.

"He smells," Marcia said.

"Let's try to keep the anthropocentricity under control," Donovan said. "We probably don't smell so great to him. Besides, we're taking him away from his home."

"Donovan, I believe you have developed a sentimental side."

"I have not."

"You talk to a snapping turtle. You even play his favorite music."

"I liked jazz when he was just a gleam in his mother's shell," Donovan insisted.

Clint looked up from the laundry tub, and Donovan thought he saw a sentimental side to Clint, too. "Look at it this way, old man," Donovan said. "A freshwater pond smells better than either my bathtub or me, and frogs are better company. Better tasting, too."

He poured two inches of water into the tub, enough to keep Clint wet, then tried to lift the tub. "I'll need your help," Donovan said to Marcie, and grabbed her before she could flee the room.

When they had struggled to carry Clint to the *West Wind* and had left him in a safe spot on the afterdeck, Donovan lingered, staring west. "What's up?" Barnes asked.

"She's gone."

"Who?"

The *Christoper E.* You know, Ashton's boat. She's not there."

Marcia glanced at the empty berth, then back at Donovan.

"That's funny," she said. "It's not like him to leave without saying good-bye."

"I really wanted to be called '*lef*tenant' one more time," Donovan said.

"Wait, there's a note taped to the wheel." Marcia opened the note, and read, "Dear William and Marcia. So sorry we had to leave early, but it will be a long slog to Perth and I felt it best to get an early start. I realize that it's a bit much to expect, but I do hope to see you at the trials. All best, Francis, William, and Kevin Ashton."

"Well, well," Donovan said.

"The 'trials' are the America's Cup trials?" Marcia asked.

"Right-o," Donovan said. "They begin in October."

"I hope he makes it on time."

"I'm sure he's keeping to his schedule," Donovan said.

Marcia crumpled the note and stuck it in her pocket. "I'm going below to make something to eat. Will warmed-up Chinese food do?"

"Next to cold pizza there's nothing I like better."

"Why don't you ask D'Amato to watch the boat while we're gone?"

D'Amato had *Tosca* playing. Donovan went to the man's boat and stepped on board. When he returned to the *West Wind,* the heated-up Szechuan menu was ready.

After dinner they sat on the bow with a single candle providing light. For a Friday night, the last Friday in May, it was unusually quiet at the Seventy-ninth Street Boat Basin. Only one party was in progress, and it was a small one on the northernmost pier.

Curiously, Donovan's wounds had stopped hurting. The demolition of the BMW and its occupants had drained him. While some things were still haunting him, he felt a sense of relief. Maybe it was the end of that hated car. Maybe it was the prospect of seeing family, his aunt, whom he hadn't visited since Christmas. Maybe it was just the chance to get away, to a place that could be called country.

# DONOVAN LOOKS OVER A FOUR-LEAF CLOVER

The Saturday was perfect. Even the driving wasn't bad. It only took them two hours to make the drive from the city to Aquebogue, a hamlet on Long Island's North Fork just past Riverhead. Clint sloshed around a bit, perhaps sensing adventure, but otherwise caused no trouble in his tub on the back seat.

Donovan's aunt Elizabeth, a sprightly woman in her late sixties who looked much younger, lived in a large house by a pond on the South Jamesport Road. She supported herself by renting out the half-dozen cottages that lined the pond, and amused herself by doing charcoal sketches of the pond and Peconic Bay, a broad expanse of water just across the road.

She gave Donovan and Marcia the guest room that overlooked the pond and the bay, as well as a lunch fit for half a dozen people. They also had a briefing on the births, deaths, marriages, soon-to-be-broken marriages, real estate deals (plans were afoot to build a McDonald's on scenic route 25a), and other events of major significance that had taken place since Christmas.

After tea they took a stroll around the pond, something they hadn't done in twelve years. And they found the grassy knoll overlooking the pond where they had first declared undying love twelve years earlier. Inspired, Donovan got a bottle of wine, two glasses, and Clint, still in the laundry tub in which be had made the journey out from the city.

As Marcia uncorked the wine and poured it, Donovan hefted Clint and set him down half in and half out of the water. The turtle contemplated the pond, then looked back at Donovan. "Go forth and procreate," Donovan said, and gave Clint a shove. He hesitated, then dived for the bottom of the pond.

"I'll miss him," Donovan said.

"Oh, *please,*" she said.

"Seriously. He's been my roommate for a long time."

"Your new roommate is a lot prettier and has a better disposition, too."

"I'll drink to that," Donovan said, and did so.

She laughed. "I can't believe you'll miss that turtle."

"I'll miss Flanagan too. For all his faults, he was a good conversationalist."

"He was smuggling guns to the IRA," she said. "Those guns killed women, children, and British soldiers."

"There are two sides to every argument. My grandparents gave to the IRA in 1916. So did everyone in Ireland then."

"William, 1916 was seventy years ago."

"Damn!" he swore. "Flanagan died before he could pick me a four-leaf clover, the bog-trottin' sonofabitch!"

"There must be one around here somewhere," Marcia replied, scanning the knoll.

While she leaned against a maple, Donovan prowled the grass on his hands and knees. A flight of broadbill ducks came in off Peconic Bay and landed in the pond. To the north end of the pond, a large white egret stood in the shallows, looking for prey.

After about fifteen minutes Donovan found the clover, and gently plucked it. He rolled onto his back and held it up for inspection. Marcia joined him, lying by his side.

"See . . . it wasn't that hard," she said.

He twirled the stem so the clover rotated in the spring afternoon sun.

"They're good luck," she said.

He stared at it, and quickly his expression changed from mellow satisfaction to wild speculation.

"What's the matter?" Marcia asked.

## . . THAT HE OVERLOOKED BEFORE

"There are four of them," Donovan said.

"Of course there are four leaves," she replied. "That's why it's called a four-leaf clover."

"No. I mean, there *were* four of them: Francis, William, Kevin, and Christopher."

"The Ashtons?"

"Yes, I saw them in a photo in Captain Ashton's cabin. There was a picture of him, Kevin, William, and another young man."

"Christopher? The boat is named Christopher."

"In his memory, no doubt," Donovan said.

"But . . ."

"Don't you see? Christopher is dead—almost certainly killed in Northern Ireland by an IRA bullet. The kind of bullet supplied by Flanagan and Ciccia."

"And Andrea Jones?" Barnes asked.

"She must have been close to Christopher somehow. When I was on Ashton's boat yesterday, he seemed rather keen on the subject of frontier justice. I also asked him how he managed to get William and Kevin—two on-duty military men—eight or nine months' leave so they could sail with him. His explanation was unconvincing. And there's the matter of Jones using British expressions and dispensing *real* frontier justice."

"Ashton also left abruptly after having said he was staying for the Fourth of July celebrations," Marcia said.

"Yeah, why go a few thousand miles out of your way just to sit on the Seventy-ninth Street Boat Basin for a couple of weeks? And another thing: D'Amato told me he heard a woman's voice aboard the *Christopher E.*"

"Andrea Jones?"

"Who else?" Donovan said. "Any other woman wouldn't have to be hidden from our view."

"Can all this be true?"

"There's a way of checking. Come with me."

# EIGHTEEN

The office of the *Peconic Bay Herald* was on Route 25a not far from the projected MacDonald's. The weekly newspaper served the needs of half the North Fork, from Aquebogue to Greenport, and had done so for nearly a century. It was an anachronism as newspapers go: it still used lead type and huge presses out in the back shop, not the cheaper, and cheaper-looking, offset process employed by most other papers. Donovan opened the door and let Marcia inside. There was a stirring in an inner office, then a slender man with horn-rimmed glasses appeared, saw Donovan, and smiled. "Bill Junior, my Lord!"

"Hello, Joe. How's the fish-wrapping business?"

Joe Cooper had always joked about his paper, which actually was quite good, being useful mainly for wrapping fish.

"Pretty good, all in all. And you? Come to see your aunt?"

"Yeah, and to check out the bay and relax for a few days. You remember Marcia, don't you?"

"Of course. The two of you created quite a scandal when you first showed up. Now, nobody notices. Remember Tad Schuyler? I think you used to race against him."

"He sailed," Donovan said, "I raced."

''He's married to a Vietnamese girl he met during the war. They have two lovely kids. Now, isn't he about the last person you'd expect to marry out-of-town?''

''Just about the last,'' Donovan agreed.

''So what brings you to the paper? Nobody's broken the law hereabouts, have they?''

''Not that I'm aware of. I need your help.''

Cooper asked what he could do.

''I need to contact the editor of the weekly paper in Riverton, Virginia,'' Donovan said. ''I'm assuming the town has one.''

''Come into my office,'' Cooper said.

Once inside, he pulled from his bookshelf a thick, red paperback book. ''If Riverton has a paper, it will be listed in *E & P.''*

*''Editor & Publisher,''* Donovan said to Marcia. ''It's a listing of newspapers and editors worldwide.''

''Here we go. The *Riverton Times-Messenger,* founded in 1885. The editor's name is John Cummings.''

''Think he'll be in today?''

''If not we can get him at home. Weekly newspaper editors can't afford to have their home phones unlisted. That's a shame, because I get sick of hearing from the parents of kids who were arrested for drunk driving and got their names in the paper.''

''Can you give him a call?'' Donovan asked.

''Sure. What should I say?''

''Tell him you're trying to track down relatives of one Andrea Jones of Riverton. She had a traffic accident while passing through town.''

''That's it?''

''No. Draw him into a conversation about her, if you can. See if she was engaged to be married a few years back.''

Cooper made the call, and, after a few tries, located the editor of the *Times-Messenger,* who was at home, cutting the lawn. The two men talked for a while, came up with a mutual acquaintance, a one-time weekly newspaper editor who had gone to work for the *Washington Post,* and Cooper made copious notes.

When he was done, Cooper hung up the phone and said, ''Andrea Jones is dead.''

''Is she now?'' Donovan replied.

''Her uncle called from D.C. and had an obit put in the *Times-Messenger*. It will run next week.''

''I'll bet her uncle's name is Sam,'' Marcia said.

''And as for being engaged, yes she was. According to Cummings, she was engaged in 1983 to a British Marine named Christopher Ellis Ashton. They met at a horse show near Norfolk. He was in the U.S. while his ship was making a port call at Norfolk. According to the story the *Times-Messenger* ran at the time, the couple planned to settle in England.''

## THE ARROGANCE OF THOSE WHO THINK THEY OWN THE WORLD

Donovan sat in the room he used to live in during the summers he spent as a child at his aunt's house. In front of him was a thirty-year-old globe of the world, roughly basketball-sized, that squeaked when it rotated. He studied it while waiting for the phone to ring.

Marcia sipped tea and watched with growing awareness of what her lover was up to. She didn't want to disturb him; Donovan was deep into thought, and inclined to be irritable if interrupted. She knew his moods well enough to let him alone while this one passed.

Donovan rotated the globe and made some notes on a steno pad. He looked at New York. He looked at Australia. He went to his old bookshelf and got out an atlas that, in the back, had a chart showing the great explorations of man, which included all the voyages of discovery made by European captains.

He consulted a small, thick paperback, *Royce's Sailing Illustrated,* and his pocket calculator. He did some math on the steno pad.

At last he looked over at Marcia and said, ''It's impossible, hydrodynamically speaking.''

''What is?'' she asked, pouring him a cup of tea.

''A standard-displacement hull can make no better than 1.34 times the square root of the waterline length,'' Donovan said. ''Figuring that the *Christopher E.* has a waterline length of sixty feet, that works out to slightly more than ten knots. Beyond that, no matter how much sail you add, you simply can't push the water out of the way fast enough.''

''Meaning?''

''Meaning that sailing flat-out, with only three port calls along the way, with optimum wind and weather conditions, there's no way that Ashton can make it to Perth in time for the America's Cup trials. At best he'll get there in February—well after the finals are over.''

''He said in the note he left on the *West Wind* that he was leaving early.''

''He should never have been in New York if he meant to go from England to Australia,'' Donovan went on. ''In sailing to New York he took himself three thousand miles out of the way. It's like going to L.A. while en route from New York to Boston. In my opinion, he never had any intention of going to Australia.''

''He came here so William and Kevin could help Jones,'' Marcia said.

''Yeah, and considering Ashton's importance to the Royal Navy—he had commendations from several First Sea Lords in his cabin—it means that British secret service is in on it, too. Anglo-American cooperation and all that.''

''You're not saying that British and American intelligence agencies collaborated to encourage and support Andrea Jones in her quest for revenge?'' Barnes asked.

''That's what I'm saying,'' Donovan replied. ''From their point of view the plan was perfect—her fiancé is killed by the IRA, she wants revenge on the people responsible, and they want the same people out of the way. So they support her and in the process keep their hands clean. If she's caught they can stay out of it. It looks to all the world like a case of a woman from an old Virginia family out to save family honor. The use of the odd weapon added to that."

Marcia shook her head in grudging admiration of the plan. "In a weird way I can understand her thinking. I'm sorry I didn't get the chance to meet her."

The phone rang. Donovan picked it up and entered into a long conversation with Jefferson, who was at the Unit in New York. The phone call went on for half an hour, during which time Marcie went to join Donovan's aunt in the kitchen, which like kitchens in all country homes was mission control for the entire household.

After a time, he joined them, pulling a chair up to the large, round kitchen table. He laid out a passel of papers, and asked his aunt if she had an Orient Point ferry schedule. One was produced.

"You're taking the ferry?" she asked.

"Yes. Marcia and I have some business to clear up this evening."

"In New London?"

"In Newport."

"I have dinner planned for six, but . . ."

"We'll have it cold tomorrow afternoon," Donovan said. "After that, I promise you that we'll stay for a week."

"We will?" Marcia said excitedly.

"Sure. We'll fix up the cottage Aunt Elizabeth has been saving for me . . ."

"For when he makes up his mind to settle down and help me run the business," she said. "Neither of us is getting any younger, William."

"Don't remind me. Anyway, we'll take the wraps off my sailboat and putt around Peconic Bay. What do you say to that?"

"Terrific," Marcia said, "but what business do we have in Newport?"

''To catch the Ashtons.''

''And you think they're in Newport.''

''I know that they are,'' Donovan said. ''If the British have a major fault, it's tidiness. Ashton filed a course plan with the Coast Guard as he was leaving New York Harbor. He's en route to England with a stopover for provisions in Newport.''

Marcia said, ''I can't believe . . .''

''. . . In the arrogance of those who think they own the world,'' Donovan said. ''The sun may have set on the British Empire, but Ashton hasn't been paying attention. He and his crew are laying over at Newport until tomorrow afternoon.''

''What are the arrangements for Newport?''

''We'll have a bite and then leave in an hour. Jefferson has worked out the reciprocal agreement with the Newport P.D. and will be joining us there. We'll meet at the P.D. and plan our moves. Newport has promised us fifteen men if we need them.''

Aunt Elizabeth said, ''William, are you going to go and get shot at again?''

''Hopefully we'll do most of the shooting.''

''You'll need a good meal first,'' she said. ''After all, you *are* my only heir, and I don't want my land turned into condominiums or whatever they're called. I expect you to take over the place when I'm gone. The *both* of you.''

Marcia gave Donovan a kiss on the cheek. ''Look at it this way,'' she said, ''you can't leave Clint all alone out in the country.''

## SATURDAY NIGHT ACROSS THE SOUND

Donovan and Marcia sat on wooden benches, sipping coffee, while the car ferry made its way from Orient Point, Long Island, to New London, Connecticut. Donovan's car was tucked safely below with dozens of others, but laden with pistols, shotguns, and ammunition.

The sun was setting behind some high clouds, and halfway up from the horizon, a military jet from Westhampton Air Force Base left twin vapor trails as it roared through the upper atmosphere.

"I take it my aunt and you have my future figured out," Donovan said.

"Almost. Give us a full week and we'll have the wedding announced."

Donovan harrumphed.

"Come on, William, we were just talking."

"Sure. And Hitler was just having stomach distress when he planned the invasion of Russia."

"I'm not sure I care for that comparison."

"I'm not sure I like having my future planned," he said, adding, "except, maybe, by you. You did catch the 'maybe' in there, didn't you?"

"Frankly, my love, I've watched you try to run your own life for over a decade, and it isn't one of your strong points."

"What do you mean?" he asked.

"I mean that in twelve years you've wrecked two relationships that I know of and successfully raised a snapping turtle," Marcia replied.

He started to open his mouth.

"Don't say anything," she said. "I like you better when you're quiet."

"Can I get you a donut from the snack bar?" he asked, trying in vain to change the subject.

"No. Watch the sunset and tell me that you love me."

He watched the sunset, and, by way of telling her that he loved her, let her pull his head to a rest on her lap. Donovan put his feet up on the bench.

"When will we reach Newport?" she asked.

"About 8:00 P.M."

"And Jefferson?"

"About the same time."

"What's the plan?"

"To hold the Newport P.D. in a backup role. I want *us* to take the Ashtons, not out of pride but because they'll least expect it. That's assuming their sponsors bought our false messages. Even if we don't take them by surprise, I have two Coast Guard Boats on standby. The *Christopher E.* isn't going anywhere."

Donovan and Marcia were quiet for a long time, until the sun was well below the horizon and lights were turned on aboard the ferry. The lights of the Connecticut shoreline were nearing.

"Jefferson also checked ship movements into and out of Norfolk," Donovan said. "The HMS *Worcester* paid a month-long port call to Norfolk in April 1983. She carried royal sailors and marines."

"One of whom, being of aristocratic birth, had an interest in horse shows."

"And Jefferson's library research of the records of the fighting in Northern Ireland show one death of special note: Corporal Christopher E. Ashton, killed by a sniper, February 10, 1984."

"Did they catch the sniper?"

"They didn't catch the man who pulled the trigger," Donovan said. "But those who supplied him with ammo are now pushing up daisies."

"I'll be glad when this is over," Marcia said.

# Nineteen

Newport was part tourist attraction, part museum, but only a little bit home.

Donovan felt certain that somebody must live there, but apart from servants and waitresses there was little sign of permanent habitation. Of course there were the big mansions, carefully marked on a "Map of the Mansions" available at the Tourist Information Bureau. Maybe somebody lived in the mansions, but with all the tour groups coming and going, Donovan couldn't imagine places less homey.

The main drag of downtown Newport ran past the yacht clubs and piers for the tour boats, and also the police station, which wasn't far from the tourist information place.

As they drove up Donovan said, "Maybe we can get my aunt to put up a sign saying 'Teddy Roosevelt Slept Here' and make a fortune selling souvenirs."

"I don't think she'll go for it," Marcia replied.

There was plenty of traffic, which the Newport police seemed to spend a good deal of time directing, and that might have accounted for the interest taken by the police chief in Donovan's arrival.

A portly man of about fifty, Chief Robert Williams had the ruddy face of a dock worker, which told Donovan that the man preferred the piers to the mansions. So did enough of his men that Donovan felt that, if nobody lived in Newport, at least some real people came to work there.

After the introductions among Williams, Donovan, Marcia, and Jefferson—who had ripped up I-95 all the way from New York to meet them—the chief asked what he could do.

"Tell us where the boat is," Donovan said.

Williams handed Donovan a map of the harbor with the position of the *Christopher E.* marked in red. Also marked were the two Coast Guard boats that lay at anchor about a mile offshore, guarding the channel from Newport to the Atlantic Ocean.

"How far from shore is Ashton's boat?" Donovan asked.

"Let's see," Williams replied, consulting the map. "About a quarter of a mile. I have a launch standing by if you need it."

"No. I'll row out, if you have a rowboat."

"A rowboat?" Williams laughed.

"I could use the exercise," Donovan said. "Besides, I don't like boats that have engines in them."

"A sailor, huh? I *thought* you looked a bit like Ted Turner when you walked in."

Donovan twirled an end of his mustache and smiled at Marcia, who looked away. "Actually, I'm taller," he said modestly.

"And a lot poorer," Barnes added.

"You won't need a boat of any kind, at least not for a while," Williams said. "We've had the *Christopher E.* under surveillance ever since Sergeant Jefferson called. Three of the crew—two young men and a woman—are ashore. The older guy is still aboard."

"A woman?" Barnes exclaimed.

Donovan said, "D'Amato showed me how he could hear conversations spoken inside other boats moored at our pier at the boat basin. Living in a fiberglass boat is like living inside a guitar. He heard a man with a British accent talking to a woman—

two hours after we totaled the BMW.''

''Andrea Jones?'' Marcia said.

''May be. Forensics went over the bodies in the BMW and confirmed two men and a woman dead, but said positive I.D.s on the bodies would take at least a week.''

''Yet somebody phoned the newspaper in Riverton with an obit for Jones.''

''Her 'uncle,' '' Donovan said. ''He wanted anyone who was paying attention to think she's dead. I think she's sailing to England with the Ashtons, her mission here having been accomplished.''

''Do you know where the three who came ashore have gone?'' Marcia asked.

''They ordered provisions this afternoon, and went back to the boat for a while. About an hour ago they came back ashore and went to a party at the Overseas Yacht Club. They don't look especially dangerous, Lieutenant.''

''So far they've killed at least five and as many as several dozen people, depending on how many bodies are found in the wreck of a certain warehouse,'' Donovan said.

Williams was impressed. ''You'll need help, then,'' he said.

''I don't think so. We know how they operate now. The two young guys are British commandos and devious as hell. The woman—well, she's a whole other story. We can reach you on channel two if we need backup?'' Donovan brandished the walkie-talkie that Williams had lent him.

''We'll be ready,'' the chief said. ''And two of our guys were U.S. Navy Seals, so if things get rough . . .''

''I appreciate it,'' Donovan said.

''What are you going to do?''

Donovan shrugged, and said, ''Take 'em by surprise, which in this case will be to walk into the Overseas Yacht Club and ask for a beer.''

''That's your plan?'' Williams asked.

Donovan explained: ''These guys were trained by machines and think like machines. The last thing they'll expect from me—

if they expect me at all—is something really stupid like walking in and asking for a beer.''

''When reason fails, be unreasonable,'' Marcia said.

Donovan patted her on the hand. ''We may indeed have a future together,'' he said.

## THEY'RE SELLING POSTCARDS OF THE HANGING

The Overseas Yacht Club was an old building of at least thirty or forty rooms, with six piers and a motorized tender on call from eight in the morning until eleven at night to ferry members and guests to and from their boats. At least two hundred boats were hitched to moorings in the harbor, the *Christopher E.* among them.

Donovan drove up to the parking lot attendant and flashed an old, laminated card. He said, ''Captain William Donovan, Peconic Bay Yacht Club. I'd like guest privileges, please.''

''Yes sir, Captain,'' the attendant said. ''Have you checked in with the club secretary?''

''Of course not. I just got here, as you can see. My boat will arrive in an hour.''

''Okay, sir, park in any spot you like.''

Donovan drove off.

''*Captain* Donovan?'' Jefferson asked.

''In yacht club parlance, anybody who's ever skippered a dinghy is entitled to call himself 'Captain,' '' Donovan explained.

Donovan parked, and the trio conferred while distributing arms. Marcia hid her shotgun in a zip-up tennis-racquet cover, while both Donovan and Jefferson filled their pockets with speed-loaders for their pistols. Each of the loaders held six bullets in the proper position for simultaneous insertion in the pistol's cylinder.

''If the woman sailing on the *Christopher E.* is Andrea Jones, how did she get out of that car?'' Marcia asked.

''She was never in it,'' Donovan said. ''I only saw a woman

with long hair. The NSA claims it doesn't have field agents, but do you believe anything they say? They could have male and female field agents. The BMW could have belonged to the FBI, the CIA, the NSA, or British intelligence.''

''I ran into a paper wall when trying to trace the origin of the car,'' Jefferson said.

''And if you were in charge of one of these agencies, would you want Andrea Jones caught while in your BMW?'' Marcia said.

''By George, I think she's got it!'' Donovan replied.

He surveyed the club. ''It's fairly dark around the back perimeter,'' he said. ''The main lights are in the dining room and den and on the deck and docks. Stay away from them, Thomas, while circling around the back and taking up a position on the far side of the deck.

''Barnes, you look respectable enough to be a guest. Walk in with me. I'll sign us in and you go out onto the deck and find a table. I'm going straight for the bar.''

''What a surprise.''

''It's pure business,'' Donovan said. ''If the two Ashton kids are anywhere, it will be in the bar or the den. Andrea Jones also seems to have a fondness for bars. I'll look for them.''

''And if you find them?'' Marcia asked.

''I'll holler. Both of you come in, and, well, take your best shot.''

They left the car, and, in the busy parking lot and even busier yacht club, had no trouble blending in. All three were dressed for the occasion: Donovan and Barnes wore shabby genteel, while Jefferson looked like the yachting department of Brooks Brothers. There was no way they could be mistaken for cops, except, perhaps, by the people they were after.

A Dixieland band was playing on the deck, and signs announced a fund-raising party to benefit the New York Yacht Club's *America II* Cup challenge. Donovan duly presented his old yacht club credentials and a fifty-dollar contribution to the club secretary and signed in.

Barnes went to the deck as she had been told, and soon found a table at which she took up residence.

Donovan pushed his way through the crowd, doing his best to keep his magnum from peeking out from under his blue blazer. A young woman who was slightly tipsy gave him an imitation straw boater advertising the America's Cup challenge. He reluctantly put it on.

Neither Kevin nor William Ashton was to be seen, and Donovan looked around the entire room for them. He made his way to the bar, which had only a few seats but did a brisk business as milling customers picked up drinks to take outside or into the den.

Donovan went to the center of the bar and procured a bottle of Miller Lite. He barely had time to take a sip when he saw her.

Andrea Jones was sitting at the bar, staring into a glass of white wine. She was alone, which considering her looks and the number of available men was unusual. Donovan called the bartender over.

"Who's the blonde?" he asked.

"Forget it," the man said. "She's a human refrigerator—won't talk to anybody."

"I'm a good electrician," Donovan said. "I'll fix her up."

"Good luck," the bartender said.

Donovan made his way over to where she was sitting. Perhaps she sensed another guy about to come on to her, for Jones lowered her head and stared more deeply into her glass. She didn't even look up when Donovan stood beside her. He sensed that she was trying to block out all sensations.

The Dixieland band was playing its version of the downbeat "St. James Infirmary Blues."

Donovan said, "Sorry about your horse."

She still didn't look up.

"You haven't been listening to the radio," he went on. "Gamesman finished out of the money at Belmont this afternoon. I guess you lose."

Andrea Jones looked up, and Donovan saw the same look he had seen in his apartment, after he snatched the strands of her hair. It was a look of surprise, confusion, and hatred.

"Donovan," she said.

He moved the magnum to where she could see it. "You're under arrest. Let's leave quietly and not make a mess of these people's party."

The surprise, hesitation, and hatred lingered a moment, then dissolved into something like futility. She picked up her glass of wine and took a sip.

"I got your message," she said. "What did I leave in your apartment?"

"A strand of your hair . . . and some fingerprints," Donovan said.

"So you really *didn't* make a pass at me."

"Disappointed?"

She offered a gallows smile. "I gave up on sex when Christopher was murdered."

"Tell me something—why all the showmanship? Why leave clues all over the landscape? Why come to my gym, my bar, my apartment?"

"Why not?" she asked.

"Was it to divert attention away from Washington and London?"

"You'll never prove any of that."

"Was it to show off? Why didn't you just bump off the bastards and blow town?"

"Terrorists are cowards," she said. "You don't kill cowards by being cowardly."

Donovan thought for a moment, then said, "Let's go. I suspect you're about to start acting noble, and I prefer to remember you as just another loser with a gun."

The look of hatred returned to her eyes, and she looked around for Kevin or William Ashton.

Donovan read her mood perfectly. "Keep your hands where I can see them," he warned.

She didn't respond. Angry, Donovan said, "Okay, so we'll do it the hard way: put your left hand behind your back, keeping your right hand on the bar."

He reached behind for the handcuffs that were hooked to his belt, and as he did so, Jones tossed her drink in his face and then drove her elbow into his solar plexus. Donovan went down in a heap of barstools and people, and there was some laughter from those who assumed that another man had struck out with the blonde at the bar.

As she ran toward the deck, shoving people aside, Donovan got to his feet, wiping the sting of wine from his eyes. He raised his handgun and yelled, as loud as he could, "Police! Everybody down!"

Jones made it halfway to the deck as the party dissolved in screaming and chaos. Then, in the doorway leading to the deck, she saw Marcia Barnes, her feet set and ready, the shotgun aimed in the air. Jones halted, looking around frantically.

Kevin and William Ashton were pushing their way through the crowd, moving as efficiently as when they demolished Facci's warehouse. Jones looked to them, then turned and ran toward Donovan, fumbling for her Dragoon as she did.

Donovan aimed his magnum at her; Barnes aimed her shotgun. Jones spun about, looking at them both, caught between them, her old Colt now at the ready.

Kevin Ashton was the first through the crowd. He sailed through the air, over the heads of ducked-down party-goers, and hit Donovan with a flying kick that sent the lieutenant back to the floor. The magnum fell from his hand.

There was another shout. Jefferson hollered, "Police! Freeze!" but William Ashton wasn't listening. He went to his inside jacket pocket for an automatic, and then there was the blast of a .38 that caught the young man in the side, piercing his heart and dropping him to the floor. Jefferson leaped over the body and toward the other Ashton.

Donovan got back to his feet just in time to duck a left-hand chop. He drove his right hand fist deep into the other man's stomach, then grabbed him by the hair and brought his head crashing down onto a rising knee. Kevin Ashton crumpled to the floor, his face an abstract portrait done in blood.

A moment froze in time: Donovan stood over the bodies of the two young Ashtons, staring down the barrel of Andrea Jones's gun. She had chosen her final target, and it was him. Then there came a roar that shook the windows and the glasses. Jones was hit in the middle by a single shot from Marcia's shotgun. What was left of her fell atop her two would-be brothers-in-law.

The only sound in the room was a click as Marcia pumped another shell into the breech of her shotgun.

Donovan found his own gun and stumbled to a barstool. He had his head down on the bar, the magnum in front of him, some of Jones's blood dripping down his cheek. Gradually, his eyes began to focus on the mess that had been made of the Overseas Yacht Club.

Jefferson was on the radio to the Newport P.D. while everywhere, people were picking themselves up and stumbling out of the room, away from the carnage. Then, down the grand staircase came an old gentleman, wearing a commodore's insignia on his blazer and a look of benign intoxication on his face. He didn't see the bodies on the floor, or, if he did, assumed they were drunken yachtsmen who had fallen down—an often-enough occurrence at any yacht club.

Weaving up to Donovan, he straightened his blazer, and stared the lieutenant in the eye as Donovan raised his head.

"Ted, old man," the commodore said, "you've come to win back the Cup from those damn Aussies."

## FOR QUEEN AND COUNTRY

The rowboat was old and wooden. Paint chipped from its sides. It leaked a bit, and an old tobacco can, rusted from years of use in bailing out the boat, rolled back and forth in the bilge.

Donovan rowed the boat straight and true on a course for the *Christopher E.* He had no doubt that Ashton knew what had happened. If he hadn't gotten a call from Washington or London, much could be deduced from the display of lights and sirens onshore. The fact that no official boats had swept down on him would itself tell Ashton that the end was to come gently, but it was to come.

Donovan pulled the rowboat up to the stern of Ashton's yacht and clambered up the landing ladder, taking with him the rowboat's bowline. He tied the line to a cleat and paused a moment to look around the deck of the yacht. Everything was neat, tidy, shipshape, and even the lines were coiled. It looked as though preparations had been made for a wake.

He took out his magnum and walked slowly to the main companionway, from which lights could be seen. Donovan used the muzzle of his Smith & Wesson to push open the door, then peered down the steps.

It was like a museum on a holiday, when nobody was around but the ghosts. Donovan descended the stairs, and heard music. Francis Ashton was in his personal cabin, listening to Mozart. Donovan walked slowly into the cabin, and when he stopped in the door, Ashton barely acknowledges his presence.

"Lieutenant," Ashton said, pronouncing the title in the British manner.

Ashton was finishing a note. He did so, sealed the envelope, and then left it on the desk. "You'll see that the letter is mailed, won't you? It's to my wife, and is only of personal concern."

"I'll see to it," Donovan said.

"I heard shooting and saw the lights. Tell me about my sons."

Donovan said, ''William is dead. Kevin is on his way to the hospital. He'll recover.''

''I see. And Miss Jones?''

''Also dead.''

Ashton closed his eyes briefly, then opened them. ''How did you find us?'' he asked.

''Among other things, you filed a course plan with the Coast Guard.''

Ashton sighed. ''An old habit, like coiling lines. I must have done it out of instinct. Of course, you deduced that I never had any intention of going to Perth.''

''Of course,'' Donovan said.

Ashton looked at Donovan's gun and said ''That won't be necessary.''

''You don't mind if I make my own conclusions?''

Ashton turned to face Donovan, and, as he did so, swept a small revolver from under some papers. Donovan raised his magnum. ''There's been enough of that lately,'' he said.

''True,'' Ashton agreed. ''But I've lost everything. You Yanks have won—you always do.''

''Not always. The flow of arms from New York to the IRA has been stopped . . . for a time. And Christopher is avenged.''

''But at what cost,'' Ashton said, fiddling with his revolver.

''Put that thing away,'' Donovan said.

Ashton ignored Donovan and swung open the cylinder, removing all the cartridges but one and throwing the unneeded ones away. Ashton closed the cylinder and cocked the pistol.

He said, ''Lieutenant, would you pleas allow me a minute by myself?''

Donovan nodded, a bit sadly.

''There *was* a reason, you know,'' Ashton said. ''Apart from avenging Christopher's murder?''

''I know,'' Donovan replied. ''But I'm a simple cop with a simple beat to protect. I can't have people—no matter how just their cause—fighting wars on my territory. I'll see to it that your letter is mailed.''

Ashton thanked Donovan and handed him the note. Donovan backed out of the cabin and went up on deck.

The Newport P.D.'s tender was approaching. Jefferson stood in the bow, looking like Washington crossing the Delaware. The sound of a single shot came from within the *Christopher E.*

Jefferson didn't hear it.

When the tender pulled alongside and cut its engine, Jefferson said, ''Well?''

''Ashton shot himself. I couldn't prevent it.''

''It's just as well. Kevin didn't make it to the hospital.''

Donovan asked what he meant.

''Someone in the crowd at the yacht club shot him as he was being carried to the ambulance. We haven't caught the shooter.''

''You won't,'' Donovan said, looking up as a military jet roared through the upper atmosphere.

# TWENTY

Donovan and Marcia sat on the grass overlooking the pond by his aunt's house. They had just finished the dinner that was left over from the day before, and were relaxing with rums and Cokes, the traditional Sunday afternoon drink at the house.

It was a gorgeous day, the start of what promised to be a gorgeous week, the first week off they had spent together in twelve years. There was a slight breeze coming off the bay, keeping the mosquitos down and carrying with it the scent of salt air. The white egret was back at the northern end of the pond, where Donovan had seen it the day before.

"I don't think that 'Teddy Roosevelt Slept Here' will sell after all," Donovan said.

Marcia agreed, noting that it had been fifteen minutes since the last car passed on the South Jamesport Road. "Maybe we should open a vegetable stand?"

"There are already too many on 25a," Donovan said.

She sighed. "I guess we have nothing to do but relax and enjoy the week," she said.

"We'll sail tomorrow. Remind me to fill the boat with water this afternoon so the planks will swell overnight."

"You're not going to sink on me, are you?"

"I'll try not to," Donovan said. "In any case, Peconic Bay is so shallow that you can walk ashore from most spots."

Marcia laughed, and said, "Jefferson's been calling himself 'Captain' ever since he piloted that tender out to Ashton's boat."

"He didn't pilot it," Donovan said. "All he did was stand in the bow and look important."

"That's what most captains do at most yacht clubs, isn't it?"

"I suppose," Donovan allowed.

"In that case, you can call me 'Captain Barnes.' "

"Is there some meaning to this?" Donovan asked.

"Yes, Donovan, there is. I decided to keep the boat."

"Keep the boat?"

"The *West Wind.* I have the option to live on her year round if I want. I've decided to exercise that option. I like living on the river."

"It gets cold in the winter," Donovan said.

"When winter comes we'll just have to move up to your apartment," she said.

"I guess *we* will," he replied, a bit sharply.

"And I've decided to apply for transfer to your Unit," Marcia went on. "I think the West Side Major Crimes Unit could use a woman's touch."

Donovan said nothing, but watched the pond. The head of a turtle broke the surface and looked around. Donovan thought that it might be Clint. "What do *you* think?" he yelled.

The turtle disappeared.

"Who are you talking to?" Marcia asked.

"My adviser on the subject of women. He had no comment at this time."

"And you?" she asked. "Do you have a comment at this time?"

Donovan thought for about a quarter of a second, then stood, helped her to her feet, and tossed her over his shoulder.

"Where are you taking me?" she asked.

"To a shady glen."

"I don't know of any shady glens around here."

"This one is an old family secret."

"Donovan!"

"Generations of Donovan men have used this glen to good purpose."

"What purpose?"

"Mainly to produce more Donovans."

They passed through a blueberry patch and an acre that was crisscrossed with vines. Soon they were quite removed from the prying eyes of humanity. He laid her out on the soft grass of the glen and deposited himself next to her.

"Donovan, are you out of your mind? What if your aunt . . .?"

"My aunt was begat in this very spot," Donovan said. "So was I."

"William, is this for real this time?" Marcie asked. "I mean, are you and I for real at last?"

By way of reply, Donovan drummed his fingers on the grass.

She looked at the shady glen, at the sky, and at him. She thought of the generations of Donovans who were begat on that grass. "Right," she said, "ask a silly question . . ."

She began to unbutton her blouse.